WHAT SURVIVES

WHAT SURVIVES

A NOVEL

PHYLLIS M SKOY

IPBOOKS.net
International Psychoanalytic Books

International Psychoanalytic Books (IPBooks),
New York • http://www.IPBooks.net

What Survives: a novel

Edited by NY Book Editors
nybookeditors.com

International Psychoanalytic Books (IPBooks),
25–79 31st Street Astoria, NY 11102
Online at: www.IPBooks.net

Interior book design by Maureen Cutajar
www.gopublished.com

Front cover design by Kathy Kovacic
Back cover design by Lawrence L. Schwartz

ISBN: 978-0-9969996-2-5

to Arthur
for his love, support and patience

ACKNOWLEDGEMENTS

My sincere thanks go to Lynn Miller, PhD, my writing coach, mentor, editor and dear friend;

Thomas H. Ogden, MD, my psychoanalytic mentor, for his friendship and years of support, encouragement and reading;

My sister, Gay Lasher, for her love and support;

Lisa Lenard-Cook, mentor, editor and dear friend;

Elizabeth Hadas for editing and consultation

Hilda Raz for her loving support and reading;

Lynda Miller, PhD, for her loving support and reading;

Ayşegul Hurder, my Turkish consultant and friend, with thanks to your anneanne for the apartment on Steep Street;

BJ Firestone and Debbie Newborn for their critical eyes;

The members of my wonderful critique group led by Lynn Miller

and all my many readers.

PART I
AVANOS

CHAPTER 1

It was the second time that someone had painted graffiti on Adalet Ulusoy's red Fiat Palio. The wide blue splashes crisscrossing its stubby body meant nothing to her in any language other than the unspoken one of Avanos; that it would be better for her and for her neighbors if she were to just pick up and move on.

Avanos was beautiful but harsh country. The summers were hot but dry; the winters were cold and generated enough snow to attract skiers. The house Adalet lived in was four hundred years old and not easy to heat comfortably with coal. It would never have occurred to Adalet to live in such a place, but the evening of November 12, 1999, changed everything and forced her hand.

The potters and weavers who populated Avanos had been there for centuries. Most of the homes that were as old as Adalet's had developed with extensions built onto cave dwellings. The only people who could afford to build homes that far back in time had been quite wealthy families like that of Yasar, her ex-husband.

Women on their own here were an anomaly, even among the more modern women working in the tourism industry. And those few single women were not divorced, as they'd never been married, and stood in a class of their own. They stayed only to guide foreigners through the fairy chimney rock formations and deserted underground city caves of Cappadocia. They came and went during the heavy tourist seasons and could not have cared less what the locals thought of them. They dressed and dated as they pleased, provocatively and promiscuously, or so it seemed to Adalet. They drank and smoked too much, and as far as her brief experience of them informed her, they did not pray or read the Koran. Ironically, she knew that this was exactly what the local villagers suspected of her.

In any event, Adalet thought, the Fiat would have to be repainted. She'd have to call Temel to see when he'd be able to do it. In the eight months she'd lived in Avanos, Temel had been the closest she'd come to a real friend. She'd gotten his name from Fatma Celik, the nearly blind widow of a successful potter whose sons had taken over the family business after his death from lung cancer five years ago. Adalet had wandered into their shop. From the street, she'd seen exquisitely woven traditional *kilims* spread over benches and tables, a perfect stage for the reddish clay Hittite wine jugs, hand-painted pots and plates set between a stunning variety of succulents and flower arrangements. Behind the display room was the factory where the Celik family had been making pottery for eight generations.

A shrewd Fatma Celik watched over this empire, her visual impairment impeding her not in the least. Her throne was an ancient wooden rocker covered with a couple of antique *kilims*, probably worth a small fortune, and situated at a convenient spot between the display room and the factory. After Adalet had made half a dozen trips to the shop without making a purchase, Fatma motioned her to a seat by her chair and called to someone in the back to bring black tea.

"Please sit and talk to an old woman. You don't seem to have anything else to do." Adalet had laughed. She liked the old woman instantly but knew enough to be cautious. Gossip spread like uncontained wildfire in Avanos, and this woman had access to the whole town. But she took the seat she was offered.

"Thank you, I will. The pottery here is some of the most beautiful I've ever seen. And the displays—"

"Yes, my sons take special pride, like their father. He used to say that the poorest of food could have been served to sultans on his plates. So tell me, what are you doing in Avanos? Are you a guide?"

"No. I'm deciding."

"Deciding what?"

"What to do."

"Hmmm. Do you like to read?"

"Yes, I read a lot."

"Come read to me. I'll pay you."

"I don't need the money, thank you, but I can read to you."

"Call me Fatma."

"I'm Adalet."

The black tea arrived and an agreement was reached. Adalet offered to come a couple of times a week to read to Fatma. And when Adalet mentioned that she needed house repairs, Fatma recommended Temel.

"He's reliable at a reasonable price," she said, "and he knows what he's doing."

Temel had repaired the roof, plastered and painted the house and would eventually upgrade the kitchen and bathroom. He was as reasonable and reliable as Fatma had promised. Temel was in his late thirties, married, with two children. This took some time for Adalet to learn, as Temel worked much more than he spoke. But when Adalet had come down with the flu and could barely get up from her bed to make her way to the bathroom, Temel had called his wife and asked her to make some soup for Adalet. She'd arrived later that day with a large pot of chicken soup with vermicelli. She'd handed the pot over to Temel and left before Adalet could even meet her, let alone thank her.

"She's shy," Temel had said, handing a cup of heated soup to Adalet. "Just sip it slowly. Only broth for now."

As Adalet had eaten the healing soup, she'd felt some of her bitterness leave her body, along with the flu. Temel came and went, plastering, painting, and Adalet slept. When the chicken soup was finished, Temel took the empty pot home and brought it back with a hearty stew. She'd learned how much she could trust Temel when she'd finally felt well enough to return to Fatma for her readings.

"Where have you been?" Fatma had asked, concerned, but a bit annoyed as well.

"I was ill. I thought Temel would've told you."

"Temel? I don't think he's said more than ten words to me in all the years he's worked for me. Well, you seem well enough now. What should we read today?"

This was a rhetorical question. Fatma always chose exactly what she wanted read to her. Adalet had given up hoping for a good classic or even current fiction. Fatma was attracted mostly to human interest and crime. She insisted that Adalet read the international and national news and local business developments, but she'd doze on and off, emitting the occasional snore. But when Adalet read stories about immigrants crowding into Istanbul, Kurdish conflicts, liberals protesting Islamic fundamentalists, men beating and killing their wives for disobedience, writers being arrested for protesting censorship, Fatma would right herself in her chair so as not to miss a word. When one of Fatma's sons would interrupt to consult with her, she'd shoo him away with a brisk, "We're busy here. Later."

Although seeing her defaced car had not been a good start to Adalet's morning, it was an unseasonably warm day and Adalet decided to walk to Temel's home instead of calling. She knew that Temel would be working at this hour. And so Emine, Temel's wife, would probably invite her to stay for tea. Dogu and Devrim, their five year-old twin sons, could make her forget her troubles with their antics and games. Only their parents could tell them apart, and even they could be fooled. The twins already knew their unique power and used it precociously to the amusement and frustration of the adults in their lives. Soon they would be starting school.

When Adalet had first been exposed to Temel's family, she'd thought she'd be overcome by envy. But it was impossible to hold on to these feelings for long. Emine welcomed her with kindness and an interest that no one had shown in some time. And the children were irresistible, in spite of the pain of her loss. They called her *Adalet teyze*, as if she were their mother's sister.

Adalet loved to walk the back route along the winding and rocky pathway that led to Temel's house. She leaned on a wooden staff for balance. Autumn wildflowers and weeds pushed their way to life from behind clumps of dirt, jagged rock and the snarled roots of thirsty juniper. Tiny lizards perched on rocks, waiting for a single one of the loud chorus of insects to come within reach of their outstretched tongues. It astonished her that life could thrive in these desolate places. Today her legs felt almost normal, and she took pleasure in every step without pain. There had been so few of these days since the fire.

When Adalet opened the wooden courtyard gate, the boys ran to greet her.

"Look at the fort we're building, *Adalet teyze*."

Adalet surveyed the pile of rocks they were pointing to and nodded her head.

"It will be hard for the enemy to get through that, won't it," she said. "Who's the enemy?"

Dogu and Devrim looked at each other and one of them, Adalet could never be sure which, shrugged and said, "We don't know yet. Do you have a good enemy for us?"

Emine opened the cottage door into the courtyard and stood in the doorway.

"Good morning, Adalet. Will you have some tea with me?"

'Give us an enemy first," one of the boys pulled on her arm.

"Careful, Devrim. You'll hurt her."

"Sorry, *Anne*." He dropped his hold on Adalet's sleeve. "But we need an enemy."

"What about whoever is painting my car?"

"That's not an enemy. We need an army." This came from Dogu, Adalet now knew, since Devrim's mother had already tagged him.

"I'm sorry, but that's the only enemy I have."

"What about the Kurds?"

"Dogu, your grandmother is a Kurd. My *anne* is a Kurd. Where did you ever get that?" Emine flushed with embarrassment.

"Just wait until they're in school," Adalet said.

"Come," Emine gestured toward the kitchen just beyond the door, "I'll put the *çaydanlik* on." Adalet shrugged her shoulders to the boys and followed Emine inside.

"So they got your car again," Emine said as she filled the double Turkish kettle with water in the bottom and tea on the top.

Adalet glanced around the small but fully equipped kitchen. Temel had remodeled it completely. How lucky Emine was to have him. The cottage was hundreds of years old and much the same as Adalet's. It was constructed from local stone and heated by a coal stove located in the center of the house. The floors were tile and covered with an array of old carpets handed down by both sides of the family, in typical Turkish tradition. In addition to the kitchen, there were two small bedrooms, a central room and a Western-style bath Temel had installed after tearing out the old one. It was warm and inviting. Adalet sat down at the large wooden table.

"Can you believe it?" Adalet shook her head in frustration. "This is the third time. I can't drive it like that."

"Why not? If they see it doesn't bother you, maybe whoever is doing this will leave it alone. You should act as if you like it."

"But it does bother me."

"Well, that's the thing, isn't it?

"What do you mean?"

"I think whoever's doing it knows that it bothers you or you wouldn't be in such a hurry to repaint it. I don't know. Maybe they want to get your attention." Emine took the kettle from the fire and poured tea into two small glasses. She set the kettle on the table between them.

"Attention for what? I don't see them. If they want my attention, why don't they knock on my door and just tell me to leave."

"Is that what you think this is about?"

"I don't know what else." Adalet took a sip of steaming tea.

"Who would want you to leave?"

"Burcu and Erol."

"Why would they care?"

"I moved them out of their house."

"No, you didn't. It was never their house. They were renters. Okay, so it meant they had to find another place, but they got a great deal on a bigger house in town near their travel agency."

"How do you know?"

"They hired Temel to help them move some of their things."

"He never told me."

"Did you ever tell him you thought they were the ones painting your car?"

"No. I thought he would think I was paranoid."

Emine took two small oranges from a large bowl of fruit. She peeled them both and handed one to Adalet.

"Do you think I'm paranoid?" Adalet asked, breaking off one of the slices and biting into its juicy sweetness.

"Well, there is paint on your car. And unless you're doing it in your sleep, someone is making mischief with you. Let's find out who it is."

"And just how are we going to do that?"

"We'll be a lookout."

Adalet laughed. "I would never have thought you had something like this in you. A lookout. You don't even have a television. And all this time I've been thinking you're so quiet and shy."

"Makes me a good lookout, eh?"

"And what about the kids? And Temel?"

"We can take turns. I could bring them with me sometimes, and I can put them to bed and Temel can watch them. And Temel can be a lookout, too, if he wants."

"You have it all figured out. Let me think about it. It could be dangerous."

"Come on, if they were dangerous, they would be doing much worse things."

"Do you think so?"

"Of course."

They finished their tea and oranges, and Emine promised to send Temel to paint the car as soon as possible. Adalet hugged Emine as she left.

"Thank you, Emine. It's nice to have a friend."

"It is nice, isn't it?"

Emine walked out the door and into the front courtyard with Adalet to check on the twins. They'd managed to pile up quite a large number of rocks.

"*Anne, Adalet teyze*, look. We have a fort to keep out the Greeks."

"It's beautiful," Emine said, "but why do you need to keep out Greeks?"

"Grandpa says the bad guys are the Greeks. Alp and Isik say the bad guys are the Kurds, but if your *anne* is a Kurd, they can't be the enemy."

Emine shook her head and hugged each child under a different arm. "That's old history," she said. "We aren't enemies with the Greeks anymore." The boys broke away from her grasp and ran back to their rocks.

"It's just pretend, *Anne*," one of them called back to her.

"It's just play," Adalet agreed.

"Yes, but it's still important that they know. I don't like this enemy thing. Alp and Isik are Temel's brother's children. Whenever they play together, they come up with these things."

"As I said, just wait until they start school."

"Do you think we should send them for religious school in the summer?"

Adalet was surprised that Emine would ask her, of all people, for advice about the children's education. She didn't have any children of her own, and she was afraid of intimidating Temel and Emine if she talked too much about her university experience.

"What does Temel think?"

"He doesn't know. I think he feels that boys should play in the summer. I worry that they'll learn bad things."

"They'll hear bad things no matter where they go to school. It doesn't mean they have to learn them."

"Yes, it's true. I can't protect them from the world. I'll tell Temel to go and paint the car. Then we can start the lookout."

"I'll think about it, I promise. Thanks for the tea." Adalet waved good-bye and started the walk home. It was too much for her to walk all the way to Fatma's shop, so she would have to drive the branded Fiat into town. The walk home felt a bit more difficult. Her legs began to ache, and she had to lean harder into her walking stick. This was how it was now. She could feel fine until she didn't, without a moment's warning. She was afraid of the pain medication the doctor had prescribed. When she took it, she felt dull, the way she'd been after her surgeries and during her long recovery. She would rest today and go to Fatma tomorrow.

CHAPTER 2

Temel didn't come that day, and so the next morning Adalet was faced once again with driving her car into town, as it was, with wide blue streaks on its bright red body.

She considered Emine's question. Why did it bother her so much to drive a scarred car? She'd become so self-conscious since her marriage and divorce from Yasar. His family, his friends, Yasar himself, they dressed, spoke, behaved so perfectly. She imagined that any one of them would fit in anywhere in Europe, the States, in New York City. And here she was in Avanos, living on her own as a divorced woman and ashamed of the blue paint on her car. She laughed out loud at herself, something she could not remember ever having done.

Fatma grunted when she saw Adalet. She didn't like to acknowledge how much she looked forward to her visits. Fatma greeted her sons in much the same manner, and Adalet knew they meant the world to her.

"My car was decorated again."

"I hope it's a nice color."

"It is. It's a deep royal blue."

"Very nice. Maybe Temel can paint the whole car this color."

"I think I prefer the red."

"What difference does it make?"

"Easy for you to say. You don't have to drive it or look at it."

"If only I could see red or blue, I'd be happy with either."

Adalet picked up a copy of *Aksam*, one of the more widely read Turkish newspapers, and began to read. She'd gotten Fatma's point. She was grateful for her sight, but the fact remained that someone was vandalizing her car. Perhaps Fatma thought she was taking the whole thing too seriously.

"And then what?' Fatma was tapping her fingers on Adalet's arm.

"I'm sorry. Where was I?"

"You were reading about the demolition of the buildings on the Ayamaya River."

"The floods?"

"Yes. Go on."

Adalet read without taking in a word of it. Then there was another plot to overthrow the government and the press was in some sort of trouble again. She used to follow the news so closely. Back then, she felt that she would become an active citizen of Turkey, effecting change, doing things that mattered. Yasar was designing buildings, creating the future Turkey, and she was reading the news to an old woman at the end of the world. Yet, here she was.

Fatma was soon asleep, and Adalet ducked out of the shop before she could wake up and ask her to go on with the reading. The more she thought about it, the more she wanted to know who was painting the car. When she surveyed her little Fiat parked across the street, she had to smile. The brush strokes were comical, playful. They went up and down and around in an abstract form of sometimes thicker, sometimes thinner lines, here and there disappearing into nothing and then reappearing in thick clumps. A good artist, at least, she thought.

Later that evening, Adalet took a long, hot bath. She perched her feet on the edge of the tub to submerge her upper body completely. Her fingers traced the outlines of the scars on her legs. There were images, patterns there as well. She could identify a bird's wing, a seashell, the dotted trees of an ancient Chinese landscape.

Adalet added more hot water to her bath and lay back with a hot, wet washcloth over her face. Her marriage to Yasar had never been easy. If she forced herself to be honest, the challenges that the engagement dinner and wedding party had presented should have set off the sirens she'd sensed in the distance but had refused to hear. Her mother always used to say how easy it was to look back and see the truth.

For several generations now, both sides of Adalet's family had lived out their lives in Duzçe, a village too small to be seen on a tourist map of the Black Sea Coast. A trip to Istanbul was a major undertaking for Adalet's parents, and they admitted that they were uncomfortable in the large city. In the several years that Adalet lived away from home and attended university, it was rare for Adalet to ask them to visit her. They had not met Yasar or his family until the evening of the engagement dinner.

Adalet's parents didn't want to make the trip to Istanbul. They would have preferred to make a party in their home. The question of where it was to be held led to several telephone calls from Duzçe to Istanbul. Adalet hadn't told Yasar that her parents wanted to have the event in their home. In truth, she'd been afraid. Part of her felt ashamed, but only in front of Yasar's family, of their old-fashioned ways and their quaint stone home. The house was over three hundred years old, and Adalet's parents had seen no need to do much in the way of upgrades. Adalet's father, Selim Ulusoy, had grown up in this house, and her mother, Eda, had grown up in one very similar. They didn't see the need for Western plumbing, modern appliances or decorative furnishings. They were happy with carpets and pillows and things the way they'd always been. Adalet privately found it beautiful.

So Adalet had told her parents that there wasn't enough room to accommodate everyone. Her mother argued that there were many carpets and pillows and rooms in the houses of the village. Adalet pictured Yasar's parents sleeping on the floor with strangers and wept. So she'd begged her parents to accept, and finally a date was agreed upon for the two families to meet at the Sultan's Seafood

Palace in Kumkapi, Istanbul's famous seafood district. The restaurant was owned and operated by Yasar's father's older brother and was a well-known tourist attraction.

If Adalet could have known how awkward the evening would be, she might have relented in spite of her shame. When she rescued her parents from the train station, she hid how dismayed she was by their appearance. Yes, they'd been traveling for several hours, but they knew they'd be going straight to the restaurant and there would be no time to freshen up at the hotel. Her father looked much older than his forty-five years, although he still had a full head of thick, salt and pepper hair. It wasn't so much that they were shabby as they appeared disheveled, worn, bent, used. Her mother looked young next to her father, but tired and second-hand, though still pretty. She wore a headscarf that made her appear more countrified and less appealing than she would have with her dark waves of hair released. But Adalet knew she never would've had these thoughts before Yasar.

The rows of restaurants in Kumkapi looked very much the same. Simple wooden structures with a posted menu outdoors with several tanks of fish swimming frantically back and forth, as if announcing their freshness and ready availability, as well as their anxiety to get the inevitable over and done with. Long wooden plank tables surrounded by simple wooden chairs hopefully announced the promise of better food than décor, not that the surroundings were atypical of most seafood establishments located by the water.

Yasar's Uncle Erol was waiting by the door to greet them. He held out his hand warmly to Adalet's father, "Ah, Selim Bey, Hanim Eda, and you must be the lovely Adalet. Selim Ulusoy returned the handshake. "Thank you, Erol Bey. How thoughtful of you to meet us at the door." "It's no trouble at all," Erol Ozbek assured him. He took a stack of menus from a table next to the door and ushered them to one of the larger tables farthest away from the kitchen in a corner of its own. Yasar and his family had already been seated. A large bottle of *raki* sat on the table surrounded by glasses partially filled with ice. A pewter pitcher of water was placed nearby. Large murals of fishing vessels and their crews in the various acts of procuring what might end up being their dinner covered the wall space on all sides. Since the Ozbeks had seated themselves next to each other on one side of the table, Adalet seated herself between her mother and father on the opposite side. Yasar excused himself to help Adalet and her mother with their chairs.

The names of the dishes on the menu were foreign to Adalet's parents. They couldn't have known that they were often given fancy names that had little or nothing to do with the actual food being prepared and were solely created for the tourists. Sultan's Mullet or Sultan's Bed from the Sea not only gave few hints as to content (other than "mullet" or "sea") or manner of preparation, and not a single price was listed. Although it was understood that Yasar's family would assume responsibility for the bill, Adalet's parents were afraid of choosing something too expensive, and so they sat exchanging furtive glances, paralyzed to order.

Yasar's mother, clothed in a skin-fitted sleeveless pink silken sheathe that stopped at her knees and allowed elegant legs to be further enhanced by soft Italian pink leather heels, thoughtfully suggested that she had some favorites here, if they'd like to try some. Innocently assured that she would respect their unstated wishes and refrain from selecting anything at the high end, they immediately agreed to let her order for them.

When the entrées arrived, after much *raki* and many *mezze* were consumed, (the *raki* only by the Ozbek family) and the Ulusoys realized that they'd been served the seafood platter special, possibly the highest-priced item in the list of entrées, they looked at each other in confusion and dismay.

The conversation up to this point had been stilted. Yasar's sister, Belgin, had done the majority of the talking. Not one to suffer silence for very long, she asked many questions of everyone which frustratingly led to either one-word or one-sentence responses.

Yasar's father was an intellectual, a writer and poet, and Yasar's mother had been a model and a recognized face, if not name, in

Turkish film. And although all four parents made some attempts to initiate conversation, it would falter.

"So then, Selim Bey, I understand you are quite the craftsman. Yasar told us about the armoire you made for Adalet. He said it was beautiful, absolutely beautiful."

"Yes, it is a good piece, more due to the quality of the wood than my talents, I'm afraid."

These comments were followed by an uneasy silence, broken by the next person willing to venture forth, even though there was so little in common between the two families that Adalet began to wonder how she had ever attracted Yasar in the first place. Belgin had once hinted that Yasar was smitten with Adalet's looks and charmed by her innocence and her lack of sophistication. This had been in response to some frustration Adalet had expressed when Belgin had gone shopping with her to help her to pick out a dress to wear to dinner with Yasar's boss and his wife.

"I wish I had some of your fashion sense, Belgin. Yasar isn't exactly crazy about the way I dress."

"Oh, I don't know, dear. I think he likes it. You're so pretty and sweet, and you're not in the least –and she made a motion with her forefinger, pushing her nose upward into the air. "You know how obnoxious some of the women he's known can be."

Adalet didn't know much about the women Yasar had known, but she hadn't wanted to show her ignorance or curiosity to Belgin. She'd smiled and said nothing, but she did think of it at this dinner where their families, at least, seemed so mismatched.

At 24 years of age, Yasar was decidedly more worldly and experienced than she. Adalet's 21 year-old peers at the university would smile at one another and say, "Isn't it amazing how naïve Adalet can be?"

Adalet knew that she was a pretty girl, even by Istanbul standards. Her features were small with the exception of two: a prominent nose which some said gave her character and made her look exotic, Egyptian perhaps, and wide almond eyes that seemed to fill the whole of her slender face. But Adalet could not yet think of herself as a woman.

Yasar was a full-grown man who could occupy a room. He wasn't tall; maybe five foot ten, but he possessed a bearing connoting intelligence and power. His was not a handsome face, but formed the kind of rugged features that will bring a woman to pause and turn, and then go out of her way to be introduced. Adalet watched women watching him, and she was proud that Yasar had chosen her.

An old friend of Yasar's sister's who'd taken a Turkish Sign Language (TSL) class with Adalet thought they would look stunning together and arranged to introduce them. The friend had been correct. The women who might have looked back and attempted to meet Yasar before Adalet came into his life, now looked at her and turned away. They made a striking couple.

It had been Yasar who'd insisted they marry in a secular ceremony in Istanbul, where his family and Adalet and Yasar's university friends could easily attend. Her parents had accepted this, but unhappily. Adalet knew that it was not the way things ought to have been, but even then, she was so unsure of Yasar.

Adalet was the only child of only children, and this would have been her parents' single opportunity to host a wedding celebration. But they'd reluctantly taken a back seat in the planning, handing over control to Yasar's modern and wealthy family.

Adalet removed the now tepid washcloth from her eyes, and slowly began to push herself up from the large but ancient hexagonal marble tub that looked like something from a tourist ad for the Turkish bath. She was pretty sure that it had been an expensive whim of Yasar's mother and not something that had come with the house. The simple tub of her parent's home came to mind. Then she thought of the squat toilets they'd never replaced and sighed. What she would give to be able to return to those toilets now.

CHAPTER 3

Temel showed up early on Sunday. The red paint he brought was not a match.

"It was all I could find, sorry." He shrugged his shoulders. "It's close."

"But it's not the same. Can you take it back?"

"If you want me to, sure."

"I want you to."

Throughout the day, Adalet found herself returning to the car, looking at it from different angles, noticing images in the brush strokes she hadn't seen, and then not being able to look at them without squinting or altering her vision in some way to recreate them, much as she and her *anne* had played with the shapes of clouds when she was a little girl.

A week passed. Fatma didn't ask about the car when Adalet came to read to her, and Adalet didn't mention it. Temel stopped by once to say that he hadn't found the right red. Adalet told him there was no rush.

"Are you sure?"

"Yes, no hurry."

"Emine said something about all of us taking turns to find this guy?"

"I don't think it's necessary. Please tell her I said thank you." If Temel was surprised at her change of heart, he didn't express it.

The coolness of fall came with the end of Ramadan. Fasting came easily to Adalet. She ate little during the day in any event, having almost nothing but tea until evening. Temel came by during the last week to invite her to celebrate Bayram, the holiday of sweets marking the end of Ramadan, with his family.

"We'll pick you up and go to the grandparents. Our brothers and sisters will be there and all the little cousins. My mother will cook a feast. You can meet everyone."

"I'm sorry," she told him. "Another time. Bayram is difficult for me since my parents died. I like to keep it simple. Please come to visit me instead. I'll have treats for the children. I must visit Fatma first, so if you can, come later in the day."

"Sure, we will. We'll come after we see my family. By the way, I still haven't been able to get the paint."

"Don't worry, I'm getting used to it."

"Alright then. I'll see you in a few days."

Adalet took her paint-dabbled Fiat into town to pick up sweets. Bayram had been her favorite holiday as a child. Her mother had always bought her a new dress and coat and shoes. They would visit her mother's parents first, and then her father's mother, her paternal grandfather having passed away before Adalet was born. She'd had the three grandparents for the first six years of her life, and her mother's mother had lived until Adalet was fifteen. Bayram had always meant strong ties of family and tradition.

Adalet parked on a cobbled side street in between the pastry shop and the candy store. The shops were tiny in comparison to newer sections of Istanbul but not so different from the old city. The family who ran the pastry shop had been there almost as long as Fatma's husband's family had been making pottery. The candy store was much more recent. Adalet made her pastry purchases quickly, taking longer to think about what candies the children would like.

When she turned the corner where she'd parked the car, she saw several teenage boys leaning against it. They were dressed alike;

knockoff designer jeans, fake black leather jackets, fake leather Italian boots, matching cigarettes dangling from their lips. She thought about turning back the way she'd come, but one of them spotted her.

"Bayram treats for us? You shouldn't have." He reached out an unwashed hand with dirty, bitten fingernails and took the candy package away from Adalet.

"I'm sorry. They're not for you, but you're welcome to try one. They're for my friend's children. Please give them back and let me into my car."

"This is your car?"

"Yes, it is." She stood firmly in front of them with her hand outstretched to claim the sack of candy. The boy handed the bag to her without reaching inside. He threw his cigarette to the ground within inches of her foot and stamped it out with the toe of his boot.

"Lucky for you," he said, "we've been watching it. Looked like it needed watching." The other two backed away from the car.

"Thank you. I guess it does." Adalet got into the car and saw them watching her as she drove away. She was glad she'd offered the boy candy. They were just little boys trying to be tough, but the encounter left her shaky and vulnerable. It would never be easy here to be a divorced woman living on her own.

When she arrived home, Adalet arranged the candies in separate little colored cloth bags she'd started making last year just for this purpose. She closed each bag with a shiny satin ribbon that she finished off with a bow. She smiled at her handiwork. The children would be delighted.

Adalet gathered some garlic, onions, carrots, celery, lemons and parsley from the refrigerator to make her daily meal. She had soaked Roman beans overnight so that they'd be ready to cook. She chopped the vegetables and set them aside on the small, tiled counter. She placed the beans in a large pot with water and set them on the fire to cook for an hour. She settled into an overstuffed chair in her living room with a mystery novel she'd picked up to read to Fatma to wait for the beans to finish cooking.

But the pot on the stove brought her to another time and place, and she was unable to concentrate. She set the book on her lap, put her feet up on the ottoman and thought back to her wedding and then, inevitably to just two years later, and the worst night of her life.

The wedding day had been spoiled mostly for Adalet by the wedding dress while it had been spoiled for her parents by the wedding itself. Her mother had been visibly offended when Adalet informed her that she would not be able to wear the dress her mother had worn when she'd married her father.

"It's beautiful, *Anne*. I'm so sorry. It's just not right for this particular wedding." Her mother laid the dress on her bed next to a clear plastic box filled with pins. Adalet had been making one of her weekend trips to visit her parents and clearly, she realized, her mother had planned to have Adalet try it on so that she could fit it to her more slender figure.

"What's wrong with it? Why isn't it right? Look at this lace. You couldn't find it more beautiful in Italy. My mother made the lace herself. She learned it from her Italian friend, Silvana, who helped her with this dress. They designed the dress without so much as a pattern. I promised my mother that if I had a daughter, she would marry in this dress, too. It took my *anne* from the engagement to the wedding to make this dress."

"I understand, but it's a simple wedding, *Anne*. Yasar wants me to wear a suit." Adalet couldn't bring herself to tell her mother that Yasar's mother had already taken her shopping, picked out the suit, and they'd been to her seamstress for a fitting. The suit was smart, Belgin told her, when she'd accompanied Adalet and Mrs. Ozbek to the fitting. And Adalet, even before confessing to her mother that she could not wear the dress, something her mother had taken out and showed her, even modeled for her when it still fit when she was just a child, felt her stomach lurch as if she'd eaten pork.

But after Adalet's pronouncement, her mother hadn't uttered a word. She'd simply folded the dress back into the storage bag and hung it into its place in the back of her closet. Neither of them had made reference to the dress again, and the topic never came up between Adalet and her father. The dress had been one of the few items Adalet later rescued from the remains of her parents' house. And even though it was destroyed by smoke, Adalet kept it in the back of her closet. Who knew why some things survived and others didn't.

Adalet was surprised when the timer went off for the beans. She'd been daydreaming in the chair for an hour. She slowly lifted her legs from the ottoman and made her way back into the kitchen. Even though her legs still felt tired, Adalet was glad that she'd rested them. Cooking was an effort since her ordeal, so she had to do it in stages. Standing for any length of time was not possible. There were days when she called Hazan, the woman who sometimes came to help her clean, to go and bring her prepared food, but she preferred her own cooking when she could manage.

Now she hesitated before she lifted the heavy pot and poured the beans into a colander. Adalet wondered if she would ever be able to accomplish this sort of task without flinching. She left the beans in the sink to drain while she sautéed garlic, tomato paste, carrots and celery in a large pot with heated olive oil. After she added the beans, salt and pepper, potatoes and lemon juice to the pot, she let it simmer for fifteen minutes while she found a serving dish and sliced some lemon wedges. Adalet transferred the mixture to the serving dish to refrigerate for one hour. She then stretched out on the chair and ottoman with a glass of *raki*, ice and water, a habit she'd acquired with Yasar, and returned to her reverie.

Her parents had attended the wedding. Somehow it had felt more like a rebuke to Adalet than a show of love, even though she knew at some level that she was dead wrong about this. The wedding itself had been a short, civil ceremony followed by a much longer party at the Ozbeks' fashionably renovated Istanbul building. The building went back to Yasar's great, great-grandparents, and it seemed, according to them, that there was no more appropriate place to hold the celebration of the marriage of their only son.

But Adalet, who had attended the weddings of her village, was left in a state of confusion. She should have felt sophisticated and modern; instead she'd felt terribly cheated. Both she and the white suit, or so she'd been told, could have been on the cover of *Vogue*. She'd missed the satin and lace, and the whole affair had felt more legal than celebratory. Now she felt ashamed for her parents and relieved that no villagers had been invited to make the trip.

Her parents had not returned to Istanbul since the wedding, and Yasar had accompanied Adalet to visit her parents only twice. He'd been traveling quite a bit to evaluate various projects for his company and when he was at home, the last thing he'd wanted to do was to drive to Duzçe.

Once she'd married, Adalet had stopped seeing her friends from the university. They were still single and their lives were so different from hers. The women who were married to Yasar's friends were merely social acquaintances, not women she called on the phone to chat or to meet for lunch. When Yasar traveled, she would often go to Duzçe for a day or two. She would cook with her mother and often bring food back to Istanbul. But her mother would always broach the topic of pregnancy, and so there were times when this price was too high for Adalet.

The timer went off again, and Adalet rose to take the marinated food from the refrigerator. She removed the lid and garnished it with parsley and lemon wedges. When she'd made this dish with her mother, they had served it with grilled lamb. Sometimes neighbors had joined them, bringing breads and salads and sweet desserts.

CHAPTER 4

The last Bayram before her parents had been killed in the earthquake had been the first Bayram Adalet had neglected to spend with them. She'd been struggling with the news that she was pregnant, and looking back, Adalet felt guilty and selfish. Even if she hadn't been in the mood, she should have visited her parents.

On the afternoon of November 11, 1999, Adalet had driven the 228 kilometers east from Istanbul to Duzçe to visit her parents and to tell them she was pregnant. She'd been married to Yasar for two years now. Yasar Ozbek had stayed in Istanbul. He'd said he had meetings to attend on the architectural contract he'd recently been hired to oversee. And he did not yet know that Adalet was pregnant.

It wasn't that Yasar had ever said he didn't want children. It was more that he seemed to push it into some unknowable future whenever the subject was raised.

"We're so young. Let's have some fun first. Let me get more established." This he would say to Adalet. To his mother he would say, "Let me get more established."

"But you *are* established," his mother would insist.

"This is Turkey, Mother. The economy swings back and forth like a pendulum. We'll have children, just not right now."

Yasar's father never commented on such things, but his mother never stopped. And Belgin liked to think of herself as a modern Turkish woman. Her baby brother was already married and she had no one lined up as far as anyone else could observe. When she heard her mother inquiring as to when she'd become a grandmother, she'd laugh and tell her, "You'll never let yourself look like one anyway."

So after a couple of years, Adalet stopped using her diaphragm without mentioning it to Yasar. She convinced herself that she'd handle it when the time came, maybe tell him it had been an accident. Now she needed some advice from her parents, and she knew her mother, at least, would be happy. Her father would be far more critical of her deceit.

Adalet had arrived very late at night and awakened refreshed to the rhythmic sound of her mother's morning prayers. How long had it been since she'd joined her? Perhaps it was sometime during her second year at university, after she met Yasar and his friends. The sound of her mother reciting the *takbir*, "Allah is great," brought Adalet back to the purpose of her visit. For a moment she'd forgotten, but then it was there again, gnawing at her stomach, where she thought she could already feel the insistent murmur of that tiny heartbeat.

They spent the afternoon making spicy lamb filling and dough for *manti.* The part that Adalet loved most was watching her mother spoon filling into the little dough pockets and seal them so perfectly that they never broke or leaked when she boiled them. Adalet had not been able to develop this skill. Hers invariably exploded or came apart in the cooking.

After the dumplings were sealed, Adalet took out the large soup pot and filled it with water. She placed it on the stove and set the fire on high to bring it to a boil. As the water began to hiss, it occurred to Adalet that if she didn't come out with the news right then, she would leave Duzçe without telling her parents. This had already happened so many times with Yasar. The words pressed up against the edge of her tongue, and in the next moment, they completely dissolved. She forced herself to speak.

"*Anne,* I have something to tell you and *Baba,*"

"After we eat, we can talk."

"No, *Anne,* please, let's do it now." Adalet's mother sighed deeply. She didn't like to disturb her husband at his workbench until the food was ready. His relationship to the wood he turned into mass-produced furniture in the factory was nothing like the one he had with the wood in his workshop at home. Next to prayer, it was his most beloved practice. On the other hand, her time with Adalet was limited and ran on such a strictly timed clock. Preparing food together always brought them closer, and Adalet's mother didn't want to change the mood by refusing her daughter.

" Okay then. Watch the water. I'll go get him."

Adalet pulled a stool up to the stove. Her parents had often lamented the fact that they were both only children and therefore had no means of keeping her marriage within their family. They would be so happy that she would have a child, but how would this child share holidays with both families, with two sets of grandparents who were from such different walks of life. Maybe it would be good, she thought.

And then the stool she was sitting on in front of the stove began to tremble under her. She grabbed onto the stove to regain her balance, and saw the pot of boiling water rising to meet her. The tiles on the floor began to crack and split apart, and Adalet could not let go of the stove. When the bubbling and steaming water hit her face, all at once like a bolt of lightning, she immediately fell off the stool and onto the floor unconscious.

When Adalet was once again able to open her eyes, she couldn't remember the initial pain, thanks to Allah, but she still didn't know how she'd survived those first terrible nights and days. She was unconscious so much of the time, passing out whenever her burns were treated. A woman appeared in and out of the shadows of Adalet's brief waves of consciousness. And when she'd truly awakened, this same woman came to sit by her.

"Good, you're awake. I'm Daliah. I'm with the Israeli medical team. Do you remember what happened to you?"

Adalet couldn't remember anything consciously, but instinct prompted her to touch her face.

" No, dear, your face was not affected."

"I felt the water on my face. Yes, I remember that. It's the last thing I remember." Adalet continued to run her fingers over her cheeks, her eyes. Thank God she hadn't lost her sight. Thank God her face hadn't been burned.

"There was an earthquake," Daliah continued. You must have been cooking. They found a big empty pot near you. The hot water spilled on your legs and burned them. You had some minor cuts and bruises from the fall, but the house didn't collapse where you were. It collapsed everywhere else. The kitchen was the only room intact. The outside shed was destroyed. I'm afraid that your parents did not survive. It was actually the equipment and the stored wood inside that crushed them, probably instantly."

Adalet wanted to turn away to hide her face, but her legs were wrapped and elevated, her arms attached to needles. She was unable to move her body, but her fingers traced a line around her belly.

"It's all right, you'll be okay. You have some nasty third-degree burns on both legs, but you'll be able to walk. There will be scarring." Dalia's eyes followed Adalet's fingers. "There's one more thing I must tell you. I'm so sorry to say, you lost the baby. Maybe the fall, the shock of the burning."

Then Adalet remembered.

"Has my husband been here?"

"Yes. He wanted to move you to Istanbul immediately. We advised him that it wasn't a good idea just yet. We told him about the baby, and I'm afraid he was terribly upset."

"He didn't know I was pregnant."

"I see," Daliah said, although, of course, she couldn't have.

When Yasar came to move Adalet to the rehabilitation center in Istanbul, he was as polite as a stranger. It was a warm day, and Adalet was wearing a long, loose skirt and a short-sleeved blouse. She'd been lying on her bed waiting for Yasar and when he walked into the room, she swung her legs over the side of the bed, causing her skirt to lift above her knees.

"For heaven's sake, Adalet," he said in a low but forceful tone, "I don't want to see your legs. Hide them, please."

"I'm sorry, Yasar."

"I wouldn't think you'd want anyone to see those legs." He turned away from her in disgust.

Adalet went into her suitcase and pulled out a pair of pants. She took another glance at Yasar, noted his displeasure, and went into the bathroom to change from her skirt. She hid her tears from Yasar in there, sobbing silently into her hands.

When Adalet emerged from the bathroom, Yasar was speaking to Daliah about Adalet's aftercare. "Ah," Daliah said. "You've changed." Then she noted Adalet's teary eyes and quickly added. "You look so nice. Daliah helped Yasar to lift Adalet's legs into the car.

"Are you comfortable?" he asked.

"I'm okay," she said in a whisper. He seemed so distant.

Once they were on the highway, she said, "I'm so sorry, Yasar. I was going to tell you about the baby. You were gone so much. There didn't seem to be a right time."

"Did your parents know?"

"No." She didn't say that she'd never gotten the chance to tell them. If she hadn't been so impatient, perhaps her mother would have survived, still next to her in the kitchen.

Adalet knew she had crossed an irreversible line. She could hear her mother's voice in her head, warning her in the kitchen, if she'd only had the time to tell her. No, Adalet, you can't keep this from Yasar. You must tell him now.

Even though she knew it was too late, she turned to him, "We could try again."

"I'd rather not do this now," Yasar told her, looking straight ahead at the empty expanse of highway. They barely spoke during the rest of the drive.

*   *   *

The rehabilitation center was new and made its institutional attempt at being cheerful. The challenge was to keep Adalet free from infection and to begin the slow and painful process of skin grafting. She would also begin physical and occupational therapy, as much as she could tolerate.

Adalet refused to look at her legs since Yasar had turned his eyes away from them. He stopped by every few days to check on her, and then he started sending his mother in his place. He offered no explanation for his absence and Adalet didn't ask.

Adalet started to pray again. At first she cursed Allah for letting her live and killing her parents and her child. She wanted to curse Allah for the excruciating pain and suffering she had, if not for the fact that she began to believe it was a punishment she'd earned. The large doses of pain medication altered her sense of reality. Gradually, Adalet began to see the death of her child and her parents as God's just retribution for her desertion of Him. The pain and the scars were there to remind her. Sometimes she'd allow the morphine to take her back to her childhood, and she said prayers with her mother in opiate dreams.

When the doctors allowed her to go home, several months later, even though they told her she would have to return for further skin grafting, Adalet was not surprised by Yasar's reluctance to have her come back to live in the apartment with him.

"You know I work so many hours, and then I'm on the road too much. It won't be good for you to be there alone. I think you should stay with my parents. My mother can take better care of you." He stood staring at a photograph of the Sea of Mamara hanging on the wall of Adalet's room in the rehabilitation center.

Adalet almost protested. She wanted to go home after so many months. She longed for something familiar. But she heard the decisiveness in Yasar's tone. Things were not the same. And her own mother was not there to care for her. So she accepted and went to live in the Ozbek household.

The following eight months went by slowly and painfully for Adalet. All her activity revolved around her medical condition. She had never been one to sit around and do so little, even after she'd married Yasar. Although she hadn't had a real job, she'd consulted with parents of deaf children, visiting their homes and helping them to make educational and social decisions for their children.

When she'd left her parents and gone to school in Istanbul, and before she'd met Yasar, she'd thought of herself as independent and sophisticated. She'd paid her way through university by working as a liaison between families and their deaf children for the Yeditepe School for the Deaf. She'd majored in Education and Early Childhood Development and dreamed of being someone instrumental in making changes in a Turkey that she often felt moved backward as quickly as it moved forward. She never intended to work with the deaf, but she'd become intrigued with sign language, which had never been officially taught or even sanctioned in Turkey. The little she learned, she picked up from the children who practiced it among themselves. She hadn't been shocked to learn that a significant number of these deaf children had parents who were first cousins.

"Can you believe that these village idiots are still marrying their relatives?" The Head of Admissions had said this to her on her first day. Adalet was secretly offended. If she'd had any first cousins, she might herself have been one of those "village idiots."

Instead she was learning to walk again, in a strange home with well-meaning but somewhat indifferent in-laws. They did everything they were supposed to do, but only Yasar's sister's visits cheered her. Belgin made Adalet laugh, something no one else could do.

Yasar visited regularly. He also did what he was supposed to do. He paid her medical bills, asked her if there was anything she needed, and then if she did, he would assign the purchase of whatever small requests Adalet made to his sister or his mother.

And then when she was finally able to be on her own, Yasar told her that he wanted a divorce.

"Is it about the baby?" she asked him. "I'm not even sure why I couldn't tell you."

"Maybe you didn't trust me."

And even though this was true, Adalet could not admit it.

"You had reason not to trust me." Yasar looked her in the eye. "A few months before the earthquake, I started seeing Aysun. I don't love you anymore, Adalet."

Aysun was the final blow, a blow that sucked all her air away. Adalet wondered if Yasar had ever loved her, or if she'd been some kind of novelty that he'd grown tired of after the newness had worn off. So often she'd experienced twinges of jealousy when Aysun flirted openly with Yasar. She'd accused him on one occasion of being attracted to her. He'd laughed. "You're so beautiful and so silly. We've been friends for years. We were children together, and so we're familiar. Why would you even think something like that?"

She'd believed him then, but he was right to say that she didn't trust him. She hadn't told him about the baby because she was too afraid that he wouldn't want it. But she told him nothing of any of this. Instead she sat quietly, thinking back on the lonely ride to the rehab center, his silence and his disgust, the dusty barren road that had now led her to a dusty, barren future. Without her parents, without her husband, without anyone or anything at all. Her parents had left her no debt, but they'd been unable to afford insurance. A divorced woman in Turkey with no money and no one to help her.

That was when Yasar suggested that she take his family home in Avanos, and to be fair, he hadn't been obligated to offer her anything. Although she'd never seen the house in Avanos, Adalet decided she had little choice but to accept the offer. She had to wait for several more unpleasant months at the Ozbeks' before the rental lease on the house expired and the couple who were living there moved out. They had no desire to relocate, as they both led guided tours in Cappadocia, and bitter words were exchanged. She heard from Yasar's mother that they had to take a smaller, less well-maintained house not too far from Adalet. She had to wonder now if they might not be responsible for some of the mischief aimed at her.

Yasar and his family were generous. They gave her the house, a new car now fresh with graffiti, and a decent monthly allotment.

Combined with her medical disability, she was able to manage more than a simple life. But Adalet's legs had not healed well. There'd been complications due to scar tissue that left her in chronic pain.

And if she'd chosen to stay in Istanbul? Yasar's older sister, Belgin, had been the one to deliver her family's stipulation. She'd tapped lightly on the door of the guest room where Adalet had been staying.

"How are you feeling, little sister? I came by to see Mama and Papa, and I thought I'd look in on you as well." Belgin was a university professor of Literature married to a university professor of Mathematics. They were both political liberals and prideful Westerners. She addressed her parents as "mama" and "papa," not the traditional *anne* and *baba*. Certainly Adalet had noticed this before, but now it made her feel more than ever like a village peasant.

"I'm well enough, thank you."

"I'm so glad to hear it. You must be excited about the move then."

"I'm not sure I understand."

"To the house in Avanos."

"Your mother mentioned it to me, but nothing's been decided. There are tenants living there now. And I may want to stay in Istanbul."

"But how would you manage?"

"I could find a small apartment on my disability and the monthly stipend from Yasar. I might be able to work, I don't know."

"I guess Mama wasn't clear, or maybe she just assumed you'd agreed to move to Avanos."

"What do you mean?"

"They won't give you even one *lira* if you stay here."

Adalet knew she'd never make it on the government disability alone. She had nowhere to turn, and the unpredictable pain from her condition prevented her from telling them all what they could do with their house and their money and striking out on her own. Even the house was only hers as long as she continued to live in it. Selling it and moving back to Istanbul was not an option. Nothing was in Yasar's name, so there wasn't anything she could claim in the divorce. And even though some laws had changed, the courts were not sympathetic to women. In all fairness, she acknowledged, they could have left her with nothing.

And so Adalet started her new life in Avanos with two enemies and no friends.

CHAPTER 5

When Adalet walked through the pottery shop's open door and found Fatma sleeping in her chair exactly as she'd left her a couple of days earlier, she covered a giggle with her hand. Only the change of clothing indicated any movement on Fatma's part.

Adalet tiptoed backwards to the doorway where she stood quietly looking out on the early morning sky. Soft water color brush strokes of pink and orange wafted through puffy white clouds wandering slowly against the bluest of backdrops. A heavy blanket of heat would soon smother the cool morning breezes and stifle the smell of wet mud before it was hardened into clay. This was Adalet's most optimistic time of the day. The initial stiffness she suffered as she first got up from bed and began to move around had time to dissipate, and then she had until the full heat of the day, sometimes as late as four o'clock, before the weariness in her bones returned. A sharp, young voice interrupted Adalet's reverie.

"Can I help you with anything? We're not quite open yet, but that's okay."

Adalet turned to face a slender slip of a girl, she guessed anywhere from 14 to 17, hard to tell these days. Her features were sharp, a long sculpted nose set between large dark eyes that would have swallowed her cheekbones had they not been so prominent.

She wore an "I Love New York" t-shirt in a soft pink with black lettering over two small, firm breasts, and a pair of black flared shorts that emphasized her giraffe-like legs. Her thick dark brown hair was straggly at the ends, but pulled back in a high ponytail, the bottom of which reached her upper back. As she motioned Adalet back in the doorway, Adalet could see a black lace tattoo on her right wrist.

"Come on in," she said, and Adalet saw that what she'd thought was an ankle bracelet in the shape of a snake was another tattoo on her left ankle.

"Oh, thank you. I'm not shopping, though. I'm here to see Fatma."

The girl looked over at the sleeping woman.

"My grandmother? My *anneanne* sleeps so much more now than I remember. Would you like to wait? I can bring you some apple tea or black tea. I don't like the apple much, but *Anneanne* says the tourists all love it."

Adalet smiled. "You're her granddaughter. I didn't know. Yes, I'll join you in a cup of black tea. It's true what she says. The tourists all think we drink apple tea. It's okay, but I prefer the black."

"I'm Meryem. I'm here for a visit." She held out her right hand, the one with the lacy tattoo.

"Hi Meryem. I'm Adalet. I come to read to your grandmother."

"Oh yes," her wide eyes crinkling into a smile that made her less statuesque and almost pretty. My *anneanne* told me you'd be coming. Come back here to our little kitchen so we don't wake her."

Adalet followed Meryem back through the beaded curtain that separated the shop from the workroom and facilities to a small but full kitchen also sectioned off from the rest of the work area by a beaded curtain. Fatma's two sons, Ahmet and Bekir were too busy working and supervising their four employees to notice them passing through the little corridor that lead to the kitchen area. Fingerprint splotches of mud spatter on the walls in the corridor indicated that hands were not always washed so well on the workers' bathroom breaks. Adalet could detect a slightly bitter odor from the ever-churning kiln.

Water had already been poured into a large brass kettle and was sitting on a single gas burner. Meryem lit the burner and motioned Adalet to take a seat at the small, round tiled ceramic table that could only fit three chairs. The pattern of the tiles was a large peacock assembled by an intricate pattern of tiny tiles on a background of mostly sky and a patch of green.

"I haven't been back here before." Adalet ran her fingers over the tiles. "This table is beautiful."

"*Anneanne* brought it back from Italy, and she's promised it to me when she dies. My *anne* has been gone for two years now, or she would have left it to her."

"I'm sorry. I don't think I knew Fatma had a daughter."

Meryem set two cups and saucers on the table. She arranged some biscuits on a small plate and filled the *çaydanlik* she removed from a shelf just over the tiny sink. The biscuits smelled of freshly squeezed lemons. Meryem didn't respond to Adalet's comment.

"Oh, I can't eat anything until later this evening," Adalet pointed to the biscuits. "Ramadan."

"That's okay, I was just setting them out to cool. I just made them this morning."

"So when did you arrive?" Adalet was concerned that Meryem's mother might not be a safe topic.

"A few months ago." This unannounced visit surprised Adalet.

"Fatma didn't tell me you were here."

"She wouldn't."

They were both silent while Meryem poured hot water into their cups and placed the teapot back on the burner. She sat down across from Adalet with a grace that belied a 14 year-old child. Adalet recalculated her to be older than first appearances. They both sipped from their tea. Adalet wanted to pick up a biscuit. She imagined something lemony and thick, with a bitter taste of rind to offset the sweetness, and she had to wonder if Meryem had really only set them there to cool or that she didn't observe Ramadan.

The girl and the young woman sat quietly sipping tea. Adalet waited for Meryem to speak again, but she remained silent. Adalet was trying again to guess at her age when Fatma's older son leaned through the beaded curtain.

"My mother is awake now," he said. "She's ready to see you any time. Finish your tea."

"I will," Adalet told him. She didn't consider that she had to jump up from her chair and run immediately to Fatma. She was curious about Meryem, and she didn't consider herself to be an employee of the Celik household, even though she was sometimes addressed as if she were. These were old-world villagers who had most likely never lived anywhere but Avanos, and may have never even traveled as far as Ankara, the nearest large city to the region of Cappadocia, of which Avanos was a part. And even though it seemed that Fatma had made it to Italy, if she had indeed brought the table back, it was more than likely that she had stayed with relatives in another village much like Avanos.

"So you're just visiting your grandmother?" Adalet asked.

"Sort of, yes." Again she offered nothing further and Adalet decided not to ask. She finished her tea and thanked Meryem; then Adalet rose from her chair.

"I'll see if your grandmother would like me to read to her now. It's nice to meet you. I hope I'll see you again."

"I hope so, too," Meryem did not stand up or give any inkling that seeing her again might even be a possibility, but after Adalet got up, Meryem shifted the plate of biscuits to the counter next to the stove. She hadn't eaten any herself.

Fatma was clearly waiting for Adalet. She had a popular magazine in her lap.

"A customer left this here," she said. "It might have something interesting in it. There's a story about a woman being stoned to death near the Iranian border."

Adalet was used to Fatma's lack of small talk or even formal greetings. She knew from experience that if she suggested anything else, it would be ignored. Fatma had already asked someone to read her the contents of the magazine, and she'd decided that the stoning incident was the most tantalizing. Adalet took the magazine from her arthritic hand and sat down in the wooden chair that Fatma now kept close to her own for just such occasions.

"I didn't know you had a granddaughter," Adalet said. "She says she's been here for a while, but this is the first time I've seen her."

"She came here by herself for a visit. Stays with my sons' wives and helps them around the house. She'll help me in the shop. We keep her close by."

Adalet thought, No chance of her ending up stoned to death.

"How old is Meryem?"

"She just had her 17th birthday not too long ago. Please, read to me. I haven't seen you in days." Adalet chose not to refute this since it had actually been two days. Since she no longer had parents or grandparents, she took some pleasure in making Fatma's days more enjoyable. She regretted being what she considered selfish with her own family, once Yasar had entered the picture, and so she sought some retribution through Fatma. Adalet began to read:

Wednesday, June 12, 2002, Yaylim, Turkey. It was a long and terrible day for the Dal family. Asli Dal, aged 17, pregnant and found guilty of adultery, was stoned to death on Monday, June 10, 2002. Her lover and the father of her child, Burak Kaya, was also found guilty of adultery and was hanged until dead on Tuesday, June 11, 2002. As Turkey increases efforts to join the EU, these honor killings are questioned but not yet outlawed. Pressure continues to accelerate to introduce legislation that would prevent shariah law.

"What are you reading, *Anneanne*? Do you think this might be my future?"

Fatma's unseeing eyes turned to the angry voice in the doorway where Meryem was now standing.

"If you keep on behaving so that your father has to send you here to have us watch after you, I don't know what might be in your future. That is for you to decide. And this is not a discussion we need to have outside of the family."

"So why are you having her read this to you when you know I'm in the next room?"

"It's my reading time, not yours. It's not for you to be standing in the doorway listening to us. I didn't invite you. Go away."

Adalet squirmed in her chair. She was uncomfortable being in the midst of this family drama. Fatma did not turn her sightless gaze from her granddaughter's face and Meryem didn't move. Adalet started to close the magazine and rise from her chair.

"Perhaps I should come back another time."

"No," Fatma demanded. "Sit. Okay, then, Meryem, stand there. Hear what you must hear. Maybe it will knock some sense into that stubborn head of yours. Go on, Adalet. Read."

"Yes, read on, Adalet. I want to listen." The slender figure made her way completely through the beads and into the room.

Adalet sat back in the chair, clutching the magazine with both hands.

"There's really not much more," she said. "It just talks about Europeans not liking these killings and it being one of the things that keeps Turkey out of the EU. That's all. There's no more about the family. I didn't even think stoning happened here anymore. I thought it was ancient history."

"Well, we can be grateful for that, at least," Meryem clenched her teeth.

"Don't be so quick, child. Clearly they do happen. They don't happen here in Avanos, but the farther east one goes, the more ignorant the villagers. It could happen in your father's village." Fatma leaned back and turned her blind eyes to Adalet.

"I've never heard of anyone being stoned there, *Anneanne*. Those are old wives' tales to frighten young girls like me. They do that in Iran."

"Don't be naïve, child. You'd do well to be frightened. I won't even say why you're here."

"Oh, come on, *Anneanne*, we were just holding hands. I didn't even kiss him."

"Allah, keep me patient. This girl speaks of things she shouldn't even know."

Adalet rose. She laid the magazine by her chair. "I really must come back tomorrow," she said. "It's getting late."

"Just tell me," Fatma said, "do young girls hold hands in Istanbul? Especially when they're already promised in marriage?"

"I don't know anyone promised in marriage in Istanbul, I must be honest. In my village there were, but my parents didn't choose a husband for me. I chose for myself."

"You see," Fatma uncannily pointed her finger at Meryem. "And that didn't work out so well, did it?"

"I'll see you tomorrow, Fatma. I'm going now." Good-bye, Meryem. See you again, I hope."

"*Maşallah*," Meryem said.

"*Maşallah*," Adalet repeated. She thought to herself, as she made her way to her Fiat, how odd her country could be. Here was a young girl trying to be so modern, and yet she used such an old term of respect to say good-bye. Adalet loved her country deeply, but the time she'd spent in Istanbul had irrevocably opened her eyes. She knew that some barbaric practices that kept Turkey from coming into its own were forging their way into existence again with the surge of fundamentalism that was sweeping the politics of the country. She often thought Ataturk would turn over in his grave if he saw the women covering their faces again in the bazaar in Istanbul. Who could have imagined it would ever be that way again?

Adalet backed out of the small driveway slowly. As she started to turn around, Meryem came running out of the door, heading towards the driver's side and Adalet's open window. She had a paper bag in her hand.

"Adalet," she called. "Wait."

Adalet put her foot on the clutch and braked.

"Meryem, what is it?"

"Here, some biscuits for later." She thrust the paper bag at Adalet through the window.

Before Adalet could thank her or place them on the passenger seat, Meryem spoke again. "Please have tea with me tomorrow.

Come early again. I want to talk to you." The pleading look on her face flashed a warning to Adalet.

"I won't get in the middle of you and your grandmother," she said.

"No, no. I wouldn't ask that of you. I just want to talk. I never met anyone who lived in Istanbul. I have so many questions for you."

Adalet hesitated. She felt stuck in this village and certainly didn't want to antagonize Fatma, of all people. She knew everyone in town. But Adalet couldn't ignore the girl's sense of need either. Adalet knew only too well what it felt like to be alone.

"Okay," she said. "But keep in mind what I've told you. And make sure it's okay with your grandmother."

Meryem sighed. "Thank you, Adalet. I will make sure she doesn't object."

Adalet gave the car some gas and slowly released the clutch.

"Then I'll see you tomorrow," she said as she pulled away.

CHAPTER 6

Bayram would be here tomorrow and Ramadan would end this evening, and so when Adalet got home, she sorted her packages of sweets, wrapped them together in colored paper and tied each of these larger packages together with a ribbon. Through all of this, she was unable to check her racing thoughts about Meryem.

There were other teenagers in Avanos, of course. Adalet had run into them here and there, as she had at her car the other day after shopping, but she didn't know any personally. There was no one Meryem's age to whom Adalet could introduce her. Her neighbors either had young children or were elderly and their children had gone to the bigger cities a long time ago.

Did Meryem even fast for Ramadan? Adalet had no idea. She knew Fatma did, and so she suspected that Meryem would while in Fatma's home. Now in the cities, people often went to cafés and ate during Ramadan. Even here in Avanos it happened, but people tried to go where their neighbors wouldn't see them. Adalet drank tea and water, but she still fasted until sundown, and it hadn't been sundown when Meryem served her biscuits.

In Adalet's childhood village, no one would have risked being seen in a café during this holy time. She wondered if the standards had been lowered there, too. As modern as Yasar's family was, they had always observed Ramadan. Adalet wondered if Yasar and Aysun would be celebrating Bayram with his family this year. Aysun certainly fit in with modern Turkey and Yasar's family better than she ever had. Like Yasar, she'd grown up in Istanbul in a similar kind of complex of relatives all occupying a large building split up into apartments to accommodate each immediate family.

But quickly her thoughts darted back to Meryem. Why did Meryem's request for Adalet to come for tea feel so urgent? And why tomorrow? She would simply have to put it out of her mind and wait.

Adalet was just about to go into her kitchen to heat up some dinner she'd saved from the night before when she heard a funny noise outside. It almost sounded like a baby crying, but it was something wild, she thought, not human. Whatever it was, it seemed to be in her front courtyard. How had it managed to get in through the wooden gate or over the stone wall? She crept quietly to her front door and eased it open slowly, just a crack. She could see nothing from her angle of view, so she stepped lightly into the courtyard and looked around.

Adalet stood there waiting, and there it was again, emanating from bushes pushing out against the courtyard wall. She crouched down and finally could make out something rolled up in a ball, hard to distinguish from the reddish-brown shadows of the bushes shifting in the evening breeze. The ball unfolded slightly, and a tiny head emerged, making small whining noises. It raised its head in a stretching movement, revealing four spindly legs rising onto four wet, scrawny paws.

"How did you get in here?" Adalet asked, reaching into the bush with one hand to let it smell her fingers. "You must belong to somebody. I'm going to get you some milk; then we'll see what we do with you."

Cats wandered loose everywhere in Avanos, but this was the first to venture inside this enclosure in Adalet's time. She poured a bit of milk into a small bowl, thinking that even this size was probably too large for it. When she came outside again, the kitten was still hidden in the bushes. She set the bowl on the ground and called to it. "Come little baby, I have something sweet for you." Nothing happened, and Adalet put the bowl in the bushes. After a couple of seconds, she peeked in and saw that she was right. The bowl was too large.

Adalet went back into the house, opened her medicine drawer, and found an eyedropper. The kitten had tried to stick a paw into the bowl and had knocked it over, but still some remained. Adalet rescued the bowl and filled the eyedropper with milk. She reached into the bush and grabbed the kitten by the scruff of its neck. She smiled to see that it was most likely a girl, she couldn't be sure. She rested the kitten in her lap, still holding onto her, and stuck the tip of the dropper in her slightly opened mouth. At first, she didn't seem to know how to suck, but then after Adalet squeezed a few drops into her mouth, she began to get the hang of it. Adalet stroked her belly and whispered, "We're going to have to find your home, silly girl. You left your *anne* too soon." Fatma might know whose cat had just had kittens, and Fatma might also be able to verify the kitten's sex.

Adalet carried the kitten inside and found a shawl to wrap around her. It was one she had made during her marriage to Yasar while he was away on a lengthy work trip. The shawl was a deep wine and pink and as soft to the touch as this kitten who fell asleep immediately and would not wake until morning.

Adalet threw yesterday's leftovers into a pan and reheated them on the stovetop. All the crouching for the kitten had strained her legs, and she thought she might need a pain pill. She thought more and poured herself a shot of *raki* instead. Day-old food always tasted better to her than it did right after it was cooked. She liked to allow the food time to soak up the sauces and seasonings. Adalet tended to undercook her vegetables initially so that they wouldn't be soft when warmed.

After she finished her dinner, Adalet put the remaining food away and looked at the kitten. She would bring her along to Fatma's in the morning. The kitten had climbed into the shawl just before falling asleep and only her head peeked out from the layers of loosely knitted wool. Adalet lifted up the shawl and kitten from the rocking chair where she'd set it down and cautiously slid into its seat, placing the bundle on her lap. The kitten seemed content even though she'd had so little to eat. The shawl could be washed, Adalet thought. It was too late to find a box or kitty litter. In any event, she was so tiny and drank so little that it couldn't matter.

Adalet shut her eyes and rocked slowly back and forth, humming a melody that her *anne* sang to her as an infant and young child. She wondered about what her baby would have been like; a boy or a girl, it didn't matter to her. Yes, she realized suddenly, it did. She remembered her delight when she thought the kitten might be female. Yes, she felt it deeply, humming quietly to the tiny life she had with her now; yes, she would have wanted a girl.

Meryem immediately came to mind. Adalet found it somewhat ironic that Meryem had said she'd never met anyone from Istanbul before. Living in Istanbul certainly didn't make her Aysun. She stopped rocking and humming: Aysun. She was like a Turkish Marilyn Monroe, blonde and full-figured. Adalet felt like a child standing beside her. Heads turned to stare at her always, assuming her to be a foreigner. In one of those rare times that Adalet had been alone in a restaurant eating lunch with Aysun while Yasar was away, some Turkish men spoke to Aysun provocatively and laughed amongst themselves, until Aysun had shocked the hell out of them by telling them off in perfect Turkish. They'd apologized, said they hadn't realized she was a Turkish woman, but she hadn't let go. Why, she'd wanted to know, did they think they had the right to be disrespectful to any woman?

Aysun most definitely leaned towards the European side of the Bosphorus, the river that runs through Istanbul and separates the Asian side of Turkey from the European. She'd majored in Western Literature and knew many of the modern, as well as classical, books and films. Her family was well connected and lived not too far from Orhan Pamuk's family home. The parents knew each other socially. It was most likely an Aysun that Meryem was hoping for, and Adalet was concerned that she would disappoint her.

She stood and carried the kitten-filled shawl to her bedroom. She laid it down on the carpet next to the end of her bed. She took off her clothing, threw on her sleep shirt and laid down. What kind of mother would she have been? Her own mother was kind and loving but ignorant with regard to the world around her. Adalet knew that her father had loved her dearly, but he had distanced himself once she'd reached puberty. In many ways, he was also ignorant to the larger life percolating outside his village.

Adalet remembered vividly the terror and disgust she had experienced when she'd gone to the bathroom at school and found her underwear soaked in blood. She was quite alone in the restroom, so she'd gone to the sink and rinsed her panties out, but the blood kept coming. She'd gone back into the toilet cubicle and squatted there until her teacher had come to find out what was wrong. The teacher had helped her to clean up and had sent her home to her mother.

"*Anne, Anne,* what's wrong with me? I'm bleeding down there." Adalet had rushed into the house, confronting her mother. "My teacher said this is supposed to happen. Is that right? I'm so scared."

"Yes, your teacher is right. You bleed so you can have a baby. No, not now. When you're all grown up. The bleeding comes now, but the baby comes later."

"How does the baby come later, *Anne*?"

"When you're older. But now you must stay away from boys." Her mother had shown her what to do but had not continued the conversation. Adalet had asked an older girl at school who also appeared to need more time in the bathroom. She was too shocked by the responses to ever talk to her mother about any of them. It took some time before she could accept that what this girl had told her was true.

Adalet would tell her parents about what was going on in Istanbul when she visited, but they rarely had much to say. She never knew if she was telling them things they hadn't heard or that they weren't particularly interested. Changes in government, social issues, the flux of villagers into the larger cities, what she was studying; none of this elicited much comment. Her mother would shift the conversation to neighbors and what their children were doing, as if Adalet was still seeing them every day. Her father would say something like, I watch the news but I don't have time to read the paper, and then turn his head away. If he had any opinions, he was unable to articulate them. Perhaps he had felt the same shame that Adalet always felt around Aysun. Funny how Aysun knew much more about literature and film than Yasar, but Yasar took what he didn't know in stride. It never made him feel stupid or embarrassed or even afraid to ask Aysun what she was talking about. Adalet thought that she shouldn't have those feelings, but she could never seem to rid herself of them.

Adalet knew that as large as Istanbul was, Yasar's family didn't want her anywhere near where they could be reminded of his mistake. They had treated her kindly but with distance. They'd never accepted her, and so the family home in Avanos had been the perfect solution for them. Maybe she should be grateful that they hadn't thrown her out the door and just forgotten her. Would she have been a mother like her own or more like Yasar's? She looked over the bed at the kitten and thought, I'd like to think I'd be like my mother, but there's a sad part of me that isn't so sure.

CHAPTER 7

A skeletal wisp of sunlight sleepwalking across her face announced to Adalet that it was probably past the time she was expected for tea with Meryem, but when she checked the hour on her bedside alarm, she was relieved to see that it was still early. The weight of the warmth on her bedspread meant that it was likely to become an uncomfortably hot day.

Adalet spotted the empty shawl bunched at the bottom of the bed and remembered the kitty. She picked up the shawl with her fingers, surprised to find it dry. She crouched on her knees and peered under the bed where the kitten had at some point left a puddle that had partially dried but no trail as to where she might be. Adalet glanced into the bathroom on her way to the kitchen and spied the kitten crouching behind the toilet bowl and next to the wall. She went on to the kitchen and retrieved a small saucer where she poured a bit of milk. She brought it to the bathroom and set it down a foot away from the kitty.

"Come out, little one. Have a drink. I'll feed you some of my cereal, and then we'll go to visit Meryem and Fatma. But first we must eat and I have to shower and dress." Now that Ramadam had ended, it was important to eat a healthy breakfast.

While stirring her oatmeal over the stovetop, Adalet thought how natural it seemed to be talking to a cat in such a way. As if the cat could understand Turkish. It had been quite a long time, it felt to Adalet, since she'd had any living entity to speak to besides herself.

When she returned to the bathroom, the kitty had drunk most of the milk and curled up near the saucer. Adalet picked up the saucer with one hand and the kitty with the other. She stopped for a moment to shift her into the crook of her arm. "There you go, little baby, let's get some food." She placed some of the oatmeal into the saucer and the rest into a large bowl for herself. Adalet touched the oatmeal with her finger to make sure it wasn't too hot. She opened the door into the courtyard and set the dish next to her outside table and chair. The kitten sniffed, backed away, and gradually approached the dish again. She stuck her nose into the food, jumped back, and then made her next reconnoiter to the saucer. This time her tiny teeth went in and she flung a bite into her mouth which now looked like the largest part of her. She swallowed quickly, thought about it, and began to eat. Only then did Adalet sit and eat her cereal, once she made a quick run back indoors for a handful of dried fruit and nuts to sprinkle on top. It was only 9:00am and already hot.

After a quick shower, Adalet dressed, picked a few flowers from the garden, and made her way to the Fiat with the kitten once again in the shawl. She stopped in town for a box and some litter before parking on the street in front of the old wooden painted sign that read Celik Family Pottery in vivid blue Turkish lettering with English spelling beneath. It was just July and the pavements were cooking, but they would soon be packed with tourist groups, and even Fatma would be too busy for Adalet to read to her. Fatma's job was to play the part of the old Turkish village woman, inviting customers for apple tea and chatting lightly with them in broken English until they felt obligated to purchase something, anything. The Celik family was proud of their work and hardly viewed this with cynicism. They were doing the silly tourists a favor. If they let them go, they would only buy something elsewhere and the workmanship would not be as good. And it might even be more expensive. They saw it as their duty. They would barter on prices, but if the tourist crossed the line below what the brothers found acceptable, some words would be spoken softly between them in Turkish, and then the product would be placed back on the shelf. The customer could then leave in disgrace or apologize and offer a few more dollars than the lowest price originally accepted. The brothers never cursed or raised their voices. "This is first class," they told their visitors, "good enough for the sultan," and it was.

Fatma was not to be seen in the store, but Adalet heard voices coming from behind the wall that led to the tiny corridor separating the workplace from the display front. And then she heard Meryem call her name, "Adalet, come. We're back in the kitchen making the tea."

When Adalet came in, Meryem was making the tea and Fatma was seated at the table. She did not smile at Adalet, or even nod to her. She patted an empty chair next to her. Adalet started to sit but remembered she'd left the kitten in the car.

"Ayyyyyai," she muttered, "I'll be right back. I left something in the car."

The kitten was waiting patiently on the passenger seat, still curled within the shawl. Adalet was relieved that she'd remembered. The heat being what it was today, she could have perished. Yes, surely, what kind of mother would she make?

Back in the kitchenette, she placed the shawl and kitten on the table.

"What is this?" Fatma leaned in more closely and surprised Adalet by softly caressing the kitten's face with her fingers.

"She showed up in my courtyard last night. At least I think she's a she. I found her crying under a bush." Meryem turned away from the tea she was brewing. She stepped away from the kettle and came over to the table to see. "Oh, what a tiny little thing." The pleasure from Fatma's fingers caused the kitten to roll onto her back where her sex was not so easily identifiable, at least to Fatma.

After gazing at the kitten's sex for a few minutes, Fatma agreed. "I think she's a she, too, and she's older than she looks. I'd say somewhere between six and eight weeks. She just hasn't had enough food to grow."

"Do you know where she might have come from?" Adalet asked.

"Ach, you grew up in a village. How many cats did you have wandering around?"

"It was smaller and no foreigners—not like Avanos," Adalet said. "We often could find the mother of lost kittens. Not always."

"Here it is impossible," Fatma scrunched her lips together in disgust. "They don't take care of the cats, let them roam everywhere, and then they show up pregnant after they've done who knows what in the spring." She continued to stroke the kitten but suddenly spoke sharply to Meryem. "See that it doesn't happen to you. No one has room for your kitten."

Adalet misunderstood the last comment to be directed at her. "I'm so sorry, Fatma. I didn't bring her here expecting you to keep her."

Meryem grimaced, rolled her eyes and said, "She wasn't speaking to you, Adalet. Her warning was meant for me."

"Oh," Adalet sputtered under her breath. She wondered why Fatma seemed to be crashing her morning tea with Meryem, and now they seemed to be entering territory she'd quite deliberately abandoned yesterday.

"Don't worry," Meryem raised one eyebrow, "my anneanne has promised not to upset you. She's here to lay down the rules of our conversations and our friendship, if we are to have one, correct, Anneanne?"

"She is like many young girls today, Adalet," Fatma drew her fingers away from the kitten. "She thinks she knows more than all of us who have lived so much longer. I am hopeful from your behavior with me that you are not like her. I think you have been raised well and that you're in your present circumstances through no fault of your own. Is that true?"

Adalet stared at the kitten, now rolling around on its own as Meryem began to pour the tea and Fatma had more serious issues on her mind. "I don't think, Fatma, that it can be through no fault of my own. None of us are in our circumstances through no fault of our own—except perhaps this kitten."

"Ah, a good answer," Fatma exclaimed. "I hoped you were not a complainer who just hadn't begun to complain yet. I haven't known you for so long. You could be one of those who blame the world for your misfortune, and I would never want my Meryem to spend time with someone like that. Not a stupid, ignorant person. Do you have a litter box for this cat, by the way?"

"Yes, it's in the car," Adalet responded.

"Go get it, Meryem. I think this one doesn't know how to use the bathroom."

Adalet could sense that Meryem was about to protest, but then she changed her mind. "Is the car locked?" she asked.

"No," Adalet said. "But please do lock it now. I forgot."

"Sure," Meryem's voice took on a slight edge, "You seem to be forgetting a lot today." And she was gone. Adalet's eyes gazed at a pattern of the floor tile, as she began to trace it with her foot.

"Don't mind her," Fatma said. "She's not a bad girl."

"I didn't think she was." Adalet rose and began to pour the brewing tea into the cups Meryem had set next to the stove, as she sometimes did when she visited Fatma.

"Meryem says I must give my permission for the two of you to meet and talk? Did you tell her that?"

Adalet thought for a minute. "Yes."

"Why?" Fatma drummed two fingers on the slightly shaky table.

"Because she's your granddaughter and it seemed the respectful thing to do." She placed one of the cups of tea in front of Fatma and removed the shawl and kitten from the table, setting them underneath.

"Do people in Istanbul think about what is the respectful thing to do?" She nodded thanks to Adalet for pouring the tea.

Adalet poured the other two cups, arranged them on the table, and sat back down.

"Some of them do," she answered. "Istanbul isn't Sodom or Gomorrah. There are still people there who honor their elders and have respect for others."

Fatma made an unpleasant sound as she slurped her tea.

Meryem came into the room with the box and the litter. "Here you go," she said. She spotted the tea on the table. "Thank you, Adalet. I'll just fill the box for the kitten and then join you. Oh, look, she's right here." Fatma stared at Adalet while Meryem opened the litter and filled the box, placed the kitten inside, and set the box in the corner. She threw the shawl over the back of Adalet's chair, then felt it before she sat down. "I can't believe you had her on that beautiful shawl," Meryem said, taking her first sip of tea. "She's a smart little kitty. She didn't soil it at all."

"There's a puddle waiting for me under my bed," Adalet smiled, realizing she'd forgotten about that as well. "I made that shawl some time ago, when I was married and living in Istanbul. I have several. Would you like to have it?" Adalet couldn't help but be moved by how lovely the bright pinks of the shawl would look against Meryem's sun-baked skin and wine-streaked black hair.

Meryem looked at Fatma, and Fatma shook her head. "Take the shawl and she'll leave the cat in it, too. It's up to you, if you like it. The cat can live in the shop. We don't want to leave her with someone who forgets her in the car."

Adalet knew that Fatma was teasing her, but her words still cut beneath her skin. Even though she felt some relief—perhaps she wasn't capable of caring for a living thing—she had enjoyed her brief conversations with kitty. "Thank you, Fatma," she managed.

"But kitty can't have the shawl anymore." Meryem rose, yanked the shawl from the back of the chair, swirled it around her shoulders while peeking into a small mosaic mirror attached to the wall. Observing the look on Fatma's face, she removed the shawl, sat back down and placed it in her lap. "Thank you, Adalet, but only if you're sure."

"I'm very sure. If you come to visit me at my house, you'll see that I have more of them."

"Will I be allowed to visit Adalet at her home, Anneanne?" Meryem asked.

"We'll see. It will have to be before the tourists come. I'll need your help to serve them tea. It's not so easy for me anymore." Fatma shifted her rather large bottom in her chair and winced.

"We can all help," Adalet offered. "But perhaps you can come before then. I can drive you both and take you back."

Fatma shook her head. "If you promise not to leave her in the car, you can take her. I'm too old for these things. Just don't forget to come to read to me."

"I promise I won't forget, Fatma." Adalet wished that Fatma had not mentioned the car again, but she kept it to herself. She knew she'd come far with Fatma today and she didn't want to say or do anything to spoil it.

When it was time for Adalet to leave, Meryem walked her to her car.

"Why didn't you ever paint it?" Meryem asked, as Adalet settled down behind the wheel of her Fiat.

"I don't know. First the red was wrong, and then I just got used to it. It's actually pretty good work."

"Do you think so?" The eagerness in Meryem's voice alerted Adalet. "Can you find the tag?" Meryem asked.

"The tag?"

"Your car was painted by a graffiti artist." Adalet got back out of the car, walked around it, trying to find anything that might be a signature.

"No, I don't see it," she had to admit. "Do you?"

"Yes, it's here, just between the deeper blue and the almost white blue and beneath both. Here." Meryem pointed her index finger to a spot along the driver's door.

"Oh, I do see something there. It almost looks like a star and crescent moon—but not quite." Adalet squatted and inspected the tag more closely. "Yes, that's what it looks like to me."

"That's exactly what it is," Meryem stood smiling and Adalet raised herself into a standing position facing Meryem.

"That's your tag, isn't it?" Adalet was not smiling.

"Yes. It's mine. I wanted to tell you, but I was afraid."

"Promise me you'll switch to paper and canvas. It's much safer. And I won't tell your grandmother."

"Anneanne already knows," Meryem looked directly into Adalet's eyes, and they both burst into laughter.

CHAPTER 8

August simmered its way into September. Avanos was now teeming with tourists who had only been trickling into Avanos in the dead heat of summer. September and October were most likely to be busy months in the pottery shop.

Meryem had begun to sometimes occupy a room in Adalet's home which had rapidly become her studio. Fatma's desire to keep her niece occupied and Adalet's private wish to see her develop her art had opened an opportunity for Meryem in Avanos that she could never have anticipated. Fatma had reluctantly agreed to cover expenses for art supplies.

"If she doesn't have them," Adalet argued, "she'll end up painting walls or another car. It would be best if she could have a place of her own to create."

"There's no room here," Fatma complained.

"I have a guest room," Adalet had offered. "It's not like I have any guests. She can come and go as she likes and stay overnight when she's here late."

"You think you can handle her." This was a statement, never a question.

"How can I know?" Adalet responded with care. "If there are problems, I will come to you."

"Do you think you'll be able to know if there are problems?" Fatma was serious.

"She won't be living with me." Adalet thought hard before she spoke. "You'll be seeing her almost every day at the shop. I'm sure you'll know more than I if there's a problem." The kitten, now named Yetim (orphan) by Fatma, traveled back and forth between the shop and Adalet's with Meryem.

And then one afternoon while Adalet was reading to Fatma and the shop was empty, Fatma abruptly interrupted her. "I'm arranging a marriage for Meryem, you know. She has no mother and an absent father. I want her safely married as soon as I can find someone suitable."

Adalet was quiet. She knew that the next words she uttered stood to revoke every aspect of Fatma's trust in her. She was willing to concede to Fatma, but not without making her aware that life might hold other options for Meryem.

"That is, of course, between you and Meryem," Adalet said. "But you must know that she has an unusual talent."

"I don't know anything about that," Fatma nibbled on leftover Bayram candies that various friends and neighbors had brought her during the closing festivities of the Ramadan fast. She offered the tray to Adalet who shook her head.

"No, thank you."

Fatma set the tray back on the table. "You think painting on your car is talent?"

Adalet looked up from the page she'd been reading to Fatma before this conversation had begun. "I'm not sure, Fatma, but I couldn't wash it off. I'm no artist, but I knew it was special."

"If Temel had found the right color, you would have painted it." Fatma sank her teeth into the chewy nougat of a Turkish delight.

Adalet caught the essence of rosewater. "Maybe, and then again, maybe not. I wonder if I didn't want him to find the right color, now that I think about it."

"Hindsight!" Fatma spat out some candy dribbles in her disgust. "Did you think I wouldn't know who'd done it? I know what

Meryem does. She's been trained like a parrot and tells me everything. She wants me to know how clever she thinks she is."

"You love her very much, don't you?" Adalet closed the magazine and sat back in her chair.

"Of course I do. She is my only daughter's child."

"Do your sons have children?"

"Babies, one each, both boys. I had my daughter, Pinar, for seven years before I had another child."

"Does Meryem look like her mother?"

"She's a little like her mother and a little like her father. Personality is more like her mother. She knew everything, too." Fatma shifted her feet on the stool and leaned back in her chair. "Always too smart to listen to me."

A harsh question detonated in Adalet's mind. What if her mother had lived and Adalet had died? Would her mother be sitting and telling someone how Adalet had refused to wear her wedding dress; that Adalet found her mother-in-law's selection of a suit more appropriate? Would Adalet's mother say that she was too smart to listen?

Adalet's finger fiddled with the handle of her teacup. She wanted to ask how Meryem's mother had died, but Adalet was still a bit afraid of Fatma. And what if Meryem's mother had come to some terrible ending because she hadn't listened to Fatma? Adalet's parents had always taught her not to ask personal questions, "People will tell you what they want you to know," her mother would respond to Adalet's childishly prying questions about the various adults in their lives. Her father would say, "That is not our business." Now Adalet sat back and waited for Fatma to either beckon to her to read or continue to speak.

"One of these days I'll try to remember to bring you a picture."

"I'd like that," Adalet said.

"Now read more," Fatma broke the mood, "I want to know what this stupid fellow is going to say next. Idiot!" Fatma was referring to an extremist leader in the current government in Istanbul. As conservative as Fatma could seem, she loved Ataturk, and she didn't like to hear about anyone attempting even one step backward, except perhaps, when it came to her granddaughter.

Adalet picked up the paper and began to read, even though she realized she'd made no headway with Fatma. Adalet's lips moved and sounds came out, but her thoughts were elsewhere. As backward as her parents had been, they had wanted her to have an education, something neither of them had been able to have. It was true that they were almost a generation younger than Fatma, but certainly her parents had been more isolated. Their village, Duzçe, was not a tourist attraction, and they'd never had the influence of so many outsiders as Avanos had. Fatma was as confusing to Adalet as Ataturk, a man who'd brought literacy to the uneducated and then announced three times to his wife that he was divorcing her. Adalet wondered while she read if she was as confusing to Fatma, one foot firmly planted on the European side of the Bosphorus while the other sank into mud on the banks of the Asian side.

"What do you think?" Fatma was asking.

"I don't know what to think," Adalet answered, a safe answer even if she had no idea what Fatma was asking. "I think we live in a complicated country."

"Hmmm, you are still thinking about Meryem?"

The woman could be uncannily correct. "I'm sorry, I was." Adalet set the paper back in her lap. "I think she'd love to go to art school."

"You talked to her about this?"

"Oh, no, Fatma. It's only a guess on my part."

"Probably a good guess." Fatma shifted her weight in her chair, causing her feet to rise ever so slightly from her footstool. "School hasn't done much good for you, has it?"

Adalet took in a deep breath and let it out slowly. She'd never told Fatma much about herself, and even now she didn't wish to tell her more than she needed to know. But the fact remained that if she didn't open up to Fatma and give her the whole story as to why she was in Avanos, Meryem might end up in some awful marriage having babies and endlessly cooking and cleaning for her mother-in-law. She would never have the chance to test herself, to make her art. On the other hand, Fatma might not be at all moved by her story and think only less of her. But how much less could Fatma think of her? Fatma knew that Adalet was divorced.

"School was good for me," Adalet began. "My husband, Yasar, never wanted me to work. His mother had sometimes worked as an actress, but Yasar's father hadn't liked it. And after she had Yasar, the calls weren't coming so often and she stopped. Yasar's father was delighted. And this influenced Yasar. If I'd gone to work in Istanbul, I don't know if I'd be living here now. If only I'd had a job to go back to. After my legs were burned and my parents were killed in the earthquake, and Yasar didn't want to be married to me anymore, I was lost." Adalet paused to breathe, unable to control the moisture forming in her eyes.

"Tell me everything, my child." Fatma gestured for the newspaper in Adalet's lap. Adalet handed it to her and Fatma laid it on the table; then she sat back in her chair and adjusted the woven carpet pillow behind her head. "I want to know everything you can possibly bear to say."

CHAPTER 9

After Adalet finished telling Fatma everything she could remember of the events leading up to her coming to Avanos, Fatma sat silently for what felt to Adalet like hours. Though when Adalet stole a glance at the clock, only five minutes had passed since she'd stopped speaking. She wished Fatma would say something

"Things don't change all that much," Fatma said finally.

"What do you mean?" Adalet asked her.

"Here in Turkey. Even in Istanbul. When I was a young girl, Ataturk was determined to bring us all into the modern world. He took away the fez and he outlawed the veil. He even changed our alphabet. But the one thing he couldn't change was the heart of the people. Turkish men can be such children, selfish and unkind. Yasar was a child."

"Was your husband unkind to you?" Adalet covered her mouth with her hand. "Perhaps I shouldn't be asking you that."

"No, my husband was a good and kind man. He was much like my great grandfather. I was thinking of my grandfather. He was a hard man."

"And your father? What was he like?"

"I never knew my father. But that is a long story, too long to tell after yours. And Meryem knows nothing of it. I think it's best now

61

that you not have secrets you have to hide from Meryem. She's taken to you, and I think it's a good thing. Maybe one day I will share my story with both of you, but not just now. I have an idea."

Adalet was curious to hear Fatma's story but she didn't press her. She was interested in Fatma's idea. "What idea?"

"I don't think the life here is enough for you or for Meryem. I was wrong to think of marrying her off. I'm just like the rest of them. When I don't know what to do, I resort to old ways, old habits. I think you would be happier in Istanbul."

"I can't go back. If Yasar's family finds out—."

Fatma swatted a nonexistent fly with her hand. "So you hide away here for the rest of your life reading to an old, blind woman?" She pointed a finger at Adalet. "What a waste!"

"But what can I do?"

Fatma lowered her finger. "You can go to Istanbul with Meryem. I will hire you as her chaperone. We'll find an apartment for the two of you. Meryem can go to school and you will keep an eye on her for me. Do you think you could do that?"

Adalet jumped up from her chair. It was as if an enormous wave had come and swept underneath her. She covered her face with her hands, moved them away and looked at Fatma. No, Fatma was serious. But how could Fatma even think she could be responsible for another human being, and one like Meryem at that?

"I don't know," Adalet said. "What do you think, Fatma?"

"I'm asking you. If I didn't think you were capable, I wouldn't have mentioned it."

"I once felt sure of myself, of my life, my family, Yasar. And even if I wasn't completely confident, I had a good sense of where I was going. So much has happened, and I know it's changed me. The terrible burns, the wreckage after; whenever I boil water, I can feel it scalding me, even though I have no memory of the quake itself." Adalet shook her head. "There are times I'm as skittish as Yetim. I'll wake up soaking wet and shaking. Although, I know I am getting stronger every day."

"And you will continue to get stronger if you go to Istanbul where you can find people your own age beginning their lives, not ending them. The job is only temporary while Meryem is in school, and that's what you will say if you ever run into Yasar or his family. And it's not really a job. You could even look for part-time work if you felt physically up to it. See what happens. When Meryem is finished with school, you can always return to Avanos. I'm not sending her alone, and I certainly can't go myself."

Adalet sat back down and tears came into her eyes. "Fatma, I don't know quite what to say. This is such an opportunity for Meryem and for me." Adalet took a deep breath and felt her strength returning. It was a surge she felt rush from the bottom of her stomach to the top of her spine. It would not be easy to keep tabs on Meryem, but they'd grown closer and Adalet saw Meryem as her younger sister.

"There will be some details we'll have to work out," Adalet added.

Finally Fatma said, "Let's just see if she gets into the program first."

"I will do it, Fatma! I will." Adalet wanted to hug Fatma, but her Asian sensibility only allowed her to get up from her chair and kiss Fatma lightly on both cheeks.

"Don't thank me yet. She's a willful child and I don't expect her to be easy." Fatma pointed her finger to the newspaper lying on the table. "Let's get back to the idiots in the government. This is what I mean. They want to go back to the 19th century. Sometimes, so do I. I admit it. In certain ways it was easier. But my mother had a hard life. I think it might have been easier for her today, but then again, I'm not sure women ever have it easy."

Adalet opened the paper, looking for the article that she'd been reading when Fatma had interrupted her earlier.

"No, enough for today. I've changed my mind. The idiots will be here tomorrow. Go home and tell Meryem what we are thinking."

"Are you sure?" Adalet asked, lowering the newspaper back to her lap.

"Yes, quite sure. And if these idiots are gone, there will be more to take their place."

Adalet smiled. She knew that Fatma understood that Adalet had been asking if Fatma was sure that she wanted Adalet to leave, but she so loved to joke about the politics of the country.

Adalet placed the newspaper back on the table and got up to leave. "*Maşallah*," she said.

Fatma responded, her eyes beginning to close.

Adalet turned and tiptoed back to Fatma, giving her a gentle hug, so slight that Fatma could pretend to be asleep.

CHAPTER 10

Adalet found it difficult to drive home from the pottery shop. She found herself going over each word of hers and each word of Fatma's.

"I will cover the expenses. You can live with Meryem while she goes to art school; that is if she wants to go and if she is accepted. She's attached herself to you. I could not permit her to go on her own."

At first Adalet had protested, but she knew Fatma would never go." I will do it," Adalet had eventually replied, as if the care of a 17 year-old in a large city like Istanbul was the easiest task in the world.

Fatma had grunted, "Don't think it's going to be easy. You'll more than earn your keep. Personally, I think she's a willful child, just like her mother was. She'll work at you to get whatever she wants, and you won't always know that's what she's up to. I will hold you responsible."

Adalet felt the hairs on the back of her neck bristle. It was such an opportunity for her and for Meryem. But what if something were to happen, go wrong? Horrible things happened every day. And Fatma's words: I will hold you responsible—it made the stakes high, to say the least. She also worried about Yasar's family discovering that she was back, and even though Fatma argued that it was only temporary, she'd be in trouble if they withdrew their funds. Aside from the obvious risks, Adalet was not comfortable with deceiving her ex-husband's family.

"You wouldn't have to let Yasar or his family know you're in Istanbul. It'll only be temporary, and we can make an arrangement to get their monthly money to you. But if Meryem makes any trouble, you must get her back to me immediately. I won't have her making the same mistakes as her mother."

Adalet's thoughts raced ahead as she drove. I was nothing like Meryem when I was 17. And why had Meryem offered her biscuits during Ramadan? Was Meryem tempting her or toying with her, trying to see if she'd break her fast or remain true to her beliefs? It could just be her paranoia. She was certainly more suspicious of people since Yasar had betrayed her. But then, she chided herself, she hadn't been honest with Yasar either.

Well, Meryem still had to put together a portfolio and be accepted. And who knew? Maybe art school had never been anything she'd wanted. A vivid picture of Meryem walking down some dirt road in her father's village holding hands with a boy with a wicked smile on his face flashed across Adalet's brain waves. How would she be able to keep a constant eye on her? It would be impossible.

Adalet was aware that she'd succeeded in reaching something in Fatma that few, if any, had ever done before. "I want to know everything you can possibly bear to say." The tone had been different. There was a kindness and compassion to these words that Adalet hadn't heard before in Fatma.

Adalet pulled her car over to the side of the road to think. This could be a once-in-a-lifetime opportunity for her and for Meryem. There certainly wouldn't be other opportunities that she could see for herself. Not many for Meryem either, especially if Fatma married her off. My God, she thought, I'd almost resigned myself to becoming a spinster without purpose or meaning in my life. She leaned back into her seat and ran over various ways she could justify any of this to Yasar's family, should she be found out. This is only a temporary position. Meryem would not have been allowed to go to school without me. On and on. Yes, there were ways she could find around their agreement with her that she not come back to Istanbul, but she knew her rationalizations were all in her favor and Yasar's family would have their own. But what if no other opportunity ever came her way again?

Adalet started the car and shifted into gear. In the short distance remaining from the shop to her home, she began to have serious questions about what she had so precipitously agreed to do. The positives and the negatives kept cancelling each other out, and then it occurred to her once again that she had no idea what Meryem would want.

When Adalet pulled into the driveway, she was surprised to see a beat up motorcycle parked next to her courtyard wall. She was even more astonished to see the pimply boy whom she'd found leaning on her car after she'd purchased her Bayram candies exiting her courtyard door. He saw her and waved, then threw one lanky leg over the bike, bounced his entire body up and down several times in order to start its ancient engine, and took off with another wave of departure. Adalet sat back in her seat, took a deep breath and tried to control her thoughts.

Had she been living in Avanos too long, she wondered? What was she thinking; that she could be responsible for a teenage girl? Adalet got out of the car and fumed her way into the courtyard. She'd left a kitten in a hot car, and now she'd left an adolescent alone in her house. How could Meryem do this to her? Wasn't there an unspoken understanding that she wouldn't have friends, female or male, in Adalet's house when Adalet wasn't at home? Did Adalet really have to tell Meryem that?

By the time Adalet shut the door behind her, she was livid. She found Meryem in the kitchen washing glasses of something. At least she was cleaning up.

"Who was that boy who just left my house?" Adalet confronted her.

"A friend." Meryem looked confused. "What's wrong? Why are you acting like this?"

"Did you ask me if it was okay to have a friend in my house? A male friend?"

"Oh, so that's how it is." Meryem flung the dishtowel onto the counter. "You're not my mother and you're definitely not my grandmother." Her dark amber eyes flashed a warning to Adalet. "Do you even think I was doing anything wrong with that ugly boy? I have better taste than that." Her stare seemed to pull her forehead upward and her chin downward, not unlike the distortion fun house mirrors will create. Or perhaps, Adalet thought, I'm just seeing her differently. "Anyway," Meryem's expression softened, "I thought we were sharing the space. I thought this was my studio." She leaned her back against the counter in a posture that Adalet found defiant. Then Meryem relaxed as if someone had stuck a pin into her tightly inflated body. "Trust me; they don't stone women here. And secondly, I'm still a virgin. I'm preciously secured until *anneanne* can find someone to marry me."

It had been so long since Adalet had been talked to in such a manner, if she ever had been, that she was unable to come up with any response. Even when Yasar had told her about the divorce, there had been no yelling or harsh words. They'd both been polite. She hadn't seen this side of Meryem.

"Meryem," she eventually began, slowly pressing out each word, "it's not about you losing your virginity. I wasn't accusing you of having sex with that boy. To me it's just polite to ask before you invite a friend into someone else's home. And you know very well that I'm answerable to your grandmother. This puts me in a difficult position with her. And honestly, even if it had been a girl, I'd want to know who was in my home. Maybe I was wrong for not setting more specific rules."

Meryem puffed out her lips and pushed air through them. "I don't see how I can follow rules if I don't know what they are." Meryem's face became inscrutable. "Honestly, Adalet, I don't think I did anything wrong."

Adalet looked directly into Meryem's eyes, but she could read nothing except the girl's purported declaration of innocence.

Perhaps, she thought, I do need to make some rules and regulations here. She walked over and tapped Meryem on the shoulder. "Okay, I think we need to sit down and talk."

"Sure," Meryem agreed, her eyes as wide as a baby bird's mouth, waiting for its mother to drop in its morning meal. Suddenly, they shifted, looking down at the wooden table where she was about to sit. "I haven't had much experience of having anyone in charge of me," she admitted, but quickly added, "No more than you've had of being in charge of anyone, right?"

Adalet slipped into a chair and watched Meryem do the same. She felt like someone who knew where the ball was heading but she couldn't get there fast enough. As soon as Meryem seemed to be falling into line, she would attack in all directions; then, as if she knew she'd gone too far, she would drop the ball into Adalet's lap. This was a game Adalet had never played.

"I'm sorry," Meryem said now, "I have no idea if you've ever been in charge of anyone or not. And I shouldn't have yelled at you like that. "

"No," Adalet disclosed, "I haven't, and no, you shouldn't have. But I shouldn't have spoken to you that way either. If we're going to go to Istanbul together, we're going to have to do a lot better than this."

"Go to Istanbul together?" Meryem slid back into her chair, all defenses down. "Go to Istanbul together?" She repeated in a whisper. "How would that be possible?"

"I'm not sure it's going to be," Adalet warned. "You and I will have to get some things straight before we go anywhere together."

"But why are you talking about this?" Meryem seemed much younger in her curiosity and excitement than she did in her indignation.

"I've just come from visiting with your grandmother. She asked me why I hadn't painted the car, and I told her that I think you might have some talent."

"Do you really think so?" Meryem now looked so childishly hopeful that Adalet found it difficult to remain stern.

"I'm no expert," Adalet admitted, almost but not quite in a Fatma voice, unlikely as it was that she would ever be able to pull that off. "But your grandmother agrees that before she marries you off to some old, ugly rich man, we should find out."

"I'd run away first." The defiant look was back in Meryem's eyes.

"That's not as easy as it sounds. You have no training and no advanced education. You can have all the smarts and talent in the world, but if you can't support yourself, how will you live? You'd have to become a housekeeper or babysitter for someone."

"It's true," Meryem sighed. "What can I do?" she slouched so far back in her chair that Adalet thought she might slide off and onto the floor or become liquid and wash away under the table.

"Work very hard to get into art school, if that's what you want. If you can make an acceptable portfolio and get into a decent school, your grandmother will pay for you. But—" and Adalet hesitated intentionally—"you will go with me as your chaperone."

"*Maşallah! Maşallah!*" Meryem sprang out of the chair she'd been drooping in and flung her arms around Adalet's neck.

Adalet allowed this for a couple of seconds before disentangling herself from Meryem's grasp. "Meryem, this is hardly a contract between us yet. We have many things to discuss. Not just between us, but we also have to discuss everything with your grandmother. And I can't hear from you that I'm not your mother or your grand-mother. I will have to earn your respect, but you will also have to learn to give it to me." It was the longest speech Adalet had made in some time and in a strange way, it felt good. But in any event, she still had to catch her breath. She did this while Meryem settled back down in her chair.

"I do have a portfolio, maybe," Meryem said. "Do you want to see it?"

"Of course, I do. But let's finish talking here first. I realize that I was wrong to think you would know at all how to use freedom. You will have to learn to treat me as your guardian and to ask permission. You won't be on your own in Istanbul, and you're not here on your own either. We can discuss things and be polite to each other. We'll both have to compromise and make concessions. Even though my marriage ended as it did, we never argued. And I didn't argue with my parents or my elders."

Meryem fiddled with a painted clay bowl on Adalet's table, alternating between turning it on its side and setting it back up straight again. She finally set the bowl down and looked at Adalet. "I know it was wrong to have that boy here. I thought he'd leave before you got home. I wanted to ride on the motorcycle."

Adalet was perplexed. It had never occurred to her that Meryem might have simply wanted to ride on the motorcycle. To want something like that and just do it was beyond her thinking at that age. It was actually quite in line with painting the car, so why did it surprise her so? She would have asked her mother if it was acceptable for her to take a ride on the motorcycle. Of course, realizing that she would have had to hold on to the boy, her mother would have said no.

"Meryem, I'm willing to try this here in Avanos to see if it's possible, but you will have to accept asking permission to do such things. You can't just do whatever you feel you want in the moment. I will be responsible. You must accept this before we can continue. Maybe you'll need some time to think. I will never be your mother, but I can be your guardian. Are you ready for that?"

Meryem put her elbows on the table and sank her head into her hands. "I don't know. My father has never been there for me, and my aunties always wanted me out of their way. Until Anneanne, I've been on my own quite a bit. No one's cared except for her." Meryem looked away, but Adalet turned Meryem's chin back towards her again with her hand.

"If we agree to try, I will care," she said, and looked long into Meryem's eyes before she released her chin and asked, "How did your *anne* die? Can you tell me?"

"Cancer. Breast cancer. It runs in the family."

PART II
ISTANBUL

CHAPTER 11

Eight months later, Adalet watched Meryem stop to pick up four stalks of roasted corn from the street vendor below their apartment. Adalet waved to her from the window that framed the small balcony overlooking the street, but Meryem was too busy managing her packages to look up. Yetim rolled slightly on the wide, flat sill to a warmer spot in more direct sunlight, her three white paws and one black one revealed against her black body. Adalet smiled to think how well they were all adapting to their new life in this second-story apartment just off Taksim Square in Istanbul.

Fatma's oldest son, Ahmet, owned the building as a business investment. He mostly rented to students and young couples, one of whom had gotten pregnant and needed more space just at the time when Meryem had received her letter of acceptance to Mimar Sinan Fine Arts University (MSFAU). The place was perfect for their needs. Fatma had taken care of everything, as she'd promised, and she'd made arrangements with Ahmet to pick up Adalet's signed money orders each month and to exchange them for cash when he did so. Adalet had taken to the place immediately. She'd always wanted to live in this lively neighborhood, at least a half-hour from the lonely residential area in which she'd lived with Yasar.

After Meryem entered the building and disappeared from Adalet's view, Adalet knew that Meryem would walk up the stairway with its cracked black and white tiles and winding wooden banister rather than risk the shaky two-person elevator that Ahmet had personally had installed for Fatma, should she ever wish to spend time in Istanbul. As Adalet left the apartment to greet Meryem, she saw her readjusting the heavy portfolio she carried back and forth to the university from her right shoulder to her left, balancing the corn with her other hand. "Here, let me help you," Adalet called, trotting down the stairs to meet Meryem halfway.

"Oh, thank you. Here, just take the corn. I smelled it and couldn't resist." Meryem handed the paper-wrapped corn to Adalet, and the two of them made their way up the old-fashioned curved staircase. A whiff of spinach or cabbage hit Adelet as she took in a deep breath. "Someone always seems to be cooking cabbage," she whispered to Meryem.

"It's either that or mildew," Meryem giggled back.

Adalet knew that Meryem loved everything about these shabby hallways, down to the dust and dirt she could see encrusted in the caulking between the tiles on the floor. Meryem called it shabby elegant, like an elderly woman who has known wealth and fashion, but whose ivory lace gloves now have several loose threads hanging from them, her velvet gown worn down in the seat, her soft leather boots marred by scratches and scuffs, the cup of good China in her hand chipped both on the rim and the gently curved handle.

Meryem told Adalet that she wanted to draw and paint everything that she saw and smelled and felt. She wanted to paint the stench of fish and the inky blackness of the Bosphorus. She wanted to draw all the winding streets off the major avenues, the complexions and faces, some so different from her own or anything she'd seen except in magazines or newspapers. But the schoolwork was so boring. Copy this and copy that and copy this again. She complained to Adalet that she could not see the point of it.

"You have to learn the basics," Adalet reasoned. "All artists copy the masters. You must know the history. It's for your degree."

"But by the time they've finished with me, I won't be able to paint anymore," Meryem argued. And although Adalet had to admit to herself that the work Meryem brought home from school was not nearly as impressive as the portfolio she'd brought to her interview at MSFAU, she kept silent. The lines and curves and endless building parts looked more like architectural design than fine art. She consoled herself with the notion that Meryem was only beginning the program, and that her frustration with what Meryem often expressed as a complete lack of creativity would pass as she moved along. Adalet already knew that Meryem was not patient. Meryem had not been completely honest with Adalet when she'd said she had a portfolio, but she certainly put one together in such short time that even Fatma had been impressed.

Now in the fading afternoon light of the small but cozy living room, Meryem flung her portfolio onto the couch and then followed Adalet into the adjoining kitchen. Adalet had taken the corn from the newspaper wrapping and was already shucking the leaves into the sink.

"Hurry, please. I'm starving," Meryem called to her. Adalet shook her head. Yes, Meryem was impatient all right, and Adalet hoped it wouldn't get her into too much trouble. But then Meryem was pulling out plates and napkins and pouring iced tea, setting the table, and Adalet thought, she's just young.

The corn was still warm but not too hot to bite into deeply. Yasar's mother had raised her eyebrows and shook her head when Adalet had suggested they get some during a shopping trip. "You eat things made on the street?" She'd wrinkled her nose in disgust. It had been one of the first things Adalet and Meryem had eaten when they'd arrived, and now Meryem would pick them up and bring them home whenever the roasting butter and corn invaded and overwhelmed her nostrils.

Meryem devoured her first ear and went for her second. "I'm so hungry," she said. "I better be careful or I'll be fat before I graduate."

Adalet waved her half-eaten first ear of corn at Meryem. "Not if you have your mother's genes. She was quite slender in the photo that Fatma keeps of her."

Meryem dropped her corn onto her plate. "Do you think I might?"

"Might what?" Adalet asked, absorbed in eating and losing track of the conversation.

"That I might have her genes?"

"You look just like her."

"Do I? I never think so. I think I look like my *baba*." Yetim jumped from her favorite spot on the windowsill to her second favorite spot on the large kilim-covered pillow next to Adalet's favorite chair. When Adalet sat there, Yetim almost always jumped into her lap.

"Have you written to him recently?" Adalet asked.

"A couple of weeks ago. But you know how he is. He doesn't like to write. He won't get a phone. Sometimes I think my father is also dead, or he's some kind of a ghost who pops back into my life out of nowhere and then is gone again before I can touch him to see if he's real. First he left me with my aunts, then with Fatma, now with you—and he doesn't even know you!"

Before Adalet could protest, a repetitive beeping noise went off in Meryem's portfolio bag. "Who would be calling me now?" Meryem jumped up from her corn to salvage her phone before it stopped ringing. Now that they were living in a big city and were apart almost daily, Meryem had suggested cell phones. "Everyone here has one. This way we can stay in touch. If I'm going to be late, I can call you." It was hard to disagree with this reasoning, although Adalet suspected that Meryem had multiple other motives. Now Adalet watched as Meryem expertly retrieved her phone and answered it as if she'd been doing this all her life.

"Professor Aronson, yes, it's Meryem—oh, I didn't realize—yes, I will need it today. I live close by. It's only a five-minute walk— that's so kind of you to let me know. It must have fallen out of my portfolio. Yes, sure, I'll come and get it now." Meryem ended the call.

"That was my art history professor, Dr. Aronson. I dropped my book in his office. Come walk with me. I'm going to go and pick it up." Meryem tossed the plates in the sink. "I'll clean these as soon as we get back."

Adalet threw on a jacket and grabbed her keys from the nail next to the door. "Aronson?" she asked. "What kind of name is that?"

"He's American. He's the only professor I have that I like. He makes us laugh and he's fun. I'm so happy that you'll get to meet him."

Adalet wasn't really looking forward to meeting anyone just now. She imagined that he would be short and fat like the professors in the art videos that Meryem sometimes watched, and so she didn't bother to change from her yoga pants and t-shirt. The jacket she'd grabbed was an old and comfortable woolen shirt that did nothing to add to her appearance, but she was glad she'd chosen it because the air had cooled and the sun had gone behind the clouds in the time it had taken to eat the corn.

They just about ran down the incline of their street, a steady drop, stepping over offal left in the street as garbage or on purpose for the feral cats. They reached the bottom and the tram station just as a train of cars went rushing by. Meryem's school was only a few minutes walk from the tram, and students, tourists and businessmen hurried in and out of the gate that led to the tram platform. Adalet gripped her jacket and put her hands in her pockets as they made their way along the street next to the water.

Adalet had forgotten how lovely the grounds at MSFAU were kept. She hadn't walked here in some months. Even with the chill of rain in the air and the absence of flower blossoms and leaves, the positioning of the trees indicated that the landscaping was meticulously planned by someone who knew exactly what they were doing.

And the way the back of the school sat on the edge of the Bosphorus. During the warmer months, and even now in September, Adalet could see students gathered in small groups, chatting about their work, their lives, gossiping about their professors and each other, and smoking cigarette after cigarette.

Adalet tugged at Meryem's sleeve and pointed towards the water. "Just for a minute?" They stood silently watching the waves lap against the concrete edge and the gulls circling for fish before

Meryem nudged Adalet into the building. "I want to get there before he leaves," Meryem urged.

Meryem directed Adalet into an elevator in the glass-walled lobby of the modern structure and pushed the button for the third floor. They'd been quiet on the way over. Adalet thought that Meryem might be in a hurry by her resolute pace and the absence of her chatter. They exited the elevator onto a long, tiled hallway with doors on either side. Meryem stopped at a door down the hall on the right with a small sign that read: Mark Aronson, Ph.D. She knocked with three, short but determined raps.

The door opened almost instantly and Adalet was surprised to see a youthful man of slender build. He was dressed semi-casually in jeans and a gray and blue tweed jacket. His sandy-colored hair trailed down his neck and over his shirt collar in soft curls. He had a wide nose and strong brown eyes, and when he smiled, a dimple opened up on the left side of his mouth. Adalet liked his trimmed beard. She immediately thought there was something about him that she found exotic. She wished she'd combed her hair and changed her clothes.

"Hello, Meryem," he said. I was just leaving. I thought you were going to pick up your book from the secretary. I was about to drop it off with her now." His eyebrows crinkled. He looked a bit confused by Meryem's appearance at his office door. He went back inside and appeared a minute later with a large textbook. He handed it to Meryem and was about to close his door when he noticed Adalet. Since he hadn't seen her at first, he didn't assume they were together.

"I'm sorry," he said in Turkish, "can I help you?"

"She's with me," Meryem responded quickly in English. "This is my roommate and friend, Adalet."

"Hi, I'm Mark Aronson," the man said. He extended his right hand. Now he opened the door wider. "Would you like to come in?" He spoke in halting Turkish with a strong accent, and it took a minute for Adalet to understand what he was saying.

"Hello, Professor." Adalet was startled by the change in his manner, not knowing many Americans, even when she'd been at school. But she took his outstretched hand and felt a quick squeeze before he dropped hers. "But you said you were just leaving," Adalet didn't want to delay him. She thought he was just being polite.

"I was going home to grade these," he opened the door wider and pointed to a stack of papers gathered in a box on his desk. "They'll wait till later." He gestured to them with his other hand to come in. He used an odd word for "grade" but then so mispronounced it that Adalet looked to Meryem to translate.

"He's inviting us in. He's going to grade those papers when he goes home." Meryem giggled. "Adalet speaks fluent English. You don't have to speak Turkish to her."

"I know my Turkish is pretty bad, " he responded in English. "I should practice more."

"That's okay," Adalet told him. "We'll practice our English."

"Please, sit for a moment." Mark Aronson waved his arm towards the odd and sparse assortment of seating that was available.

Adalet sat on the small couch across from Mark Aronson's desk. It was a loveseat rather than a couch, the upholstery a worn, purple flower pattern that looked like it would be more at home in a bordello than a university professor's office. Meryem sat on a small, green chair next to it that appeared to have been taken from someone's dining room set. The professor caught Adalet examining the furniture and laughed as he sat down in his desk chair. "Charming, isn't it? Other than my desk and the chair I'm sitting on, there was no other furniture in here when I came. So I went on a hunt to used furniture stores."

"Is this the way they treat professors here?" Adalet asked, genuinely surprised.

"It seems it's how they treat newly arrived visiting American professors. In any event, it is how they treated me. To be honest, I was delighted to get this position, especially since no one seems to understand what I'm saying in Turkish. The pronunciation is impossible for me."

"Do you teach the students in Turkish?" Adalet asked.

The professor smiled. "No. It's a requirement that they speak

English in order to take my class. So many students learn English in school these days. I doubt there are many here who don't speak English. And what do you do, Adalet? Are you also here to study?"

"No, I've completed university. I'm older than Meryem, as you can probably see. I'm living with her as her guardian." Meryem shot Adalet a warning look, and so she quickly added, "Her grandmother is old-fashioned, from a village in Central Turkey. She would never have let Meryem come here on her own." Meryem smiled a thank you. "And I hope to find some work to keep me busy."

"Since when are you going to work?" Meryem asked.

"I've been thinking about it for a few weeks. I need to do something else with my time. And it wouldn't hurt to earn some money."

"What kind of work?" the professor asked.

"I know a bit of sign language," Adalet told him, "and I did some consulting work with parents of deaf children. I will go back to the Yeditepe School for the Deaf where I worked before to see if they have any openings. I might even be able to consult again."

"And what about me?" Meryem sounded amazingly childish for someone who wanted to appear capable of caring for herself.

"Part-time, Meryem. I only plan to work part-time."

"That sounds like a wonderful plan," the professor said. "I can also ask around here. Is your degree in deaf education?"

"Educational psychology. That would be very kind of you."

"Give me a week or so, and I'll get back in touch with you."

"Why don't you come to our home for tea?" Meryem suggested.

"Yes, Professor. Please do come for tea." One of those times when Meryem's spontaneity was a blessing and not a curse, Adalet thought. She wanted to jump up and hug her.

"Please call me Mark," the professor said to Adalet. He turned toward Meryem. "But you, young lady, will continue to call me Professor. And since you both ask me so nicely, I will accept."

"Is next Thursday at this time good for you?" Adalet asked, not quite yet ready to call him Mark.

"It is, actually."

"Next week then, Professor?" Meryem added ever so slight an

emphasis to the word "professor," just enough to cause Adalet to give her an admonishing look. Her professor didn't seem to notice.

"Thank you," he said. "That will be perfect. Now I must ask you to leave so that I can get home and get to work on these papers." They all rose. "Don't forget your book, Meryem." He pointed to where Meryem had set it on the floor. She bent down to retrieve it.

"I wasn't going to forget it again," Meryem told him. But Adalet had to wonder. Before the professor had reminded Meryem of the book, Adalet had completely forgotten why they'd come there in the first place.

CHAPTER 12

Adalet poured a second cup of apple tea for the professor. Like many Americans, he preferred it to black tea. He and Meryem were munching on the sweet anise biscuits Adalet had placed on a painted ceramic plate in the center of the table in their apartment. A large bouquet of sunflowers brought by Professor Mark Aronson sat in a glass vase on the floor by the fireplace, brightening and inviting more sunlight into the room. The professor turned his attention to Adalet.

"Are the two of you related?"

"In spirit," Meryem responded.

"It's true," Adalet smiled. "We are like cousins, but without any common blood. Her grandmother is a friend of mine. Fatma is almost blind, and I spent some months reading to her."

Yetim had jumped up on the windowsill when the buzzer to the apartment had sounded the professor's arrival. Now Adalet watched her pounce onto the floor to explore the new human who was now sitting and therefore less threatening to her. She began to stalk his right foot and sniff and paw at it. "And who is this fellow?" Mark asked.

"This is Yetim. It means orphan in Turkish. And she's a she, not a he. There are only women living here." Meryem tossed her head and hair flirtatiously.

"Then I'm honored that you invited me for tea."

"You ought to be," Meryem looked at him over the top of her tea-cup. "I believe you're the first and only man that we have invited."

Adalet looked down at her biscuit in embarrassment. There were times when it was hard to believe that Meryem seemed to have so little experience in so many areas and so much experience in others. How dare she reveal so much about them in so few words?

"We've only been here since the beginning of Meryem's first semester," she countered. Then she felt even more embarrassed. Since this was her second semester, would that mean that it was now time for a long line of men to appear at their door? What an idiot I am, she thought. But it all seemed to bounce off Professor Mark Aronson, with the exception of Yetim, who was now boldly ensconced in his lap.

"Where did you move here from?" he asked, while stroking Yetim behind her ears.

"Avanos," Adalet said quickly, not leaving a minute for Meryem to speak. "It's in Cappadocia."

"Yes, I know it. When I knew I was coming here to teach, I left some time to travel first. It's geographically very like where I was from in New Mexico before we moved to New York."

"But I thought you were American. You are Mexican?" Adalet asked.

"New Mexico is in America, silly." Meryem flipped some strands of hair from her face, all adult and knowing.

The professor laughed. "Most people make the same mistake, and you did, too, didn't you Meryem, when I told the class where I was from? I seem to remember that everyone thought I was from Mexico."

Meryem tossed her hair back into her face and glowered at Adalet. "Maybe," she admitted, but then quickly added, "I don't remember."

"New Mexico has some rock formations that are similar to your fairy towers," the professor added quickly, "but there aren't as many and they're not as varied."

"Really? I didn't know that." Adalet took a sip of tea. "I don't think of America as being anything like any part of Turkey."

"It's a big country," Mark Aronson said.

"What do you think," Meryem chimed in, that the whole of America would look like New York City—or maybe like the cowboy movies? Like Clint Eastwood?" She shook her head, ending with a knowing smile.

"Actually," Mark said, "A lot of the country where I'm from does look like old western movies. Many of them were filmed there. It also looks a lot like some parts of the Middle East. We have a lot of Jordanians, Palestinians, Lebanese, even quite a few Israelis who emigrate there."

"That's funny, are they going to have a Middle East war in the United States?" Meryem asked. "Why would they move to America to live in the same neighborhood? I thought they hated each other."

"Actually, so did I," Adalet interjected. She toyed with the crumbs on her plate, debating silently whether she should have another biscuit or not.

"It's not so simple." Mark folded his napkin and set it back on the table. "Do you hate me?" Both Adalet and Meryem looked at him in astonishment.

"I'm Jewish and American. Are those reasons to hate me?"

"No, no. The Turkish people love Americans. We're a western people." Adalet insisted. She didn't know what to think. Where could he be going with this?

"Do you think that all Turkish people love Americans?" Mark struck back.

"Well," Meryem looked upset, "*we love* Americans, Professor. Adalet and I do. And as far as Jews go, I don't think I've ever known anyone Jewish. Have you?" She turned to Adalet who had stopped playing with her crumbs and had stopped thinking about another biscuit.

"Not in person, but I don't think I've known any Americans either. I met several Americans but I couldn't say if they were Jewish or not. There are still some synagogues here, but I don't know if they are still working or just preserved as museums. Do you know, Mark? I think there is one in Izmir."

"Yes, there is one in Izmir. I had to get a special pass to visit because the Jewish people there are afraid that someone will come to bomb the place. You see, even here we once lived together as friendly neighbors, but now we need special passes, even another Jew, just to visit." His tone had changed from lighthearted to serious, and Adalet didn't know what to make of this.

"I hope we haven't offended you, Mark." Adalet was not used to this kind of discussion, even though between school and Yasar, she had some experience of western thinking, she had never met a Jewish person. She rarely talked to anyone about such things since she'd been with Yasar and his friends, and even then, she mostly listened. When Fatma went on about the stupidity of the Turkish government or politics in general, Adalet just nodded except when it came to cultural issues related to women and she thought a lack of response on her part might impact Fatma's dealings with Meryem.

Meryem was shaking her head, "No, Professor Aronson isn't offended, Adalet. He's upset at what he calls 'the human stupid.' He just sounds emphatic because he likes to argue."

"This isn't arguing, Meryem, this is discussion." The professor spoke more gently.

"Whatever it is," Meryem patted Adalet's hand to elicit her agreement, "it sure sounds like arguing to us."

Adalet wished that she could think of something brilliant to say to shift the conversation, but all that came out was, "Would anyone like more tea?" This was followed by dead silence, until Meryem and the professor started to smile. "You are a diplomat, Adalet," Mark Aronson said, and all three laughed.

"I guess I am," Adalet agreed. "I'm not used to this way of speaking. Sometimes Fatma gets very excited, but it's always about our own problems here in the Turkish government."

"No, not possible, the Turkish have problems in the government? Find me a single Turk on the street who'll admit to that?"

"Maybe not to you," Adalet retorted. "We're a proud people. We like to keep our problems to ourselves."

"There you go," Mark slapped his hand lightly on the table. "Now we're in a discussion, a real conversation. Seriously, though— he shifted his body, leaning back into his chair—it is a problem when we see each other as more different than we are alike."

"What do you mean?" Adalet asked. She leaned forward, curious to hear what Mark Aronson had to say.

"Do you eat pork?"

"No."

"Do you wash your hands and feet before you pray?"

"Yes."

"Do you pray at set times of the day and face in the direction of Mecca?

"I don't always, but religious Moslems do, yes."

"So do religious Jews—who don't eat pork and wash their hands before they say the prayer to bless the bread. They face Jerusalem and in Jerusalem, they go to the Wall to pray, next to the holy Mosque and near the Stations of the Cross. The very best falafel in the world, in my humble opinion, is an Arab hole in the wall on one of the Stations of the Cross."

"So what are you saying by all of this?" Adalet knew nothing of Jewish or Christian customs.

"He's saying we're all human," Meryem answered. "That's why his classes are so special to me. He always talks about the inheritance of the arts in the world, not just the world of Turkey."

"We're just human beings, all of us," the professor explained. "In being human, of course we inherit all that is human, as well as in art and in science. So I like to point out the similarities as well as the differences, what makes art universal and what makes art Turkish, if there is such a thing. And Arabs and Jews are siblings, if you believe in the bible. You know, back to Ishmael and Isaac."

"I see. But we are Moslems. We are not Arabs." Adalet thought it important to make this distinction, one she'd heard Yasar make many times when speaking with foreigners. And because she wasn't sure why Yasar was adamant on this point, she added, "And not all Arabs are Moslems."

"And there are Arabs who consider themselves Jews," Mark smiled at Adalet. "I will share with you why I call all of this, 'the human stupid.' Whenever anyone disagrees with my mother, who is stronger in her opinions even than I am, she tells them, 'Everyone is entitled to their own stupid opinion.' Collectively, I've coined it 'the human stupid.'"

"Isn't that awesome, Adalet?" Adalet noted that 'awesome' was another new American word in Meryem's vocabulary.

"Yes," Adalet had to agree. "Your ideas are interesting to me. I'll have to think more about them." She thought to herself how insulated and narrow her thinking might appear to the professor, walled in as she was by Turkish mortar and brick that had only been penetrated by still life portraits of the outside world. "I think I could be one of 'the human stupid." She looked up at Mark.

"Oh, no, I never meant anything like that," Mark was quick to tell her.

"But stupid is ignorant, and I'm ignorant about so many things."

"Tell me about it," Meryem sighed. "I wish I knew as much as my professor does."

"And when you do, which I think might be sooner than even you could imagine, Meryem, then you can teach my art history class in Turkish."

"That will be very far from now, Professor."

As if to point out just how far, Yetim, who had been sound asleep in the professor's lap all this time, yawned and stretched and dropped to the floor.

"I see that Yetim agrees with you, Meryem." Adalet felt more relaxed now and did take another biscuit from the plate. "If you have to wait for Meryem to know all that you know to be out of a job, you might be here in Istanbul for some time."

"Thanks a lot, Adalet. Just you wait and see." Meryem crossed her arms in defiance but a smile leaked out from the corner of her mouth.

"Ah, if I know Meryem at all, I'd better start looking," he teased. "You know, I'm wondering if either of you has had time to see some of the art and sites here in Istanbul. I go wandering all over the city in my free time. And you," he turned to Meryem, as if the suggestion was being made for her benefit alone, "ought to be looking at great art. Perhaps you'll agree to come with me one day." He didn't lift his voice at the end to form a question. Then he added, "This next Friday?"

"I'm Moslem," Adalet said quietly, as if this were a new revelation. "It's a religious day for me."

"I'm Jewish," Meryem's professor reiterated, "but I'm not religious. So Saturday is okay for me. Do you think that would work?"

Adalet appeared to be deep in thought. She wanted to say yes but not too quickly. She was attracted by and frightened of this man at the same time. "No, not next Saturday," she answered. "I'm sorry, we're busy." Meryem stabbed Adalet with her eyes, but before Meryem could deny this blatant lie, Adalet relented. "But the following Saturday would be fine."

"Good, then it's settled. Now, let me help you clear these dishes."

"No, no, Professor. It was just tea. I'll do it." Meryem practically leaped from her chair, certainly faster than Adalet had ever seen her move in pursuit of washing dishes.

"Well, then, if you won't let me work, I will thank you both and be on my way. There are always papers to grade and lectures to prepare." He and Adalet moved from the table and Adalet reached out to retrieve the professor's jacket from where she'd placed it on the old-fashioned tree next to the door, but the professor got there first. "Thank you again, Adalet."

"You're very welcome." She could not quite call him Mark yet, but she watched him walk down the stairs. She wondered if he, like Meryem, was a bit wary of the condition and reliability of the elevator.

CHAPTER 13

Adalet kept her curiosity about Professor Mark Aronson to herself. She was bursting to ask Meryem a million questions. Did he have a family here? A Jewish wife? A Turkish one? A family back in America? How old was he and why was he teaching in Istanbul?

Once she'd had a little time to think about it, Adalet did not believe for one minute that Meryem had left a book in her professor's office by accident. Meryem was extremely careful with her books and materials, knowing that Fatma was footing the bill. And for all her protesting to the contrary, Adalet knew that Meryem was enjoying going to school and for the most part, she was pretty responsible. Meryem had arranged for Adalet and the professor to meet. She was sure of this. If it hadn't happened when it did, Meryem would have come up with something else. Perhaps Meryem had watched too many American romantic comedies on television.

Well, Adalet mused during the first week of waiting she'd forced upon herself, she did find him interesting and attractive. If he turned out to be a married man, on the prowl or not, she didn't have to see him again. And if he turned out to be single, at the very least, she could use a friend. She just didn't want Meryem pushing something she didn't know if she wanted or was even ready for at this point in her life.

Adalet was still annoyed that Meryem had made it so clear to Mark—she began to use his first name in her thoughts so that she'd be able to say it in person—that there was no man in either of their lives. Adalet would not be able to claim to be attached to anyone if she chose not to see him again.

Adalet was also disturbed that Meryem had witnessed her lie, so she set about making a plan for that Saturday that would include Meryem. "I've been wanting to go to the baths," Adalet told her, "so I made a reservation for the two of us. There's a good *hamam* near the Blue Mosque. I used to go there once in a while when I was married to Yasar. Then we can visit the mosque. You haven't been there yet."

"That will be fun," Meryem sounded excited. She didn't ask if this plan had come before or after the invitation from Mark Aronson, and Adalet hoped she'd safely navigated her way around that blunder.

They set out early that Saturday, taking a bus through the noisy, bustling streets that curved and stopped and started again as they neared their destination. A daring taxi came at them from out of nowhere and tried to get the bus to back up the narrow one-way street. They shouted and cursed at each other, until they both got out of their vehicles, waving their fists in the air and threatening to annihilate not only each other but all the members of their respective families as well. The scene delighted Meryem. "Who will back down?" She laughed. Adalet was relieved when the taxi driver finally agreed to back up, as he was going the wrong way to begin with. When the bus driver climbed back into the bus, he was greeted by a cheering group of passengers.

The *hamam* was exactly as Adalet remembered, but she had never seen it this crowded. A group of young Japanese women on tour had gone in just in front of them, and although they seemed quite experienced in common bathing and locker rooms, Adalet wondered if they'd ever been to a Turkish bath. They chatted and giggled amongst themselves, removing their fine clothing, stepping into the clogs that were provided, and wrapping the towels they were handed at the entrance around their perfectly shaped tiny bodies. Adalet found it difficult not to stop and stare and Meryem did. The Japanese women seemed not to even notice them.

When the Japanese women entered the bathing area, Adalet and Meryem entered with them. The lighting dimmed instantly, obscured by the steam rising from the heated rocks. It was rather like entering a large cavern with faucets on the walls, as opposed dripping streams from waterfalls. Three women waited to administer the individual washing. As they approached, they motioned the Japanese women to stools against the walls, where there were faucets and buckets. The Japanese women gaped at them, taking in their large, hanging naked breasts. They were stripped to the waist also because they would get very wet. Adalet stepped forward to serve as a demonstration, as the Japanese women did not speak a word of Turkish and clearly did not know what to make of this procedure.

When Adalet sat on one of the stools, the woman washing her poured a bucket of water over her head and body; the woman soaped her hair and then her body, moving the towel delicately as she scrubbed her private parts. As the woman adjusted her own body, her long breasts swung and dangled in the air like an African woman caught in motion and photographed for a National Geographic magazine. The woman poured more buckets of water over her to rinse her off, and then she left her at the faucet to continue to rinse or to lie on the steaming hot stones next to Meryem, who had somehow finished first. Wrapped in fresh towels, they listened to the Japanese women settle down, breathing in the steam and relaxing into the experience. Adalet felt a surge of pride. She guessed that they might have been expecting something quite different, but it was clear from the cessation of sound that the Turkish version of the bath hadn't been a disappointment.

The older baths had all been constructed next to mosques, as it was traditional to bathe before praying, or at the very least, to wash one's hands and feet. Most of the baths now served large numbers of tourists as well. Some of the newer baths were divided for men and women, but this one still kept separate hours for each. The Blue Mosque was a working mosque, and there were those who still bathed before prayer. Traditional brides also took a ceremonial bath prior to the wedding ceremony. In spite of how modern Yasar's family was, Adalet had observed this tradition and enjoyed it. She hadn't been to the baths since her legs had been scarred, but she was able to hide most of it behind towels. The woman who washed her had not reacted, if she'd even noticed. Once they dried and dressed and Adalet placed a tip in the tip jar, they walked the short distance to the mosque.

Adalet felt Meryem grab onto her wrist with one hand as they entered the outer courtyard leading up to the mosque. "It's huge," Meryem whispered, even though they were still outside and had a bit of a walk to the main entrance. They stood still for a moment, staring up at the Mosque's proud minarets from where the call to prayer came, the tall towers whose number signified the holiness of the particular mosque. They could not see all six of them from where they were standing, one had to be farther back. The six minarets of the Blue Mosque had caused quite a scandal when they were built. Another minaret had to be added to the holiest mosque in Mecca to settle the dispute. Adalet had read about this as a young schoolgirl. Every Turkish child did.

Adalet noticed several men performing the washing ritual, *abdest*, at the *Sardirvan*, a hexagonal stone structure lined with faucets in the center of the courtyard. Since Adalet had just come from the baths, she was considered to be ritually clean, and in any event, it was not customary for women to wash with the men. Their rituals were separate, including the areas where they prayed within the mosque.

Adalet and Meryem each took a headscarf from the shelves where they were provided outside of the mosque to cover their hair before going into the main mosque. They placed their shoes next to others lined up next to the entrance.

"Do you pray?" Adalet asked Meryem. Although Adalet was irregular, she did pray and sometimes read the Koran on holy days.

Meryem was respectful of Adalet's religious faith, but she had never joined her. "You don't have to," Adalet added, "I won't be long." She gave Meryem's hand a squeeze before letting go.

Adalet looked up at the giant dome. She grabbed onto a wooden rail to steady her footing. Gazing into the blue stained glass windows made up of so many different sizes, shapes and forms gave her the dizzying sensation of vertigo, of falling. She stared down at a couple of squares of carpeting to regain her balance.

It was not one of the five official times for prayer, or the mosque would not have been open, and so there were only a few men and women actually in prayer, separately facing the *qiblah*, the area indicating the correct direction for prayer, the direction towards Mecca. Adalet joined the kneeling women in a separate enclosure while Meryem took in the elaborate tile work, the enormous chandeliers that had been added in order to supplement the lighting and the incredible artistic Arabic calligraphy. Adalet joined her when she finished her prayers. Meryem put her arm around Adalet's shoulder and whispered, "It's so beautiful here. I feel like I'm being cradled in loving energy."

"You are," Adalet whispered back. "Millions of prayers."

A tour group huddled near their guide and Adalet and Meryem could hear her speaking to them in English. "This is a working mosque," the guide told them in a low voice. "Please don't take photographs here or speak loudly. There are people praying. You must not sit on the floor. It's disrespectful. It's only for kneeling, please."

"Are they American or Canadian? What do you think?" Meryem asked Adalet.

"I have no idea," Adalet smiled. "I can't tell the Americans from the Canadians or the British from the Australians. But they sound a lot like your professor, so I'm guessing American."

But wherever they were from, they tiptoed around in a small area, whispering and pointing out what they observed to one another. The women struggled to keep their heads covered, unused to the scarves that seemed to slip so easily from their hair.

Meryem whispered to Adalet, "This is all as foreign to me as it is to them."

"What do you mean?" Adalet asked her.

"I'll tell you outside." They exited the dimly lit building and stepped into sunlight. They placed their shawls back on the shelves and slipped on their shoes. They had passed out of the courtyard before Meryem began to speak.

"My *anneanne's* deep, dark secret. Fatma will never tell you this, but she knows that I will. My mother married an Armenian Christian. My *anneanne* never forgave her. My father has almost no relationship with her."

"But your father sent you to Fatma and would have allowed her to arrange a marriage for you. I don't understand."

They were passing a teashop. "Let's stop and have tea and I'll try to explain as much as I understand," Meryem told her. They entered the tiny shop, and Meryem selected a table for two in the rear. A young man in an apron served them a pot of hot tea and a plate of anise biscuits, much like the ones they'd served to Mark Aronson. When the waiter left them, Meryem took some sips of the tea before she started to speak again.

"My mother met my father in Avanos. He picked up construction jobs where he could, and he worked on a new hotel being built for tourists near Göreme. My father visited the pottery shop when my mother was just 18, my age now. My father was 21, or so the story goes. I'm not sure. For some reason I always suspected he was older. He seemed older. Maybe because he'd been out in the world and my mother's world consisted of school and the pottery shop. I don't know."

"How did they manage to get around Fatma?" Adalet was so intrigued that she let her tea get cold.

"I don't imagine it was easy. My *anne* never told me those things, even when I begged her. I was only eleven when she died, and I guess she didn't think it was appropriate. I was ten when she got sick, and after that, she was so different. She slept so often, and I couldn't ask my father anything. He wouldn't talk about it." Meryem raised the teapot and offered to pour more into Adalet's cup. Adalet shook her head no.

"And Fatma? Has she told you anything?" Adalet asked.

"Only when I first arrived. She kept saying she hoped I wouldn't turn out like my mother. Run off and marry someone without her permission. Marriage was so far from my mind, that I didn't pay too much attention, even though I didn't like hearing her say it. I knew that Fatma loved my mother because she paid for her to get treatments my father couldn't afford. And she cared for my mother as she was dying. My father brought her there. He left me with his sisters and left my mother with her mother, and so I never saw her again. I hated him for doing that, even though I understand now that he wasn't able to care for her. His family didn't have the money, and they never really accepted my mother either. But back then, I hated him for taking her away from me."

Adalet reached across the tiny table and took Meryem's hand in hers. "I'm so sorry," she said. "I had no idea. Fatma told me none of this."

"She wouldn't. My parents loved each other in their own way, but their backgrounds were so different and their families so prejudiced. Fatma was probably right in thinking it was a poor match. My *anne* went to school and my *baba* could read and write, but he was uneducated. That didn't mean he wasn't intelligent, he was, but he was a man who worked with his hands."

"My *baba* was, too." Adalet told her.

"But your *baba* wasn't an Armenian Christian."

"No," Adalet admitted, "he was a devout Moslem."

"And my professor is an American Jew," Meryem smiled, suddenly changing the topic and the mood. "What do you think of that?"

"I don't know what to think about it," Adalet admitted. "But I'm not running off with him and neither are you."

"You can never know what the future will bring." Meryem withdrew her hand from Adalet's and reached into her purse. "Let's pay and go home. I have reading to do." Adalet knew the subject was closed for now, but she wondered most of the way back to their apartment what it must have been like for Meryem, growing up between Armenian and Turk, Christian and Moslem worlds, the suspicions and prejudices on both sides, as well as the enduring power of love.

CHAPTER 14

Adalet searched in her wardrobe to find something to wear that following Saturday. She tried on a pair of rarely used jeans, but then she remembered why she hadn't been wearing them. She'd lost about ten pounds since her accident, and she hadn't been able to gain it back. She tried them anyway, but they hung on her. "You're certainly doing better at putting on the pounds than I am," she commented to Yetim who was rolling on her back, her now rounded belly poised in the air for Adalet to attend to.

Adalet scratched Yetim's belly for a moment and then returned to what she felt to be her dismal wardrobe. If she did indeed decide to volunteer a day or two at the school for the deaf, she would have to make some new purchases. She thought now that Meryem was situated in her program, she might go there to help a few children having difficulty with their reading skills, a not uncommon problem among the deaf. Now she shouted across the hall to Meryem, "Meryem, can you come here for a moment?"

"Sure, I'm coming," Meryem sang back. Adalet heard her rise from her bed where she'd been napping and reading since breakfast. She was showered and dressed in jeans and a long, bright red sweater that she'd purchased from her clothing allowance. Meryem had also acquired a pair of stylish leather boots that Adalet guessed she would don once Mark arrived to pick them up. "You could've stepped out of *Vogue Turkey*," Adalet told her.

"Thanks," Meryem smiled. "What do you need?"

Adalet sighed, motioning to her wardrobe. "I need something decent to wear."

"I told you to get something when we went shopping for me." Meryem ran her hand through Adalet's clothing until it rested on a black, silk turtleneck. "This is nice."

"But my jeans are too big." She tugged on the waistline to demonstrate.

Meryem continued to push along the hangers. "What about this?" She pulled a long deep blue wool skirt out of the wardrobe. Adalet stepped back, then took the hanger from Meryem's out-stretched hand. "I forgot I had this. Yasar's sister bought it and it was too small for her. She gave it to me."

"From the look of it, she has good taste. It's lovely. Does it fit you? It would be perfect with the turtleneck."

Adalet yanked off the oversized jeans, putting them back on the hanger to set a good example for Meryem. She tried on the skirt and then stood in front of the long mirror attached to her bedroom door.

"It fits you perfectly," Meryem exclaimed. "What will you wear on your feet?"

"That's a good question," Adalet shook her head in frustration. "I don't know."

"You wouldn't be dressing for the professor, would you?" Meryem looked directly at Adalet and then rolled her eyes. "If that's the case, you can borrow my boots. They'd be perfect and we wear the same size in shoes. Do you want to try them on?"

"Oh, Meryem, that's so kind of you, but I'm sure you'll want to wear them."

"Oh, try them on for the fun of it. Let's just see how they look." Meryem dashed across the hall to her room and came back with the boots. Adalet gazed at the long, thin heels with trepidation. "How do you walk on those things, anyway?"

Meryem held them out to her, but Adalet hesitated. "I don't think so, Meryem. I have some problems with my legs and walking in those would kill me. I have some black tights and simple black flats that will be fine, really. It will be a lot of walking for me today as it is. But I do appreciate that you'd offer them to me."

Adalet hoped that Meryem wouldn't question her further. Meryem was unaware of the dreadful ongoing pain that Adalet endured. Neither Adalet nor Fatma had told her how bad it could be. They'd discussed it and decided that even though Meryem would be sympathetic, it might end up making Adalet appear weak and thus more vulnerable to Meryem's manipulation. Adalet was adept at concealing it.

But Meryem seemed to accept her at her word. "Sure, you should be comfortable. They don't bother me too much. I guess I will wear them then." She sat down on Adalet's bed and put them on her own feet. She stood and turned around in Adalet's mirror, admiring the line of the boots and jeans. Adalet had found her tights and shoes and finished dressing. She turned to watch Meryem.

"Stunning, aren't they?" Meryem reached out and pulled Adalet next to her in the mirror. "Don't we look elegant?" Meryem moved away to allow Adalet a full view of herself.

"Not bad," Adalet smiled at her reflection. "Thanks for helping me." She turned back to Meryem, but Meryem had already sneaked away to the bathroom where she would most likely be for the next hour, fixing her hair and makeup. Adalet stared back at herself. Maybe she could use a little color on her face today as well.

An hour later, the door buzzed. Meryem had not emerged from the bathroom. Adalet was pleased that she had the mirror in her room. Now she reached for the buzzer to press. "Yes," she said.

"I'm here as promised." Mark's voice came through, along with the static of the buzzer system. "Do you want to buzz me in or just come down?"

"One minute," Adalet told him. She called to the closed bathroom door. "Mark's here, Meryem. Are you ready?"

Meryem opened the door and stepped out of the bathroom. She held out her arms, "Ta da!"

"We'll be right down," Adalet spoke back to the speaker.

"You should have let him come up and wait a few minutes," Meryem scolded.

"You watch too many movies," Adalet threw on her jacket and went out the apartment door.

"You don't watch enough," Meryem followed her shutting the door behind them.

*   *   *

"Shouldn't we take a bus?" Adalet asked this as Mark was already hailing a taxi.

"I'm sorry," Mark laughed, "after reading Orhan Pamuk, I'm a bit leery of buses here. And *Fez With A Heart* didn't help that impression." A taxi screeched to a halt and the three of them piled into the back seat. "Hagia Sophia," Mark instructed the driver.

"Oh, is that where we're going? That's what we're reading in Professor Aronson's class," Meryem looked at Adalet.

"You've read Pamuk?" Adalet looked at Mark Aronson in surprise. She didn't realize she'd ignored Meryem.

"Yup. Why do you seem surprised?"

"I didn't think an American would read—" she paused.

"A Turkish author? Why not? Turkey and art are my specialties. I think he's wonderful, even if a bit obsessive-compulsive."

"What do you mean?" Adalet asked as they plodded in winding traffic. She couldn't see the meter from where she was sitting, but she couldn't help wondering and worrying what the bill would be.

"Well, he grabs onto an idea and runs with it, and beats it into description for many pages, making his point in such creative ways, but also endlessly. Is he popular here?"

"I'm not crazy about him for the reasons you describe. I tried to read The Black Book, but I was as lost in the streets as the main character."

"I loved it," Mark said. "I felt like I was in Istanbul."

"I've never read it," Meryem sulked. "Can you tell me more about Hagia Sophia?" She directed the question to her professor.

"Not all that much more than we've read in class," Mark said. Anyway, I want to see your reaction to it physically first."

"Have you been there?" Meryem asked Adalet.

"Yes," Adalet said. "I was there once some years ago. And I agree with your professor. See it first, feel it, experience it, and then we can talk about it. It makes a lasting impression."

The taxi pulled up next to the long walkway leading into the cathedral. Adalet sighed aloud, "Four minarets," she said to Meryem. "It was a serious mosque."

Mark Aronson quickly paid the driver before Adalet could even offer. As they walked the long pathway through the surrounding grounds, they were already in an awed silence. The manicured green lawn spotted with well-placed flowering trees that were just beginning to bud. Benches surrounded the water fountains where people wandered and sat, even with the chill that remained in the air. In a couple of weeks, it would be April, and Adalet imagined that the gardens would be filled with people then.

"It's a good time to be here," she turned to Mark Aronson. It's not too cold and it's not too crowded."

"But one can't ever be sure," he smiled as he pulled three tickets from his jacket pocket. "So just in case, I got these online."

"You must let me pay for our tickets. You already paid for the taxi," Adalet insisted.

"But I really wanted this day to be on me," Mark Aronson looked serious. "But you can make us tea at the end of the day. And I hope you'll invite me to tea again."

"It will be dinner, if I'm going to accept this much of your hospitality."

"Does that mean that it's settled?" he asked, waving the tickets for punctuation.

Meryem pulled the tickets from Mark Aronson's hand and headed to the entrance ahead of them. "Sounds good to me, Dr. Aronson, thank you." She swung around to Adalet, "Don't be so old-fashioned."

"That's hardly being old-fashioned," Mark Aronson laughed. "It's actually quite modern."

Meryem shook her head with a show of disdain, "You know what I mean."

Adalet took a sidelong glance at Mark Aronson, or the professor, as she kept thinking of him. She could not quite refer to him as Mark yet. She liked that he'd defended her, something she had hardly experienced in the past. And with a thought that hadn't even occurred to her. She was being both polite and careful at this stage, not modern at all.

He wore light gray slacks, not jeans, and a light green crew-necked sweater over a blue and green striped shirt. Over that, he had thrown a fine brown leather jacket that he might have pur-chased on a trip to the Grand Bazaar. The prices were so good there, and the Americans were often willing to overlook the poor stitching for the quality of the leather and the price. Adalet thought that she liked the way he presented himself. He was confident without being overbearing.

It was dark inside the cathedral. Shafts of light streaked through the latticed and stained glass windows and hung in the center like wisps of fog. They stood under the dome and looked up, and up, past the Saints, past the tiny windows, into the glorious gold and blue tile work, Christian representations alongside the black and golden Arabic calligraphy.

"It's like being under the most magnificent night sky," Meryem marveled.

"It is," her professor agreed.

"I don't remember it being this wonderful," Adalet spoke aloud but she was talking to herself. "It was a different time in my life. I think I'm more able to appreciate it now," she added.

"How could you not appreciate this?" Meryem was still looking upward.

"I was young and too busy listening to what other, more experi-enced people knew, or thought they knew, to be able to have my own thoughts and feelings. I'm glad I was able to come back." She smiled at Mark Aronson as she said this, and he was looking directly at her. He smiled back.

An English-speaking Turkish guide caught their attention. She had a small group of Australians with her. She was giving them background information on this museum that had once been a church and had then become a mosque, as the Ottoman Empire came and conquered what had once been Constantinople. Adalet tried to follow what she was saying and moved in more closely to listen while Mark Aronson and Meryem went in different directions to examine some of the artwork and artifacts.

"Hagia Sophia is translated from the Greek as "Holy Wisdom." It was originally constructed in 537 as a Greek Orthodox patriarchal basilica. Under the Latin Empire, from 1201 through 1261, it became a Roman Catholic cathedral, but then became Eastern Orthodox until 1453, when it was converted to a mosque under the Ottomans, Sultan Mehmet II to be exact. The mosque was closed in 1931, and it was closed to the public for the following four years. The building was then secularized and opened as a museum in February of 1935. Earthquakes in 553 and in 557 resulted in cracks in the main dome. Another earthquake in 558, just the following year, caused the entire main dome to collapse. It was immediately restored—."

Adalet turned away. She knew enough about the destruction that earthquakes could cause. She'd learned many facts about Hagia Sophia and forgotten most of them. Now she just wanted to have the experience. She remembered being there with Yasar and another couple, friends of his. Yasar had studied every aspect of Hagia Sophia as an architectural student. He knew every nook and cranny and fact upon fact. He had overwhelmed them with so much information that although Adalet was proud of him, she wondered if the other couple wished he'd be more selective, as she did. She recalled this now and realized that this was the reason she hadn't been able to enjoy her last visit here. She was glad to have these few minutes to herself and pleased when she looked around to see that Meryem and her professor had wandered off in different directions to have their separate experiences. She liked to think they would share them with her later.

Adalet bent down and placed her hand on the cool marble floor, tracing the red, green and white patterns with her fingers. Marble floors, marble walls with flurries of swirling patterns that stopped suddenly here and there where some factor of time had erased them. Large cracks that Adalet imagined had been covered with carpets when it had been a working mosque. She closed her eyes and tried to imagine the muezzin chanting the call to prayer, what it might have sounded like coming from a building such as this. Now the call to prayer was recorded. She felt a strong surge of pride that it was an American who'd brought them here. And when she opened her eyes again, that American was standing next to her, respectfully waiting for her to return from her reverie.

"Meryem is busy with her sketch pad," he told her.

"I didn't even notice that she'd brought one with her."

"She'd thrown a small one into her bag. I guess she didn't want to appear too studious. She tells me she hates studying buildings, but she seems pretty taken with this one." Mark extended his arm to her. "Care to walk around and take in some of the artwork? I know a little bit about some of it."

Adalet put her arm through his and they walked together toward a display. "I think a little bit will be just the right amount," she said.

CHAPTER 15

By the time that Adalet, Meryem and Mark—Adalet had started to call him by his first name—left the large cathedral and came out into the daylight, it was late afternoon. The sky was gray and it wouldn't be too long before it became dark.

"It's too late for lunch and too early for dinner," Mark said. "Should we stop for some tea and go to dinner when we're really hungry?"

"I'm really hungry right now," Meryem complained. Adalet noticed that the longer Meryem walked in those boots the grumpier she became, but she refrained from saying anything in front of Mark. Adalet had a sense that Meryem was attempting to impress her professor and she didn't want to embarrass her.

"We could go back to our apartment, if you like," Adalet suggested. "We can have some *mezze* with some wine or *raki,* and that should hold us over until dinner."

"Great idea," Mark agreed. "And I know a couple of good restaurants close by.

I didn't think you would drink alcohol. A glass of *raki* would be welcome before dinner."

"I'm a semi-modern Moslem." Adalet admitted.

"Me, too." Meryem chimed in.

"This is true," Adalet remarked, as they slid into another taxi. Then she whispered in Meryem's ear. "A bit of *raki* might take the edge off of those boots."

Meryem slid across the seat to the far window. Adalet got in next and slid close to her. Meryem whispered back to Adalet, "You're not kidding. Stupid shoes for a museum." Meryem made a pained face as Mark got into the taxi.

"Something wrong?" he asked.

"Nothing really," Adalet said quickly.

"My feet are killing me. I can't wait to take these things off," Meryem lifted one foot in the air for Mark to see. "Adalet was smart. I offered them to her, but she refused to wear them."

Adalet was shocked at this revelation. Here she was trying not to bring the foolishness of Meryem's choice to Mark's attention and Meryem had admitted it as if it were nothing. That was something Adalet would never have said. Had Meryem been influenced by Fatma who complained about these things all the time? Didn't Meryem know that it was perfectly natural to hear an old woman complain about aches and pains, but it was something a young lady didn't do in front of a man? Or was Meryem merely showing off? Adalet often couldn't tell the difference. But for now she determined to say nothing and let it pass as quickly as possible. Fortunately, she thought, Mark made no comment.

Once they were inside their apartment building, Meryem pulled off her boots, took a deep sigh, and ran up the stairs ahead of them, waving the shoes with one hand, her bag in the other. She tossed the shoes on the floor in front of the door to search for the keys in her bag, unlocked the door and disappeared inside. When Adalet and Mark walked in, she was lying on the couch, her heels resting on top of a pillow.

"Fashion can be dangerous," Mark pointed to her feet and looked serious. He added, "And painful."

Meryem buried the soles of her feet under the pillow. "I'm sorry, Professor Aronson. I didn't mean to insult you." Meryem sounded genuinely contrite.

"I know you didn't." He turned to Adalet and winked to let her know that he had never considered that Meryem was showing the soles of her feet to him as an insult.

Adalet smiled and headed into the kitchen. When Mark joined her, he'd removed his jacket. "Oh," she said, I should have taken your jacket. The foot thing—-"

"It's okay. I never thought I'd have a Turkish person showing me the bottom of their feet. I thought for certain I'd make that mistake myself."

Adalet began to remove containers from the refrigerator. "It's not a big deal anymore."

"Can I help you with anything?" Mark asked.

Adalet was now setting small appetizer dishes on the table. "I don't think so. I'm just going to transfer these things." She emptied olives into a dish. "It's nothing fancy, just something to munch on until we go to dinner." She pulled three glasses out of a cupboard and removed ice from the freezer. She also pulled out a bottle of *raki*. "Do you take yours with water?"

"Yes, please. I'd like to be awake for dinner."

"It can knock you out if you're not careful," Adalet warned him. "It creeps up on you slowly before you notice. I'm going to make Meryem's mostly ice and water." She carefully portioned a small dribble of *raki* into a glass filled with ice water. "You can take this one in to Meryem, and I'll fix ours a bit stronger. Here, take the olives with you."

"Sure." Mark took the glass from her and picked up the bowl of olives and carried them into the living room. He handed the glass to Meryem, who sniffed it and made a face, mumbling, "Is there any *raki* in this?"

Mark placed the ceramic olive dish on the table. It was colorfully painted with various shapes and sizes of olives. He returned to the tiny kitchen area where Adalet had placed a variety of dishes with spreads and flat dipping bread on a large tray. She handed Mark a glass of *raki*. He handed it back to her, "Here, you carry these and I'll take the tray." Surprised by this, she took the glasses and carried them out behind him. Yasar would have taken his drink and plopped down on the couch, not even thinking that the tray might be heavy for her. And she would have had to come back for her own glass.

The sun had made a last-ditch effort to show itself before it disappeared, and Adalet and Mark set down the tray and their drinks and walked to the window to watch the last streaks of orange and red slip into charcoal. The hustle and bustle continued below with streetlights and neon signs illuminating the flurry of activity.

"It's live theater down there," Mark pointed to a young man in a bright red sweater holding up videos he was trying to sell from a worn cardboard box. He called out the titles to no one in particular. "Most likely bootlegged," Adalet told Mark.

Some of the street vendors were closing up for the day while others set up for the night shift. "Doesn't the noise bother you?" Mark asked.

"After living in Avanos?" Adalet shook her head. "No, I feel alive again. The streets have a pulse, a heartbeat. It quiets down around 10:00 or 11:00, and it starts up again with the call to prayer at dawn."

"Yes, it's a lot like New York, except for the call to prayer. I think that's why I can live here. After growing up in New Mexico, well, I guess I must have felt like you did in Avanos. New York has a pulse you can feel, but I think it goes 24 hours a day."

"Then it must be hard to sleep there."

"You get used to it or buy earplugs."

They both turned away from the window, as Meryem emitted a soft snore.

"I thought she'd gotten awfully quiet for Meryem," Mark took a sip of his *raki* and sat on a stack of pillows across from the couch as Meryem turned on her side, away from them. After Adalet threw a knitted afghan across Meryem to keep her warm, she pulled some pillows up and sat on the floor near him. Mark pulled the tray of food onto the floor between them. Neither of them spoke for a while as they dipped the bread into the spreads, enjoying the variety of flavors and sipping the *raki*. Adalet thought it was a comfortable silence. She suddenly realized that she had never been as relaxed as this with a man, able to eat and drink without forcing some conversation in order to feel connected. She'd always felt she had to be a certain way with Yasar to impress him, and he was the only man with whom she'd been close enough to have a meal alone together. What a relief it was to not have to work so hard. She glanced at Meryem. Well, they weren't really alone, and this wasn't exactly a meal.

As if he'd been reading her thoughts, Mark said, "This is nice."

"It is."

"Think she'll wake up soon?"

"I don't know."

"We could go and bring some dinner back for her."

Adalet hesitated, wondering for a split second if Mark had actually read her mind. "We could leave her a note and bring her something back."

Mark stood and held out his hand to Adalet to help her up.

"Shouldn't I put the food away?" She asked.

"Do you want to wake her up?"

No, Adalet shook her head. She did not. She tiptoed into the bedroom and wrote Meryem a short note and grabbed her jacket. As Adalet placed the note on the table next to Meryem, Yetim stuck her head out from under the afghan where she'd been hiding and sleeping next to Meryem. Adalet motioned a quiet shush to Yetim, and Adalet and Mark sneaked softly out the door.

The restaurant Mark chose was one that Adalet had passed many times but never entered. It was a small but lively neighborhood place. It was still quiet at this hour. It was only a bit past 7:30, and it wouldn't fill up until 8:00 or 9:00. The man who greeted them at the door knew Mark and didn't blink at his poor Turkish. He seated them at a small table in the back and sent the waiter to take their drink orders. The waiter was shorter than the man who greeted them, but he had the same large dark eyes, thick dark hair and heavy mustache.

"They're brothers," Mark explained to Adalet in English. "Their mother does the cooking which is why the food is so good." He ordered two glasses of *raki* and a plate of *acili ezme,* a hot pepper paste and bread with a dish of *cacik,* a thick yogurt with cucumber and garlic. Mark had to repeat the *acili ezme* twice, but the young waiter smiled and patted Mark on the back. He said in a heavily accented English, "Yes, yes, Professor. Soon your Turkish will be as good as my English." He turned to Adalet, "I teach him."

Adalet smiled but her thoughts were elsewhere. Here she was, almost like magic, alone at last with Mark and anticipating a lovely dinner, but she had to question her behavior. She felt a bit irresponsible running off with him and leaving Meryem asleep on the couch. What would she think if she woke up before they got back? The note she'd written didn't give a nice explanation, something like, we didn't want to wake you up, or we thought we'd let you sleep and bring you some food later. All it had said was, "Mark and I went to dinner. Will bring you some back. Adalet."

"You're awfully quiet all of a sudden," Mark commented after the waiter went off to get their drinks.

"I don't know. I don't feel quite right leaving Meryem like that."

"Why? Suppose you'd fallen asleep, would you think anything of it if I'd taken Meryem to dinner and brought your dinner back? She'll be just fine."

Adalet tried not to allow any expression of her surprise to show. Up until that moment, she'd felt a bit like a coconspirator, as if they'd silently plotted to leave Meryem so that they could be alone together. Now it seemed he was only hungry and anxious to get dinner. She cursed herself for having been so presumptuous. Apparently, she was alone in her fantasy.

"I suppose, but it just doesn't feel right. Why don't we have our drinks and the *ezme* and bring dinner back for the three of us?"

"Sure, that's fine. We'll give him the order when he comes back with our drinks."

"Let's order two things we can all share." Adalet opened her menu. She didn't know how her disappointment would get her through the *ezme* and yogurt, never mind a whole dinner portion. She'd let down her guard when she'd already prepared not to have any feelings for Professor Mark Aronson. Now she wished she could pour herself through a crack in the floor or whisk herself out a window. Clearly, he was being polite and looked on her as Meryem's guardian and Meryem as his student. Nothing more.

CHAPTER 16

"Guess who just called?" Meryem was wide awake, sketching at the table when Adalet and the professor walked in with a large bag of food from the restaurant. "Oh, good, thanks you two, I'm so hungry."

"Who called?" Adalet asked as she helped Meryem set aside her art materials so that they would have room to unpack the food onto the table.

"Fatma," Meryem announced, reaching into the bag and pulling out a take-out box. She opened it and smiled, "My favorite, *pilav* with chicken—oh, you got the good kind with almonds and pista-chios—yum!" The sweet and dusty smell of saffron puffed up by rice and nuts, chicken and dill rose from the open box and filled the air. "What else?" She set the *pilav* onto the table and reached back into the bag to lift out another container.

"Is everything okay in Avanos? Did something happen?" Adalet was used to Fatma sending brief notes through her son, Ahmet, or even verbal messages he would report when he delivered Adalet's money to her and checked on the building. Fatma didn't like using the telephone. She was like a sultan's wife, sending out emissaries and expected a lengthy description of not only words, but facial expressions and more subtle responses such as: Did Meryem look up at you when you told her that? Did Adalet push her hair over her right ear when she said that? For a blind woman, she was quite the detective and knew all the nuances of her loved ones.

"She's coming with Ahmet on his next trip here. Ah," she cried, after lifting the lid of the second box, "*borek!* What kind?"

"Spinach and feta cheese," Mark answered. "Shall I carry in some plates?"

"If someone doesn't tell me soon about Fatma and when she's coming, no one will eat," Adalet declared. She removed her jacket and took Mark's from his hand, throwing them both across the camel bag pillow, not bothering to hang them up. She stared at Meryem. "And we don't want the food to get cold."

"Okay, okay." Meryem set the covers back on the food. "A week from Sunday, Fatma said. They're going to leave very early in the morning on Saturday, and they'll get here some time in the afternoon on Sunday, depending on how many stops they have to make along the way. Poor Uncle Ahmet. That long a drive with my *anneanne* might not be fun."

"Why?" Mark asked.

"Fatma's been lecturing to Uncle Ahmet since he was a little boy, and he's been waiting on her hand and foot since he could crawl. My poor auntie has to wait on both of them. I don't think spoiling men is so good for married women. If I'm expected to do it, I'm don't think I'm ever going to marry."

"That's what you say now," Adalet retorted. "Just wait until some handsome fellow comes along and sweeps you right off your feet, right off those high-heeled boots of yours." She'd fetched plates and utensils from the kitchen and set them on the table. "Let's do buffet-style. It goes with take-out."

"We won't get away with that with Fatma," Meryem grabbed a plate and began to pile *pilav* onto her plate.

Something about the presence of Meryem and the good-natured lightness of banter and food lifted Adalet's spirits. She watched Meryem lift a *borek* from the box, set it on her plate, and lick her fingers of the sticky phyllo pastry. She envied how at ease Meryem seemed to be with life, but she admired it as well. Why had she become so tense with Mark in the restaurant? Did she need Meryem along to feel comfortable? She wasn't sure. She had been pleased when they went on to eat alone, and then she became tense and, she had to acknowledge, a bit defensive.

Adalet nodded at Mark to serve himself. And then she wondered if she should have filled her own plate first. What did they say in the West that used to make Yasar laugh? Ladies first. That was it. Not in her experience. Her grandmother had served her grandfather, her mother had served her father, and for the times they ate at home together, she had always served Yasar. She thought she might find life in America a difficult adjustment, as exciting and welcome an opportunity as it might be, not that her even traveling there for a visit was of the remotest possibility.

"Please join us," Mark sat beside Meryem. "Where are your manners, young lady? Why don't we wait for Adalet?"

"Professor Aronson," Meryem placed the *borek* she'd already taken a bite from back onto her plate, "I do apologize, Adalet. When I was growing up," she explained to Mark, "I had to live with my father's sisters and their families. If you waited for everyone to come to the table before you started to eat, you'd starve. I usually remember my manners when there are guests, but I guess I'm becoming more comfortable with you. Sorry."

Adalet wondered who had taken the Meryem she knew and re-placed her with someone who could make such a civil response to a criticism. If Adalet had said something similar, Meryem would have waved her hand at her in dismissal. Adalet wanted to laugh but she caught herself in time. Displays of politeness from Meryem needed to be rewarded, even when they came late. Instead she said, "Thank you, Meryem."

"My grandparents, my mother's parents, used to talk about the Great Depression and having to stand in line for bread. I had a great uncle who supposedly killed himself when the stock market crashed, but of course, my mother was just a little girl then. She didn't really know him. We always had plenty of food." Mark stopped there, as though his remark needed no further explanation, but Meryem shook her head at him.

"We always had enough food, too, Professor. We weren't starving in that real kind of way. My Aunties just didn't raise my cousins with any manners, so they grabbed their food, and if you weren't quick enough, there just wouldn't be any left on the table. Turkey may be a third-world country but I've always had enough to eat."

"I didn't mean—"

Adalet cut in before Mark could go on. "I've been lucky also," she said as she sat down opposite Mark and began to spoon some pilav onto her plate. "My parents weren't wealthy but we always had enough. And they saved to help me with my education. I was quite a happy child." As if to prove this, Adalet took a large forkful of the rice dish and put it into her mouth. While she chewed, she wondered if Professor Mark Aronson's idea of deprived life in a Turkish village had come from old foreign language films he'd seen as a child. But no, she thought, he's traveled to Avanos. He's seen for himself that people live well there. And why was she feeling defensive again?

"Do people still starve in America? I wonder about that." Meryem asked. "We still think of America as so rich. Everyone wants to go to America."

"I think there are starving people everywhere," Adalet said.

"Unfortunately, Adalet is right. There are poor people in America, and their families sometimes go hungry. And the numbers of people who don't have enough to eat or medical care are steadily going up. The rich are getting richer and the poor are getting poorer." Mark sighed and shook his head. "There is some government aid for people who are truly poor and have children, but it's never enough, and sometimes they don't have anywhere to live."

"Really," Meryem took another bite from the quickly vanishing *pilav* on her plate. "You mean that in America there are people who live on the street? Like the Kurds who come here and camp outside in tents and blankets?"

"In New York City there are people who live in cardboard boxes and whole families who live in the subways. You see the Americans who come here and who can afford to travel. We're not all rich." Mark leaned forward and looked at both of them. "I'm wondering why I'm feeling like I have to produce and defend poverty in America. Every time I get into this kind of discussion here, I feel like the Turkish I know are always denying that there's anything ever wrong with Turkey, and I must come up with all the problems I can possibly think of that we have in America. I think I've ended up in this conversation so many times. Do you know why this is?" He looked from one to the other, "Come on, tell me something, please. I want to understand. How will I ever understand if you don't say anything?"

"Don't be frustrated with us, Mark. We Turkish are little specks, worker bees, in the hive of the world that is run by the Queen Bee, America. We grow up comparing and finding ways to be even number 10 or 11. You grow up being number one." Adalet set her fork down on her plate and folded her hands in her lap. "Say you are the blonde girl in the Turkish high school and everyone wants to be your friend and tells you how pretty you are. We don't have too many blondes here, so a blonde girl can be very popular. But since you are already the most popular, you can afford to make your friend feel good. You can say, oh, my hair is so thin and straight while yours is so thick and curly. You can be generous because you are already number one."

"And this is where you think I'm coming from? It's ridiculous." Mark raised both his hands in disbelief. "It can't be true that most Turkish people feel this way."

"I'm sorry you feel it is ridiculous, and yes, I think many Turkish do feel this way. I told you once, we are a proud people." Adalet could feel her stomach juices churning in what she feared might soon become anger. "You ask me to explain this to you, and then you say that my words are ridiculous. I was being completely sincere with you."

Meryem sat quietly, moving her fork around the few grains of *pilav* left on her plate.

"I'm sorry, Adalet." Mark wiped his mouth with his napkin and set it back on his lap, almost as if he were wiping something distasteful away. "I guess I don't like to think of myself as the ugly and arrogant American."

"You misunderstand me again. I'm talking to you about the Turkish people."

Meryem slid her chair back and stood up. "If no one objects, I'm going to take my dish into the kitchen and go into my room to sleep. I don't think *raki* and I get along very well." She looked at Adalet and Adalet nodded.

Meryem disappeared into the kitchen and after the water ran in the sink and the dish was set into the drainer, Adalet heard Meryem quietly close her bedroom door. "Meryem has more sense than I often give her credit for. She knows when to leave. She wants us to be friends."

Mark moved his chair so that he was facing Adalet. "I thought we were becoming friends. No, I believe we are becoming friends." He gently took her hand and placed it in his.

"Then we must learn to understand each other. I want you to understand what I have to say. This is something that was not so important to me once but is the most important thing to me now." Adalet did not withdraw her hand but looked into Mark's eyes. He had to be able to listen to her. She wouldn't tolerate another relationship where her opinions were dismissed, washed up on shore somewhere like so much garbage. At the same time, she felt a tremendous wave of great power and strength sweeping her straight towards Mark, and while a sweet voice from inside told her to just let go and allow it to happen, another voice was insisting that she grab onto the nearest rock and cry out for help just as loud as she could.

But just as she thought she might pull away and escape, Mark took hold of her other hand and placed them both inside of his. "Then talk," he said, "and I will listen. And if I don't understand, I'll ask you to explain. But you must have patience with me, too. I'm also ignorant. I'm also a part of the 'human stupid.'"

CHAPTER 17

Adalet pulled her shopping cart on wheels over the uneven brick street, up the hill, and through the operatic cacophony of the Sunday open market. *"Balik, balik, balik, balik, BALIK!"* The fish vendor wagged a large red snapper at Adalet, its bulging dead eyes poking out like the shiny buttons on a doll she'd once had as a child.

"Domates, domates, domates," a boy sang out in a strong tenor. Next to him, a man who might have been his father answered "Salitalik-hiyar, salitalik-hiyar, salitalik-hiyar." . Adalet stopped to pick up a tomato and smell it.

"Good, good; please taste; taste." The older father vendor picked up a piece of tomato already cut in small wedges for customers to sample. Adalet took it from him and popped it into her mouth. "Teşekkur ederim, thank you very much," she told him, savoring the sweetness. He then handed a slice of cucumber to her as well, but Adalet felt a small presence press next to her body. She lowered her eyes from the vendor to a Kurdish waif holding out one small, very dirty hand. Adalet took the cucumber slice and put it into the little girl's palm. The vendor shook his head at Adalet, but when she quickly ordered both tomatoes and cucumbers, he ran his fingers over his thick, dark mustache and his charming smile returned.

A woman with what sounded to Adalet like a heavy British accent squeezed between Adalet and the child. "How much?" she interrupted, as the vendor weighed Adalet's tomatoes. "Five *lira*," he told her. "Five *lira* a pound."

"What about three?" It appeared to Adalet that this woman was used to enjoying a good bargain in the tourist shops. The food in the market could not be up for barter since the prices were established for the local people and were already fixed as low as the vendors could set them and still earn a profit.

"One minute," the vendor told her and handed the tomatoes to Adalet. He looked up at the interrupting woman. "You want three pounds of tomatoes?" he asked.

"No, no," she said, in a tone of exasperation, "What could I possibly do with three pounds of tomatoes? I want them for three *lira* a pound."

"Five *lira* a pound." He weighed out Adalet's cucumbers. He picked up the cardboard sign sitting in the heap of tomatoes and showed her. "Five *lira* a pound." Unlike the many carpet stores this woman had possibly wandered into, it was clear even to her that here she was not going to negotiate a discount. She shrank back a few steps while Adalet paid the vendor. Adalet moved on to a mountain of peppers.

As the crowd picked up, Adalet could no longer feel the chill of the autumn day. The sheer numbers of the tightly packed moving throng provided unnaturally moist warmth that caused her to perspire inside her sweater and rain jacket. The odor of raw, dead fish enveloped her, along with an increasing awareness of her own smell and the stronger sweat of unwashed bodies. She was tempted to take the jacket off, but negotiating the crowd, the guarding of her purchases and of her money from the running gangs of beggar children was too difficult a challenge. Every sense she possessed was on high alert, so that when she felt a tap on her shoulder, she jumped and turned quickly.

"Adalet, is it you?" She was looking directly into the dark almond-shaped eyes and aquiline nose of a somewhat familiar looking young woman whose hair was hidden under a Turkish-style headscarf. She couldn't remember anyone she knew in Istanbul who wore a headscarf, although there were plenty who did.

"It's Nuray," the woman told her. "It's been so long. I guess you wouldn't recognize me with the headscarf."

"Oh, my. It is you, Nuray." The crowd pressed on, forcing the women to the side of the street in between vendors. An older man squatted nearby on the curb, eating his lunch from a blackened pot. The start of a sprinkle of rain enhanced the stench of accumulating garbage. Adalet stepped away from the crouching man, trying to give him some privacy, and she pulled on Nuray's jacket in a gesture that remained from their days at university together.

"How long has it been?" Adalet asked. "What have you been doing?"

"What have I been doing," Nuray admonished, "you're the one who disappeared. You married that good-looking man and fell off the edge of the world."

"We're divorced." Adalet said this quickly, wanting to get it out of the way.

"Well, you're even more of a fallen woman than I am." Nuray adjusted her headscarf and smiled. "I wear this and this"—she pointed to a small wedding ring—"to keep the wolves at bay. Never married and never will. I like men to visit me, not to move in."

Adalet laughed. "Same old Nuray. Luckily, some things don't change. Where are you living and what are you doing?"

"My father passed away a few years ago, so my mother is alone. I live with her and take care of her. She's arthritic and practically blind from a rare retinal disease. I hope I don't inherit it. I'm doing some writing when I can."

"What about?"

"The life of women in Turkey. What else do I know to write about?"

Adalet took Nuray's arm and pulled her closer, out of the way of a man carrying a hefty box of goods on his head. "We're going to have to move from here," Adalet cautioned. "Let's exchange phone numbers and email addresses. We can meet for lunch or tea. I haven't had a woman friend my own age in some time."

"I haven't either," Nuray admitted. "Taking care of my mother is a full-time job, but if you can meet me in my neighborhood or even come to our home, that would be best."

"Sure. I can do that." Even as she said it, Adalet wondered how she would fit this into her schedule, but she was suddenly hungry for a companion, someone who knew her before her marriage to Yasar. There was no one in her life at present who qualified. The women each dug in their purses for a scrap of paper and a pen.

"Promise?" Nuray asked, holding out her pinky finger and bringing back another sharp memory to Adalet of who they'd been in their university days.

"Promise," Adalet said, linking her own pinky through Nuray's and kissing her old friend on both cheeks.

Adalet stuck the paper Nuray handed her into her bag and watched her make her way out of sight into the teeming street. How good it might be to reconnect. But she also remembered that Nuray had been demanding of her time and that she'd given her so little of it after she'd met Yasar. Could she even be a real friend to anyone now?

Adalet checked her shopping list. She still had to buy eggplant, cheese, olives, figs and anchovies for Fatma. She thought she might also get some pomegranates and squeeze some juice. All the other supplies she needed she could buy closer to home, but the prices here were too good to resist, even though her legs were often tired and ached after she made this trip every week.

Adalet stopped at a cosmetic table to see if there was any decent eye shadow there. She opened a package of colors to examine them against her complexion. As she was peering in the mirror that came with the eye shadow case, Adalet paused to push back a few stray strands of hair that had fallen into her face. She was startled to see the reflection of the profile of a man who either looked a lot like or actually was Yasar. She closed the case and set it back on the vendor's table, carefully turning around and walking back slowly so that he wouldn't see her moving in his direction. A large family pushed their way in front of Adalet, momentarily blocking her vision. Two little girls, sisters most likely, began to do a dance with each other, happily trying to get their parents' attention. By the time they stopped prancing and moved along in the opposite direction, the figure was gone.

Adalet backtracked for a bit before she decided to give up and complete her shopping. But it seemed impossible to get this out of her mind. Yasar never went shopping for food. True, he was on his own now, but he would just go to his family for meals or eat in a restaurant. If it was Yasar, and Adalet began to feel pretty certain that it was, what was he doing in the market? He disliked crowds. He was not one to shop for discounts. In fact, as Adalet looked around, she could not find one item that would interest Yasar. Had he seen her? Was he following her? Just thinking about this made her nervous, even fearful. What would happen if he discovered that she was living here?

Adalet finished her shopping in a daze. "Try this one. Please, try this." The olive vendor confused her when he offered her too many to taste.

"I'll just take these." She pointed to the oily black Mediterranean olives and some that were large, salty and green.

Adalet preferred the Mediterranean olives. Meryem ate them like they were popcorn. The green salty ones were something she remembered that Fatma liked. The sardines looked and smelled fresh, so she watched without seeing as the vendor filled a bag. She picked out several cheeses, one of them being Turkish white cheese, *beyaz peynir, kasar* for cooking in *borek* and a stronger *kasar* for *mezze*.

Still in a fog, Adalet made her way back through an increasingly more crowded market to *Istiklal Caddesi,* Istanbul's most famous Avenue, and the way home to her apartment. Though Adalet had never been to New York City, Mark had told her that the avenue reminded him of 42nd Street, not Fifth Avenue, as Adalet had always assumed. Mark described *Istiklal* as tacky, but since it was the street of fashion in Istanbul, Adalet could only imagine what Fifth Avenue must look like. She adored living close to this exciting avenue, right off Taksim Square, designed with snake-like side streets filled with good restaurants. Mark had also mentioned that there were good restaurants on 46th Street, but there were no winding streets or roller coaster climbs. She hoped to see it all one day.

She tugged her shopping cart behind her to the steep street that led to her apartment and began the downward climb to *Kazanci Yokuşu* 27, or *Steep Street,* as the locals often liked to call it. The English sign from Taksim Square read "Secret Garden."

When Adalet reached number 27, she was too tired to bend down to open the inconveniently placed lock on the bottom panel of the outer door. She rang the buzzer, hoping that Meryem would be home, not only to buzz her into the building but to help her to carry the food upstairs. And to be honest with herself, Adalet didn't want to be alone just now. She needed Meryem to be there so that she could tell her about seeing Yasar. She let out a deep breath when she heard Meryem's voice sing through the outdoor speaker.

"Who is it?" There was something so charming and welcoming to Meryem's voice these days.

"It's me, Meryem. Can you come down and help me with the groceries?"

"Sure. I'll buzz you inside. Be right down."

Adalet pushed open the heavy front door and pulled the cart up the one crooked step into the entrance. She leaned her body against the door so that it closed completely and locked. She had to shut the image of Yasar pushing the door open behind her from her mind. She was being ridiculous. Thankfully, she heard Meryem open the door of their apartment.

"Want to try the elevator?" Meryem shouted down.

"Not on my life!" Adalet yelled back. They both laughed as Meryem bounded down the stairway. The only person they'd known to take that clunky piece of junk since they'd lived there was Mark on his first visit. He hadn't taken it since. Adalet couldn't wait to see whether Fatma would risk the cage or the stairs.

Meryem grabbed one end of the shopping cart while Adalet took the other. They had to stop at one point with the curvature of the stairway to adjust their positions but made it through the door without spilling or dropping anything. They worked together silently until all the groceries were put away.

"Tea?" Meryem asked Adalet.

"Yes, please. I would love some tea. Do you have some time to sit and talk a bit?" Adalet asked, ever aware of Meryem's schoolwork and art projects.

"I'm not budging from this house today. I've had such a busy week. We have to talk about our plans for next weekend. I don't think we can wing it with Fatma."

Adalet placed water in the kettle to heat for the tea. "What do you think all of this food is for? We can do some prep work later as well, if you like. I suspect I'll be working at it all week. You can help me when you have the time. School comes first."

"Sure. We'll prep what we can. We'll probably have to make the veggie salads on the weekend, though, so they taste fresh."

"Thank goodness for a good refrigerator." Adalet was grateful that the kitchen appliances all worked so well. She wished for an oven, but there was only a small one to plug into the wall socket. They also had a microwave, but Fatma didn't believe in them and wouldn't eat anything prepared in one. Of course, certain things would have to be reheated in the microwave, but Adalet hoped to keep Fatma out of the kitchen so that she'd be none the wiser. Adalet kept these thoughts to herself while Meryem poured the tea and placed some cookies on the table.

"Something creepy happened today while I was shopping," Adalet said before sipping her tea. "Well, actually something nice and something creepy."

"Oh, I want to save 'creepy' for last." Meryem clicked her cup against Adalet's. "To creepy," she toasted.

"Okay, I'll tell you 'nice' first. I saw my old university friend, Nuray, shopping in the market. We stopped and chatted and talked about seeing each other again."

"That is nice," Meryem agreed. "You need some other friends besides me and Mark."

"Well, we'll see. Nuray is taking care of a sick mother. I wasn't such a good friend to her. Once I was involved with Yasar, I gave up my friends for his. It was foolish, I know. Maybe she can forgive me. But I'm a bit hesitant, as she wasn't an easy friend. She wanted too much from me."

"We must be wary of those," Meryem raised a brow and looked into her eyes. "So what was creepy?

Adalet took a large sugar cookie from the plate and a sip of tea. "I saw Yasar at the market."

"What did he say?" Meryem set her teacup down and gave Adalet her full attention.

"Nothing. We didn't speak."

"You ignored each other?"

"I'm not even sure he saw me," Adalet admitted. "I was checking the color of a lipstick and I spotted him in the mirror."

"Are you sure it was Yasar?" Meryem had a way of landing on the right question just about every time.

"Not exactly, but I'm pretty sure."

"But the food market doesn't sound like a place Yasar would ever go, from what you've told me about him." Meryem nibbled at a plain cookie glazed with some sort of pistachio topping. She pulled the glaze off the cookie and dropped the sticky topping into her mouth.

"That's what I thought. I tried to move in closer to see if was really Yasar, but it was such a thick crowd. Then I didn't see him anymore."

"Do you think he was following you?"

"That didn't occur to me until after he disappeared. I should have kept going instead of doubling back. Then I would've known."

"It was probably just coincidence," Meryem reflected. "Why would he be following you?"

"I'm really not sure. What if he just saw me somewhere and wanted to know what I'm doing in Istanbul? What if he finds out

I'm living here and tells his parents? I'm supposed to stay in Avanos according to our agreement."

"Are you serious?" Meryem placed both of her palms on the table, as if she were about to eject herself from her chair. Instead she pushed her body slightly away but holding Adalet's gaze with her own. "He has an affair and divorces you, and then you have to live where his family wants you to so they can almost pretend it never happened?"

"But Meryem, I agreed to stay there. I'm taking money from them under false pretenses. I feel like a thief about to be caught. Maybe I should—."

Meryem threw her hands up to an imaginary deity. "I don't even want to hear you say it. You are not going back to live in Avanos. And you aren't stealing any money from them. They owe it to you. You'll be back on your feet soon, and then you can thank them very much and tell them to go to hell, if you like. Yasar and his family have taken enough from you already."

"They haven't taken anything from me that I haven't taken from myself," Adalet whispered.

"And what is that supposed to mean?"

"I'm guilty here, too, Meryem. I didn't tell Yasar about the baby. And I sent my *anne* into my father's workshop to die because I had no patience and couldn't wait until dinner to tell them I was pregnant."

"And I used to think that I gave my mother cancer until Fatma helped me to see that I'd had nothing to do with it." Meryem shook her hair back from her face. Adalet supposed it was in frustration with her. "I thought that if I hadn't been so rebellious, my father would have stayed at home and my mother wouldn't have gotten sick."

"Fatma helped you?" Adalet pictured Fatma watching Meryem from the doorway, warning her about her behavior and her predictions that Meryem would end up pregnant. She was well aware of Fatma's many sides, but she was glad to know that Meryem had experienced this in Fatma as well.

"Yes. She told me stories about my parents, things that made them seem more like real people to me, with their own thoughts and feelings that had little to do with me. Fatma is giving me a life now that I never could have dreamt about without her. And she wants to do that for you, too. Don't go running away on us. Whatever happens, we'll all deal with Yasar and his family, if that's what it comes to." Meryem peered straight into Adalet's eyes, waiting for her to dare to protest.

Instead, Adalet burst into laughter. "What do you suppose they'd make of Fatma?" she asked, choking on her words. "I can just see it, can't you, Fatma standing in the doorway, facing Yasar's mother with Yasar standing just behind her? Fatma with her arms crossed or shaking one finger at them?" Adalet suddenly became quite serious, the lightness gone, her smile turned to a firm straight line across her face. "It is important to me, though, that you and Fatma don't see Yasar merely as some kind of horrible monster. I made my own mistakes and turned away from him as much as he turned away from me."

"See it whatever way you like," Meryem shot back. "I prefer him evil," and she grimaced, squinting her eyes and crunching her face to such a degree that Adalet couldn't help but laugh aloud again. Then she stopped and spoke quietly.

"I don't know how I'd feel if Yasar knew I was living here."

"Maybe it would set you free if he did."

"What do you mean?" Adalet asked her.

"Well," Meryem moved several pistachio crumbs around in her plate with her finger," you wouldn't have to be afraid that he'd find out anymore. You wouldn't have to creep around the market, seeing him in mirrors, seeing him anywhere and everywhere." Meryem hesitated, noticed that she had crumbs on her finger, licked them off with her tongue and pushed away her plate. "And maybe you want to see him," she said. "Do you?" she fired at Adalet. "Now that feels creepy." The meaning of Meryem's hesitation and her poignant question was painfully clear to Adalet. She didn't like the idea at all that Meryem would even think she was somehow "seeing" Yasar everywhere and even calling him to her by some magical means.

"No, Meryem," Adalet's tone was adamant. "Remember, I was the one who said it was creepy in the first place. I will never go back with Yasar." Adalet rose from her chair and took her teacup to the sink.

"You know what they say," Meryem said to her back. "Never say never. Never is an awfully long time."

CHAPTER 18

Adalet was both ready and not ready for Fatma's visit. So much had happened in the past week, and somehow she'd managed to shop and cook through it all. Meryem had helped as much as she could, but she had schoolwork and projects that kept her quite busy. The shopping and cooking had actually grounded Adalet. She'd been up late the Saturday night before talking into the early morning hours with Mark. At 3:00am, they'd moved from the table where they'd been sitting to the couch across the room. Mark had gone home when the sun came up at 6:00am, and Adalet had crawled into bed drained and exhausted. She'd slept most of Sunday, on and off, getting up to eat a late breakfast, early lunch prepared by Meryem who'd had enough sense not to question Adalet as to the events of Saturday evening.

The marketing had taken Adalet several days. She'd been careful not to do too much in one day so that her legs would not get too tired or inflamed. On Thursday evening, after Meryem returned from classes and they'd eaten some dinner, Adalet and Meryem worked together to clean the apartment thoroughly, moving poor Yetim from each of her resting places to clean the cat hair out from under her. "Sunday morning we'll need do this all over again before Fatma gets here," Adalet plopped down on the couch after putting fresh litter in the box for Yetim.

"Too bad Yetim can't clean up after herself," Meryem sighed. "Wake me early on Sunday when you get up to do the last-minute food preparation, and I'll clean the litter and dust one more time."

"Thank you, Meryem. And if you can help me to clean the kitchen after the cooking is finished on Saturday, that would be a great help. I'll try not to make too much of a mess and clean as I go."

"Saturday?" Meryem asked. "Will you need me on Saturday?" Meryem dropped the duster she'd been using into the dustpan and crossed her arms in front of her.

"Do you have something you want to do on Saturday? I thought you might be around to help."

"I have something I was hoping to work on and finish on Saturday for school—a project. But if you need me—

"Can you come back in the late afternoon, around 4:00 maybe? I should be finished cooking by then." Adalet didn't really like anyone in the kitchen with her when she was cooking. The only person she'd ever been able to do that with was her mother. She knew that Meryem would get underfoot, and she would have asked her to stay home for nothing, other than Adalet's own anxiety and her wish to have someone around to talk to. Better to have her there after to help clean.

"Sure, I can do that." Meryem leaned back into the couch and sighed with what Adalet thought might be relief.

"Are you behind in your school assignments?" Adalet asked her, more from concern than any thought that Meryem had been neglectful. Adalet continued to be surprised at Meryem's dedication to her work at the university. Adalet had feared having to be much more of a disciplinarian, but Meryem was fiercely proud of her grades and what she was accomplishing as a growing artist.

"Not behind. Just something I want to finish up while I'm inspired." Meryem's cheeks turned a light pink and she covered her mouth with her hands. "I feel a bit silly saying that," she said. "I don't think I'm enough of an artist yet to be 'inspired.'"

"That's silly," Adalet lifted her legs onto the couch and threw them across Meryem, rocking her with them in affection. "Even people without any talent have inspiration. And Mark thinks you have some real talent."

Meryem hugged both of Adalet's legs in her arms. "Did he really say that?"

"Now I'll give you a big head and you'll think you don't have to work so hard."

"Never!" Meryem exclaimed. "I love to work hard. I love the way oil paints smell, acrylics, even watercolors— different colors each have their own sweet essence. When I open a tube, the first thing I do is to smell it. And my brushes and tools—I love how they feel when I clean them as much as I love how they feel thick with paint. Even food isn't quite as good, although it's certainly second on my list."

Adalet loved to hear Meryem talk about her art. Adalet's mother had taught her to cherish her cooking tools in the way Meryem cared for her brushes. Adalet's mother had always oiled the wooden bowls and tools with scented oil that she made from freshly cut herbs. Adalet could remember the lingering cooking fragrances that greeted her each day when she arrived home from school. She had inherited these visceral relationships to spice and dough from her mother, the layers of sensuous mixtures that permeated her brain, soothing her mind, the feel of her fingers pressing into dough and shaping it into something new, something unlike its former self. Her joy at the sight of what she'd created reminded her of the feelings she had when she was able to help a family with a deaf child solve a problem. It might seem like the simplest of solutions to her but when the family would return and tell her how much her suggestions had meant to them, she could only imagine how Meryem felt at having her work appreciated.

Just a couple of days ago, Adalet had received a call from a family who wanted her to do an evaluation on their five-year old child. The Yeditepe School for the Deaf had referred them to her. They had also followed up with a call offering the nursery at the school and a small office where she could conduct and write up her evaluation. It was more than she'd expected. She arranged to meet the family the following week on Wednesday, knowing that preparing for Fatma and Ahmet would usurp most of her time.

"I have something to tell you," Adalet looked at Meryem.

"What?" Meryem looked back, eyes wide and staring, until Adalet had to laugh.

"No, it's not about Mark."

"What is it then? What could be more important?" Meryem gave her a mischievous look, raising and tilting her left eyebrow as high as she could.

" I have some work at Yeditepe next week." She reclaimed her legs from Meryem's lap and set them back on the floor. "What do you think of that?"

"Oh, my God, Adalet. That is amazing. You must be so excited. I'm so happy for you." Meryem raised her hand in a high five, something Adalet didn't feel comfortable with doing but it seemed to make Meryem almost joyful when she went along with it, so she smacked her hand with as much enthusiasm as she could muster.

"I am pretty excited to work with a family again," Adalet told her, feeling her enthusiasm fully for the first time in declaring it to Meryem. Meryem held out her arms to Adalet and they hugged.

Meryem pulled back and jumped up from the couch, picking up her dustpan with one hand and pointing a finger at Adalet with the other. "Now aren't you glad I painted your car? Where would you be without me?" Meryem danced off to the closet to put away the dustpan and duster.

Adalet got up from the couch slowly, stretching her arms upward and then her torso. It was true, she had to acknowledge, that if Meryem hadn't painted her car that they in all likelihood would not be here in Istanbul today. Even her legs felt stronger these days. She couldn't be sure if that was just the result of time or the change in her circumstances. Adalet preferred to believe it was a bit of both. She hadn't had to take anything for pain in several months, and she caught herself thinking about her legs less and less.

And if Meryem hadn't painted her Fiat and pranced into her life? Adalet would be back in Avanos making the best of things, which would not have been a terrible life. She missed Temel and Emine and their boys and had been most grateful when Temel had suggested that he look out for the house in Avanos for her. She had to admit that she missed Fatma, too, and was glad of her pending visit, even if the preparations were taking a full week. Adalet was actually going to have work the following week, and she knew that never would have happened if not for Fatma and Meryem.

Adalet thought about her parents. The only truly unpredictable event in their lives had destroyed them. Other than the earthquake, they'd known whom they would marry and what they would do with their lives—and in fact they were already doing it at her age now. When her mother was 28, she was already settled, married with a child. Adalet had been surprised to learn from Mark that he was 34 and had never been engaged, never mind married. How different other lives could be. Her own from her mother's. Mark's from hers. Meryem's from anyone else she knew.

Yetim jumped into Adalet's lap and Adalet stroked her just under her ear. Yetim stretched her legs, dug herself further into Adalet's lap and purred loudly. Perhaps people, like cats, could also have more than one life, even if not as many as nine. She was grateful to think she was living a second chance at life, like Yetim, who was an orphan just like Adalet. She picked up the purring creature and stared into her eyes. "We're so lucky, you and I," she whispered. Yetim squealed and broke loose, scurrying past Meryem as she entered the room, running off to be on her own elsewhere in the apartment.

"She's a lot like me," Meryem said from the doorway, now in a sleep t-shirt, her hair towel-dried but still damp from the shower. "She can only take so much affection before she has to run off and remind herself that she likes time to be on her own. Yetim is a true orphan, like me. Although, technically speaking, I do have a father. You'll never be an orphan, even though, you're as much an orphan as Yetim."

"Why do you say that?" Adalet asked.

"You create and join families wherever you go. It's natural for you."

"And you? Aren't you now my family?"

"For now, yes, of course. But you must be careful with me. I'll dig into you with my claws and then bounce off to run somewhere else. It's my nature. And now I'm running off to read and hopefully, fall asleep. Much to do before my *anneanne* arrives." Meryem blew Adalet a kiss. "Goodnight."

Adalet blew a kiss back to her. "Goodnight, little sister." Meryem disappeared from the doorway and Adalet returned to her thoughts. She knew that Meryem had spoken the truth and that it had been a gentle warning. Meryem would move on with her own life one day, and it might not be all that far into the future. Adalet would have to create a family that would stick around, or at least a life with a future. She and Mark had talked only about their pasts, their recent histories in light of becoming better friends. Mark had had girl friends, but he'd never even lived with one of them. He said he'd always been too busy, first being a student who'd hoped to be an artist, and then working towards his doctorate to become a teacher, realizing that his talent was not enough to create art alone. But she knew little about his family or their history. There was much to learn.

Thus far, with the information she had, she thought that she and Mark might not be all that different. She could imagine that art had been his first marriage and that his divorce from making art had been as painful as her divorce from Yasar. And that what he'd tried to give birth to in his art had not been strong enough to survive, like the baby she'd lost in the earthquake.

Adalet rose from the couch and went in to her bedroom. Yetim was curled up on the end of her bed. "Maybe you're more like me than Meryem after all," she leaned down and stroked her back. "You need some space but ultimately prefer to return to your loved ones, when you can." Adalet had to wonder where Mark stood on these issues. Perhaps he only looked like he belonged in Meryem's camp but would one day choose to nest along with Adalet and Yetim. Chiding herself for having such foolish thoughts, Adalet undressed and got ready for bed. As she was about to turn off the light, she heard her cell phone. She wasn't sure she'd ever get used to that irritating electronic beeping noise. Meryem had set it on the same ring tone and vibration as her own because Meryem thought it was the easiest one to hear. Adalet got out of bed and put a stop to its song and dance on her dresser by pushing the button to accept the call. She said hello in Turkish.

"Hello there," Mark's voice replied. "I hope I didn't wake you."

"No," Adalet said in English, as she settled back into bed. "I was just turning out the light to go to sleep."

"I won't keep you then," he said. "I just wanted to check in with you and say goodnight. I know you'll be busy with Fatma all weekend, but I was hoping I might see you the following weekend, if you're not busy."

"I would like that very much," Adalet found herself telling him, although she wished she hadn't added the 'very much.'" She didn't want to seem too eager.

"Good, I'm glad. I'll call you midweek to make plans. Goodnight, Adalet."

"Goodnight, Mark." Adalet switched off the phone and set it on her nightstand before shutting off the light. Scolding herself once again for having foolish fantasies, she went off to sleep to hopefully have foolish dreams.

CHAPTER 19

Fatma stood in the center of the room, looking around at the apartment. Even though her son, Ahmet, was half-owner of this building, Fatma had never had a reason to visit until now. Her clouded eyes moved as if they were as clear as sparkling lake water, gazing in silence without a hint of expression to reveal her thoughts.

"Meryem," she finally spoke, "I want to see your room now."

Meryem had been standing between Adalet and her Uncle Ahmet, as if they were servants in waiting for royalty in the Caliph's palace. As Meryem took Fatma's arm and led her into her bedroom, Adalet remembered the wrapped brown parcel that Meryem had been carrying when she'd come home Saturday afternoon. Meryem had explained to Adalet that it was a school project for which she'd already been graded but that she'd wanted to frame it and give it to Fatma as a gift on Sunday. Adalet had been curious but didn't want to ask Meryem to open the package so that she could see it.

Adalet turned to Ahmet. "They might be in there for a while. Would you like to sit down? Can I get you something to drink?"

"I will sit down," Ahmet said, and he placed his wrinkled bulk on the couch next to Yetim. Adalet thought for a moment that he hadn't seen the cat and that he might sit on Yetim and squash her. His thick black mop of hair hung down over his forehead and was as

138

tousled as his suit, both damp with sweat. Adalet wanted to offer him a shower, but thought better of it before suggesting a drink. Yetim sniffed him cautiously before putting a tentative paw on his thigh. Ahmet scratched her behind one ear and she purred before placing her other paw on his leg. "I would like a glass of water while we wait," Ahmet said, "thank you."

Adalet was handing a tall glass of water to Ahmet when she heard a loud exclamation coming from Meryem's bedroom. Adalet almost dropped the water, but Ahmet got a grasp on it before it could fall.

"What is this? What is this?" Adalet heard Fatma cry. Adalet left Ahmet and hurried to the bedroom where Meryem was holding the object in question. Fatma pointed to it and exclaimed again, "What is this? Are they teaching her to paint Christian religious images in this school?"

Adalet moved in to get a closer look. Meryem merely stood there, holding a painting which was clearly not the Madonna and child, but Adalet could see how the partially blind Fatma could recognize it as such. It was certainly a young woman holding an infant in that same loving way, gazing into her eyes as Mary looked at Jesus. But the mother's hair was a delicate blond, even though the child was dark. Adalet immediately recognized her from the picture Fatma had shown her and the little duplicate that Meryem kept with her jewelry.

"That isn't Mary and Jesus, Fatma. It's Pinar and Meryem. Come. Look closely. Pinar had blond hair, didn't she?"

Fatma leaned in to examine the images. Meryem just stood there, continuing to hold the painting in her arms. "Yes, yes," Fatma muttered. "I think you're right. Bring it into the light, Meryem, where I can see it better. Bring it by the windows in the living room. Let me have a better look."

Adalet took Fatma's arm and steered her back into the living room by the windows while Meryem, without saying a word, carried the painting into the sunlight.

"Yes, I see, it is Pinar and Meryem, but it could have been the Madonna and child. Look at the cloak Pinar is wearing and the way she's holding Meryem and looking at her. I saw many of these in Italy."

"But it is Pinar and Meryem, isn't it?" Adalet looked to Meryem to answer.

"Yes, it is. But I did base it on the mother and child. It was a project for my art history class. Professor Aronson gave me an A. He thought it was beautiful."

"But it isn't the mother and child," Adalet insisted, understanding how unacceptable this might be for Fatma, a Muslim woman, to have her daughter and granddaughter depicted as Christian religious symbols, not only because they were Christian symbols but because Muslims do not portray Mohammed, any religious figures, in portrait. Fatma and Adalet both looked at Meryem, still holding the painting.

"No," Meryem said, her voice taking on the tone of instruction, "it's not the Madonna and child. It is my mother holding me. Professor Aronson asked us to do a self-portrait based on one of the paintings we'd studied in his art history class, something that had affected us deeply in a personal way. When we studied the Leonardo da Vinci cartoon, all I could think of was my mother, missing her, wishing that she could hold me in her arms again." Meryem set the painting on the window ledge. "You don't have to like it," she said to Fatma. "It's okay."

A low moan rose from the bottom of Fatma's stomach, climbing up into her throat and finally reaching her mouth. She exhaled deeply, and Adalet was shocked to see tears in her eyes. She leaned sideways so far that Adalet was afraid she'd fall, and so she stepped in to grab onto her.

"It's the most beautiful painting I have seen in my life," Fatma managed once she'd regained her breath and could speak. Adalet felt her own breath release. She hadn't realized that she'd been holding it.

"And this is a gift to me?" Fatma looked back at Meryem who was now standing behind the couch where Ahmet was sitting, not sure what was happening.

"Yes, *Anneanne*, it is a gift to you. I wanted to thank you for all you've done for me. I wouldn't be here if not for you. I would like to make another so that the three of us would be in the picture."

"I must sit down," Fatma leaned on Adalet, and Adalet helped her onto the couch next to Ahmet. Ahmet took his mother's hand and squeezed it. "I told you she wasn't a bad girl," he said.

Adalet watched Fatma sink back into the cushions on the couch. It was not possible to read her expression. For the first time since Adalet had known her, she seemed to be without words. Her face looked softer, almost childlike, the lines less prominent, disappearing into her cheeks. "Pinar," she murmured finally. "Poor Pinar."

"It's okay, *Anneanne*, my *anne* knew you loved her."

Fatma shook her head. "I don't know," she said. "Sometimes— sometimes I wanted to smack her, even kill her, I was so angry. And then when she got so sick—I was so angry with your father for bringing her to me, I yelled at them both, said terrible things, and now I know I would've been much angrier if he hadn't." Fatma wiped her eyes and blew her nose loudly into the tissue that Adalet handed her. "Those precious last days; my Pinar was like an innocent child again. She was too weak to defy me, to argue with me. I felt the love from her then that I hadn't felt in so many years. I fed her like a baby."

Ahmet rose and gestured that Adalet should sit down next to Fatma, but Fatma was already regaining her composure. She looked around at them all, crushed the tissue in her hand and asked, "Why are you all hovering over me? I'm starving to death, Adalet. I hope you prepared some lunch for us."

"Of course we have, Fatma. Ahmet, sit back down and keep your mother company. Meryem, please put the painting back in your bedroom and you can wrap it back up for your *anneanne* after we eat. Help me get the table ready."

"No," Fatma said. "Don't put it away. I want to look at it. Leave it there by the window, child, so that I can see it better."

Meryem quickly followed Adalet into the kitchen, leaned in close to her and whispered, "I've never seen her like that in my life."

"That was a beautiful thing that you did, Meryem. She was truly moved by it."

"Do you think it's good? Really good?" Meryem clutched the silverware that she'd gathered to place on the table so tightly that Adalet was afraid she'd injure herself.

"Careful, Meryem, you'll cut yourself." Meryem loosened her grip.

"Well, do you?" she asked again.

Adalet looked straight into Meryem's doubting eyes. She could hear Meryem questioning herself as Adalet had done so many times in her own life: Had Mark given her the A because he liked her? Was *Anneanne* moved to tears thinking of her daughter and not the painting? Was it the painting of an amateur or did she really have talent? Adalet knew that her answer would matter a great deal to Meryem, and she also knew enough to know that this was no ordinary girl simply flirting with the idea of becoming an artist.

"Yes, Meryem," she said deliberately, "it is very, very good. Your *anneanne* has many reasons to be proud of you."

Meryem's eyes filled. She set the silverware down on the counter and hugged Adalet. "It's just that it means so much to me. Maybe it's not good that it means so much—that it be good—that others appreciate it."

"It's good that it matters to you. How much it matters what others think? That I can't answer for you. I hope not too, too much. Since I think you are your harshest critic, I think you will know when it's not good. Now please, go set the table before Fatma accuses me of starving her again."

"Will you always be honest with me, Adalet? I need to be able to trust you."

"I will certainly always do my best to be honest with you."

"Even if it hurts?" Meryem persisted.

"Even if it hurts," Adalet told her.

"Thank you my dear friend." Meryem kissed Adalet on both cheeks; then she gathered the silverware and left the kitchen for the dining area where Adalet could hear her arranging it on the table.

Adalet hoped that Meryem had understood what she meant by too much. She'd seen bitter young people destroyed by parents or teachers who'd warned them that they'd never be good enough, so why bother at all? When Meryem talked with her about her experiences at the art school, Adalet had seen Meryem both light up with praise and suffer harsh criticism. She hoped that Meryem would be smart enough not to give too much credence to either and to always consider the source. But most of all, she wanted Meryem to learn to value her own opinion more, certainly not to the exclusion of informed critique, but even then, to have faith in her own vision. She was thinking about these things when Meryem leaned her head back into the kitchen.

Meryem giggled softly. "Ahmet wants to know if he can do anything to help."

Adalet smiled. "Since he's most likely never carried a plate to or from a table, I would thank him for offering but tell him to make himself comfortable."

"I think he'd do just about anything to get away from Fatma. She's fussing now with her rumbling stomach and why couldn't they have stopped for breakfast, as she suggested—probably eight or nine times," Meryem added.

Adalet opened the freezer and pulled out a fresh bottle of *raki*. "Here, bring this out with some glasses and some ice and water. This will lessen the rumbles for both of them. I'm quite sure he'll appreciate this more than plain water."

"Thank you, thank you. My poor Uncle Ahmet does suffer so." Meryem took the water pitcher and filled it with cold water from the refrigerator. She took the *raki* and the pitcher with her into the living room. She returned for ice and glasses, setting them on a tray that depicted a fat and happy Dionysus stuffing several grapes into his mouth from a large vine dangled in front of him by a partially and sparsely clothed maiden. When Meryem caught Adalet eyeing her choice of tray, Meryem laughed. "Just to distract Uncle Ahmet a bit." She disappeared once more into the living room.

Adalet uncovered the dishes she'd prepared, heating several in the small oven and allowing others to reach room temperature. She wondered about Meryem. Would she ever really know her? She'd so misjudged who she was in the beginning. She'd taken Fatma's presentation at face value without giving it much thought. Meryem was constantly surprising her, swinging like a pendulum from child to adult and back again. Adalet could not recall such a time in her own growth. It wasn't that she hadn't sometimes felt like a child with Yasar and his family, but feeling like a child and behaving like one were two different things. She removed the items from the oven and called to Meryem to help her bring them to the table.

Adalet leaned into the living room. "Come, Meryem, help me carry things in. Fatma, Ahmet, please sit down at the table. Ahmet, you can bring your drinks and the water and *raki*." Adalet smiled as he fumbled to follow her instructions. Meryem was probably right. His wife must wait on him hand and foot, even though he did carry things for his mother these days. When sons grew up, they were supposed to do things for their mothers. But wives never seemed to be relieved of their duties.

The table was soon covered with a variety of mezze. There were little meatballs in a spicy tomato sauce; a yogurt and cucumber dish; ezme and dipping breads: several kinds of olives, the large purple ones, the small black ones in oil, and the medium-sized green ones; a tray of cheese *borek*, a tray of meat *borek*, a spicy carrot salad, a chicken *pilav*, tomatoes sliced with cucumber; two dishes of a variety of pickled vegetables and a large platter of cheeses.

Fatma surveyed the table while everyone waited in silence. "You've done a good job, Adalet. This is an impressive lunch. One for the sultan and his wives."

Adalet felt a rush of pride and gratitude that Fatma could express her appreciation out loud. "I'm pleased that you like it, Fatma. Would you like me to serve you?"

"Thank you." Fatma sat back as if playing the role of the sultan. She nodded her head to Adalet as if to say, you may begin. They could all relax now. The visit was meeting with Fatma's approval.

CHAPTER 20

The Tabaks sat stiffly on the small loveseat in the nursery playroom at the Yeditepe School for the Deaf. They appeared lost in the sea of toys at their feet. When they'd entered the large room, surrounded by walls of shelves stacked with toys, Mrs. Tabak exclaimed, "I've never seen so many toys in one room, except in a store, of course."

"You see," Mrs. Tabak was saying now, "Derin is our only child. I'm not able to have more. My husband—."

Mr. Tabak interrupted. "It's not certain that you won't have more children, but that isn't the point. We want the best education we can possibly get for Derin, and I'm not convinced that a deaf school is the best thing for him. We don't speak with our hands, and if he does, not only won't we be able to understand him, but what kind of a chance will he have in the real world?"

Adalet looked over at Derin who was busy placing furniture in the small, wooden therapeutic dollhouse. It was an important question but not one to be answered simply.

"That is a concern for most parents of deaf children, unless, of course, they are deaf themselves." Adalet hesitated. "Some deaf children can manage oral speech, depending on the extent of the hearing loss. Others have a great deal of difficulty ever making their speech clear enough to be understood. Some of our parents learn sign language along with their children, so that there is some dependable way to communicate, but it doesn't mean that sign language will be their only language. And some deaf children learn to lip read quite well, but that can't be their only skill either. The very best lip readers only get about 30% of what's being said. They have to fill in the rest, and so it's not always accurate." She paused here. Too much, too much, Adalet thought. She was losing them. Mrs. Tabak was staring at her son placing a line of beds in the kitchen, holding herself back from jumping up to correct him.

"What I'm trying to say is that in a deaf school, he has the advantage of learning all the things he can to be able to use language. In a hearing school, at least before we know his capacity for language, he may fall seriously behind."

"He's already behind," Mr. Tabak spoke sharply. "He's five years old and doesn't utter a word, just babbles, and even if we holler at him, he doesn't even turn his head. If we weren't desperate, we never would've brought him here. My wife thinks we should've brought him here a long time ago, but I thought he might outgrow it."

Adalet glanced over at Derin, still happily engaged with placing things wherever he liked, his spatial abilities obviously at a lower level for his age, and turned her attention back to the Tabaks. It had been some time since she'd been faced with the hard work of bringing parents to a reasonable level of understanding about a child's deafness. She had taken enough background information at this point to know that Mr. Tabak was an educated professional man, and so she wanted to assume that he was speaking not from his head but from his heart.

"Children don't outgrow profound deafness, Mr. Tabak," she said as gently as she could. "I can't imagine how difficult this is for both of you, actually for all three of you. But Derin isn't necessarily delayed. He just doesn't know how to engage with you. Are you willing to try a little experiment right now with me?"

The Tabaks shared an intense silent moment before Mr. Tabak placed both of his hands up in the air as if to indicate that he was at a complete loss. "Why not?" He placed his hands back in his lap. "Nothing we've tried so far has worked."

Adalet rose from her chair and went to a cupboard over a miniature sink. "Food is our first connection to life outside of the
mother," she said. "Let's just see what happens." Adalet pulled a box
of cookies from the cupboard. She pulled one out and got down on
the floor next to Derin, setting the box of cookies on the floor next
to her. Adalet tapped Derin's shoulder lightly to get his attention;
then she held the cookie up so that Derin could see it. He dropped
the miniature toilet he was holding in his hand, made a noise and
reached out his hand for the cookie. Adalet placed the cookie in her
lap and signed to Derin, "Want cookie? Cookie, cookie, want
cookie?" Derin moved closer, pointing to the cookie and making
more noises. "Cookie?" Adalet first signed "cookie" and then "want
cookie." She pointed to the cookie and signed it again. To Derin's
parents' amazement, Derin made an approximation of the sign for
"cookie." It wasn't exact, but he was clearly getting the meaning.

Adalet picked up the cookie and moved closer to him. Derin
grabbed the cookie from her hand and shoved it into his mouth.
Adalet made the classic motion of mmm, rubbing her stomach, and
then signed and spoke, "Good cookie." Once she had his attention
again, Adalet removed another cookie from the box and again set it
in her lap. "More?" she signed and said. "More cookie?" She made
the sign for more and then pointed to the cookie, making the sign
for cookie. Derin made the sign for cookie. "More?" Adalet persisted. Derin made a perfect sign for more. Adalet laughed and handed
him the cookie. "Good job," she signed and said aloud. She pushed
herself up from the floor and sat back down again across from the
Tabaks.

"It probably doesn't seem like much to you—."

"My God," Mr. Tabak exclaimed, "he understood you." Mrs.
Tabak's eyes filled up with tears. She got up and went over to Derin.
She looked back at Adalet. Adalet showed her how to sign, more
cookie. Adalet watched as Mrs. Tabak spoke the first words ever to
her son that he was able to comprehend.

Mr. Tabak got up and joined them. "Careful," she warned them,
"there are many more words than, more cookie. We don't want to

make him ill over his first words." But Adalet was smiling one of the biggest smiles she'd had in a very long time. The sheer joy of bringing a family together was what she loved about this work. Oh, yes, there would be many frustrations. The parents would have difficulty with the language and feel a few signs would be enough. There would be lots of resistance. But they'd had this experience of knowing that their son was capable of learning, and that would spur them on, and that meant it was a very good day.

After setting up two more appointments for the Tabaks, so that she might complete the evaluation and make recommendations to the school, Adalet straightened up the nursery room and informed the school director, a Mr. Aslan, that she had made some progress with the Tabaks and would be meeting with them again in a couple of days. He was a short, stocky man with a thick head of salt and pepper hair and a profoundly pockmarked complexion that might have spoken of a difficult time in his adolescence. He thanked her profusely and told her he looked forward to seeing her evaluation. Adalet knew that this would determine whether or not she would receive more work from them.

When Adalet exited the school, she was too energized to go back to the apartment. She decided to take a bus to the Islamic Museum and to wander a bit in the tile works there. She'd only been there once and hadn't had the time to see it all. She thought she might feel strong enough to do it, even after the stressful demands of her meeting.

The museum was located on a curved street in an old section of town, and Adalet was surprised to hear a man calling her name as she was walking up the street from the bus stop to the door of the museum.

"Adalet, it is you. It really is you. You look wonderful. It's been such a long time." Adalet found herself staring into the smiling face of a Yasar who sounded and looked to her so different that she might never have known him at all.

"Yasar." It was all Adalet could manage, as shocked as she was to see such a cheerful looking young man speaking to her in such a friendly voice. He did look genuinely pleased to see her.

"It's good to see you looking so well," she managed.

"And you are as polite as ever. Another woman would have smacked me across the face and kept on walking, or just kept on walking. And I wouldn't have blamed you if you had."

Adalet had no response to this. She'd been deep in thought about Mark. Her few years married to Yasar almost felt now as if they'd never happened. It was shocking to run into him like this, after several years. As if their roles were completely reversed and she'd run into him in Avanos, Adalet found herself asking him, "What are you doing here?"

"Business. What else? I've been commissioned to build a large office complex and they want the lobbies to be based on ancient tile. It's going to cost them, but it will be beautiful. I thought I'd stop by here and have a look. I was just leaving when I saw you. Do you have a few minutes? I've so wanted to speak with you, but I didn't have the courage."

Adalet was unable to find any words. She stood there, staring at him as if he were an apparition. Finally, she said, "You didn't have the courage to speak to me?"

"No, I didn't." He looked quite serious now, the open smile gone. "I behaved so badly to you. And the crazy thing is, I hardly gave it a thought until Aysun left me. Unlike you, she gave me a piece of her mind. I didn't get it right away. I was furious at the things she said—" They both looked up as a group of women in black with head coverings walked past them to enter the museum.

"Please, Adalet, come have a coffee with me. You don't ever have to see me again. But if I don't do it now, I don't know if I'll ever have the opportunity or the courage to say the things I so want to say to you."

Adalet looked nervously at her watch. Why should she go anywhere with him? But she was curious as to why he seemed a changed man, although she also wondered if she would still see him as changed after a cup of coffee. She wondered what Mark would say about all of this when she told him.

"I don't have a lot of time, but I can have a cup of coffee. Do you know a café close by?"

"There's one just down the street." His voice had that old tone of confidence that had first attracted Adalet to him and had later made him seem arrogant. She tried to shake off this feeling in order to be able to continue along the street with him, but it refused to go away. They were both silent until they were sitting in the tiny café just a half block from where Adalet had gotten off the bus only ten or fifteen minutes ago. A wizened old woman in a headscarf and long smock took their order. Several of her front teeth were missing and as she walked away, Adalet noticed her limp. Adalet's limp had gotten much better and was only noticeable when she was tired and experienced some pain. She felt for this poor woman. Adalet thought she must be too old to work, and yet she had given them such a welcoming smile, wide enough to reveal her missing teeth. Adalet reminded herself that she judged too quickly.

"It just occurred to me," Yasar said, "why are you in Istanbul?"

Adalet had known the question was inevitable. Why had she gone with him? Why had she even acknowledged that it was she? He might have thought it wasn't if she hadn't responded. Or if she hadn't gone with him for coffee, he might have thought she was there for the day or on a visit.

"I'm not going to lie to you, Yasar. I'm living here now, perhaps only temporarily. I'm acting as a guardian for my friend's granddaughter while she is attending art school here. It's been good for me. In all likelihood, she'll move on and I will return to live in Avanos. I have someone taking care of the house for me. He's very dependable."

"Wow, now I am impressed. I pictured you pining away in that village. I felt so guilty." He picked up his Turkish coffee and took a deep sip. Adalet watched him drink and set the cup back on the table. She thought she detected a slight tremor in his hand. Was he nervous, guilty? He should be.

"So why couldn't you tell me that, or at least tell your family that?" Adalet asked him. "I was so despondent, feeling that I'd be trapped in that village forever. Not that it turned out to be such a bad place. I made good friends there, and I did heal a good deal physically and emotionally."

"I promise not to tell them you're here. I don't want to hurt you anymore. And we all have plenty of money. I've done quite well in business. They have no use for the house."

"I've just started to work again. As soon as I feel the work is solid and that there's enough of it that I can support myself, I will tell them and relieve them of any responsibility for me."

"I promise not to say a word. If you need anything—."

"I'm doing quite well, thank you. And thank you for keeping my being here a secret." Adalet thought she recognized a flicker of disappointment that she was doing so well without him, that she needed nothing from him but silence. But even silence is something. Was he looking for redemption? "Your keeping this a secret until I'm back on my feet means a great deal to me."

Yasar's smile was back. He hadn't lost his need to be in control. Well, he could have that until she didn't need any of them anymore. She wasn't going to allow pride to destroy her chance for an independent life. But she was curious now about Aysun. How had Aysun opened his eyes to his betrayal of her? She then remembered the secret she'd kept from him. There had been betrayal on both their parts.

"Did you and Aysun divorce?" she asked.

Yasar tilted his coffee cup back and forth, moving the thick mass of coffee grains around, as if he might drink them. He set down the cup. "We never married."

"Why not?" Adalet covered her mouth with her hand. "I'm sorry. It's none of my business." She'd only taken a small sip of her tea and then abandoned it to get cold sitting there.

"Actually, it's more of your business than you think." As Yasar sat back in his chair, Adalet noted for the first time that he was a good bit thinner than he was since she'd last seen him. She had to admit that it looked good on him.

"How is that?" she asked.

"Aysun was wracked with guilt. I'd said so many bad things about you to her to pull her into the affair in the first place that she was sorry for me. But as we lived together, she began to see things differently. She began calling me selfish and saying things like, maybe she could understand now why you hadn't told me about the baby or that living with me wasn't so easy, and that she regretted so much being a part of breaking up our marriage. It got worse. When I'd come home after being away for a job, she'd cry and tell me she was a horrible person; that we were both terrible people; that she could never marry me because she could never trust me. I might do the same thing to her that I'd done to you, but that she would deserve it after what she'd done to you." He fell silent.

Yes, Adalet thought, he was looking for redemption. "We were both very young. We were both selfish," she told him. "It wasn't mature of me not to tell you I was pregnant, having some childish need to tell my parents first. And it wasn't mature of you to turn to Aysun. We were all to blame." And as Adalet said it, she knew it was the truth. She wasn't letting him off the hook; she was accepting responsibility for her own actions. She sighed. "I have to admit that it feels good to say that."

"You have grown up." The admiration in his voice was genuine. "I don't know that I have. I sort of gave up on relationships after Aysun left me."

Adalet reached across the small table and took his hand. "Don't give up, Yasar. It's in our natures to love and to be loved. I hope you will meet someone who is right for you."

Yasar pulled his hand away and clapped both of his hands together. "Ah, does that mean you've found someone who's right for you?"

"I honestly don't know, but I have started to see someone." Adalet folded her napkin and placed it next to the cold cup of tea.

"Is he nice to you?"

She smiled. "Yes, he is."

"Well then," and he motioned for the waitress to bring the check, "I won't ask you for a date." And he smiled at her so warmly that Adalet almost wished he had, even knowing full well that she would have turned him down.

They left the café together. Yasar asked, "Will you go back to the museum now?"

"No, I'll come back another time. Meryem, the young woman I mentioned, will be expecting me. Thank you for the tea and for keeping my secret a bit longer." She reached out her hand.

He took her hand and squeezed it. "For as long as you need it kept," he said. "Good luck to you, Adalet."

"And to you, Yasar." She let go of his hand and turned away in the direction of the bus.

CHAPTER 21

"Wow," Meryem exclaimed so loudly that Yetim jumped from her lap and took off for her favorite spot in the sun, the window ledge. "Are you going to tell Mark?" Meryem was eating a yogurt from a cardboard container, lying across the couch with her feet in Adalet's lap.

"Since when is he Mark to you, young lady? And of course I'm going to tell him." She picked up Meryem's feet, clad in wildly striped colored socks, and then dropped them into her lap again. "I don't think it would be a good idea not to tell Mark that I saw Yasar, do you?"

"Wish I'd been with you. I wouldn't have been so nice to him. I would've made him suffer. I'm with Aysun. That Yasar needs to be told a thing or two. He's a major asshole."

"I think he's learned some things. He's still pretty self-involved, but I think with the right woman—."

"Please, Adalet, that is such a cliché. Don't tell me you have regrets."

"Regrets? Of course I do. I wish I hadn't kept my pregnancy a secret from Yasar. I wish I hadn't been in such a hurry to tell my parents that I was pregnant that I sent my *anne* out to bring my father in from his workshop right before the earthquake. If I'd listened to my *anne* and waited for him to come in on his own, at least my *anne* might have lived." Adalet sat up and moved Meryem's legs from her lap onto the couch. "And do I regret losing my child? What do you think?" Adalet covered her face with her hands.

"But do you regret losing Yasar," Meryem persisted, "now that you've seen him again?"

"I regret how little I did to try to make things right between us. I honestly didn't know what I should do, if that makes sense. I didn't have any experience. I didn't know how to talk to him." Adalet lifted her face to look at Meryem.

"Do you think that would have made a difference?"

"I don't know." Adalet stood up and went to look out the window. She could hear the call to prayer coming from one of the nearby mosques.

"If he asked you to come back, would you try?" Meryem was certainly unrelenting in her questions, Adalet thought. She also believed she knew why.

Adalet turned away from the window and faced Meryem. "You're worried about your professor, aren't you?"

"Maybe a little, but I think he can take care of himself." Meryem answered quickly and sharply, a sign to Adalet that she was right about Meryem having some concerns regarding her intentions with Mark.

"Whether Mark and I get together or not has nothing to do with Yasar. No, I won't be going back with him. I learned a lot from my relationship with him, but we couldn't grow together. If I'm to be with anyone, I would want that." Adalet walked back towards Meryem but remained standing. "Does that answer your questions?"

"Not all of them," Meryem admitted, "but I guess it will have to do for now." Meryem stood up and began to walk toward her bedroom. Adalet thought quickly that Meryem deserved to know something more. She called to her.

"Meryem, just a moment. I want to say something else to you."

Meryem turned and walked back, settling herself down on the arm of the couch. She looked up at Adalet, her beguiling eyes tempting Adalet to want to tell her everything.

"I'm sorry, Meryem. I don't know yet if I love Mark. I like him very much, but I don't want to rush into things this time. I knew so little about Yasar when I married him. When I think back, it was magical. I watched him and listened to him and a spell was cast over me. I guess I cast it over myself. I don't want to do that with Mark."

"Ah," Meryem smiled. "When you can actually say what you're thinking and feeling, I love you the best."

"You're a lot smarter than I gave you credit for in Avanos." Adalet told her.

"And so are you. You didn't know what to make of me then." Meryem crossed her legs and waved her arms in the air, as if presenting herself to Adalet for closer examination.

Adalet laughed. "Honestly, I still don't know what to make of you. You are full of surprises."

"To myself as well." Meryem pushed herself up from the arm of the couch and walked towards the kitchen. "What shall we have for dinner?"

Adalet followed Meryem into the kitchen. Meryem opened the refrigerator door and they both peered inside. "We have enough leftovers to feed the army," Adalet joked to Meryem.

"We do have enough to feed the professor. Shall we call him? We can tell him all about you running into Yasar." Meryem winked at the shocked expression spreading over Adalet's face. "I'm only kidding, Ad."

"Very funny," Adalet pushed Meryem away from the opened refrigerator door. "I'm going to send you off to bed without supper and eat all of this by myself."

"As if you could, and I don't mean the eating part," Meryem re-torted.

"Let's not forget who's in charge here," Adalet reminded Meryem, only half joking and half serious. Meryem winked at her, pushed her way back in front of the refrigerator and began to examine its contents.

As they joined in setting the table and putting out the food, Meryem asked Adalet, "So how did it go today at Yeditepe today?"

"They're a lovely family," Adalet told her. They do want the best for their son, and it's so confusing for them." Adalet set the last dish of leftovers on the table, an ezme salad, and they both sat down and began filling their plates.

"What is so confusing for them? They should just enroll that poor child in school and learn Turkish Sign Language." Meryem spread hot pepper and tomato salad on a piece of bread, set her knife on her plate and took a large bite, sighing with pleasure as she did so.

"It's just not so simple. I wish it were."

"Why not?" Meryem asked.

Adalet placed her fork down on her plate and considered her answer.

"Every parent wants their child to be somewhat like them, to think like them, to cherish the same values, to want the very things that they've dreamed of for them. These parents don't see that their child will ever be independent from them. They don't look into the future for him and see him working at something fulfilling, living on his own, let alone having a wife and a family. And even if they learn basic sign, they see speaking with the hands as something primitive, as something of much less value than speech."

"But isn't it? How many people speak with their hands? Seems to me they should be worried." Meryem sprinkled some black olives into her salad. "It would be a lot to handle, I think. I feel sorry for those poor parents."

"So do I," Adalet agreed. "But first, this little boy must learn some form of communication, some language, so he's able to learn other language. It becomes more difficult after two years of age, but not impossible. He's smart, I think." She picked up her fork and began to eat again.

"Does he have a name?" Meryem asked.

"My work with them is confidential. But we can call him 'D.' I use initials instead of names. I have to ask many personal questions to make my evaluation, so the records are kept locked to protect the child and the family."

"When will you see 'D' and his parents again?" Meryem seemed genuinely interested.

"Next Wednesday. I sent them home with a short list of signs and matching pictures. Not ideal, of course, but it's a start. It will give them some time to think and talk to each other."

Meryem laid her fork down on her plate and looked at Adalet. "What ever made you decide to do this kind of work? How did you even know it existed? I've never given a thought to what happens to deaf kids in school. I don't think I even remember any."

"I wouldn't have either, if not for the deaf girl who lived with and worked for a family in my parents' village. I never knew how she ended up there, if she was a poor relation or just someone they found through word of mouth, but she really didn't even have a name."

"So how did she know she was being called on to do something and how did she know what to do?"

Adalet leaned toward the table and began to stack the plates and silverware. "I guess they showed her what she had to do. I don't know. But I do know they'd poke her or push her and call her 'Dummy.' So everyone in the village called her 'Dummy.'"

"That is so mean." Meryem rose and began to bring the remains of dinner into the kitchen.

"I don't think anyone thought of it as mean. She couldn't hear them anyway, and it was short for 'deaf and dumb.' She didn't have any speech. But I don't think they quite saw her as human either. The family had home signs for her, ones they'd all created together, enough to get by. " Adalet washed the dishes while she spoke. Meryem dried and put them away. "But no one knew what she thought about, how she felt about anything, if she even wanted to be there or if she wished for something else. That was awful. She was literally a slave."

Meryem shook her head back and forth in disbelief. "There should be a law."

"Ah." Adalet cleaned out the trap in the sink, dumping it into the garbage. "That's exactly what I thought. And I thought I would go to law school and become an advocate, get into government. But I was terribly discouraged by my family and their friends. Messing with the law isn't for a girl in Turkey. Why don't you become a teacher, if you really want to help, they told me."

"Are you serious? I can't believe it. Where have they been? Ataturk made women equal. What century were they in?" Meryem slapped the dishtowel onto the counter.

Adalet rescued the wet dishtowel and hung it up on a hook to dry. "It's many years since Ataturk, my dear. Istanbul has more than a body of water separating East from West. Look at your *anneanne*. She's still so afraid you'll end up pregnant like your *anne*. Look at me. I have one foot stuck in the East and the other one trying to climb into the West with a Jewish professor from New York."

" *Anneanne* can stop worrying about that," Meryem smiled. "because I'm pretty sure I'm gay."

CHAPTER 22

Adalet put her hand on Mark's and leaned in to whisper to him in the darkened theater. "I can't keep my mind on this film. Can we go somewhere and talk?"

He leaned toward her and whispered back, "Sure. Let's go." It was an old art theater that was showing a series of film noir. Since Mark's Turkish wasn't quite good enough to catch all the meaning in a Turkish film, and Adalet sometimes didn't get the humor in English language films, they'd compromised on subtitles and Duvivier's "Panique," which they both knew well enough anyway. Adalet had caught it once in the theater with Yasar and had recently watched it on satellite television, and Mark was a French film buff and had seen the movie many times.

It was Friday evening, and only a couple of days since Adalet had run into Yasar and Meryem had pronounced that she thought she was gay. Adalet's head had been spinning since, not knowing how or when or if she should share any or all of this with Mark.

"Why don't we grab some dinner and then go to my place to talk. We'll have some privacy. It's not far from your apartment, about a ten-minute walk. I'll walk you home later." He said this so naturally and easily that Adalet felt comfortable with the idea of going there with him. And she was curious to see how he lived.

"Okay," Adalet told him, "But I feel more in the mood for mezze than a full meal. I've had a surprising couple of days."

"We can go to Mezze Galore down the street from me. I think it's just what you'd like now."

Adalet had grown to love her Taksim neighborhood. Sometimes she'd take a bus or an underground train, but it was only if the weather was bad or her legs were bothering her. It seemed that nothing was longer than a thirty-minute walk from the apartment she and Meryem shared.

The air was damp but hadn't yet formed a drizzle. Adalet put her arm through Mark's. "Can we walk from here?" she asked.

"If you're up for it." Mark knew Adalet's physical limitations, and he was solicitous without hovering.

"I am," Adalet smiled at him. He instinctively seemed to know what to say and how to put her at ease. It had only been a couple of weeks since they'd talked until dawn, but since then they'd achieved a level of comfort with each other that Adalet had never known with Yasar or any other man.

Mezze Galore was a good six city blocks from the theater, but Adalet enjoyed walking with Mark. Being with him was like being with a best friend to whom she was physically attracted. A tingling sensation raced through her body as she put her arm through his to stay apace. They spoke little as they walked, but stopped to point out little shops they might come back to or to bring one another's attention to interesting interactions taking place on the street, pretty children, wandering cats, interesting food vendors. She'd always had to work hard to try to figure Yasar out. He was a logic puzzle, like the one that he'd actually sent to her on the computer once. She'd never been able to solve it —or him. And even though she'd adored her father, she'd felt the same way with him. Somehow with Mark, she had the sense that her just being there pleased him enough. Anything else was a bonus for him. Maybe if she'd had a brother, men wouldn't seem like such a mystery to her. Then again, a brother could have been even more of a mystery.

"There it is, just across the street." Mark pointed to an art deco sign that flashed on and off in red and boasted a white crescent moon. They crossed the street and entered a rather large, dimly lit cavernous space that Adalet had thought would be quite small from the outside. An eager young man hurried to greet them. He wore a white shirt, unbuttoned at the top, revealing a chest thick with dark, curly hair, decorated with a thick gold chain and shirtsleeves rolled up to just below his elbows.

"Ah, Mark, good evening," the young man said in English, grabbing Mark's hand and losing it in two of his. "And who is this lovely lady with you?" He released Mark's hand after shaking it vigorously.

"This is Adalet. Adalet, this is my friend, Mohammed. He and his brother own this place."

"But my brother, praise Allah, is never here. He is doing his military service in the North, or perhaps it's the South, somewhere, and so I'm left to manage on my own." He sighed and shook his head. "The Kurds," he muttered, as if to express a myriad of woes regarding this absent brother, military service in general, and that he'd only thrown in the 'praise Allah' in the highly unlikely possibility that it might just rescue him (or his brother) from a tragic ending. However, he did present himself as an affable fellow, and Adalet had to smile. She could also sense that he was fond of Mark, and that he would probably not have been so open with just any customer. .

"Sit wherever you like." Mohammed checked a large watch which Adalet mused might be a street duplication of a much more expensive brand. "It's just eight o'clock. We won't be busy for at least another hour."

They were well into several different kinds of *dolmasi,* stuffed artichokes, stuffed grape leaves and stuffed peppers with water and *raki* before Adalet told Mark about her encounter with Yasar. While she'd shared certain details about her marriage to Yasar with Mark, Adalet hadn't mentioned her agreement with Yasar's family. She was too worried that he'd think less of her.

"You'll need to extricate yourself from them as soon as possible," The tone in Mark's voice let her know that he wasn't going to let her off the hook. "You're not worried that he'll betray you again? Surely at this point his family might be willing to help you long enough to get back on your feet. Back then, you had no idea you'd recover this much."

Adalet put down her fork and rested her hand on top of Mark's. "I'm just afraid because I don't know what they'd do."

"What's the worst thing they can do?" Mark gripped her hand in his, let go and then stroked her fingers. "They could kick you out of the house in Avanos, but you're living here now. You're starting to work, and Fatma is helping you. It seems better to me than trusting Yasar. And if he knows that you're here and it doesn't upset him, why would they even care? The sooner you can take care of yourself, the lighter their responsibility will be."

"I know you're right. I don't know why I'm so afraid. I'm also afraid that if Yasar tells them before I do, they'll think I've been taking advantage of them. I don't think he would do that, but it feels like a hot and heavy pot of stew that I'm forced to carry around and I can't find a place to set it anywhere. It's weighing me down, and wherever I try to put it, it will drop and spill all over me."

"And you'll be burned again." Mark smoothed a few loose hairs away from her face.

"Oh." Adalet started enough that Mark could feel it.

"I'm sorry," he said.

"No, I just hadn't thought of it that way at all. Oh my God, Mark, you've gotten to the very bottom of it. The last time I kept a secret that involved Yasar—and that was my pregnancy—both of my parents and my baby were killed before I could even tell my parents that I was pregnant."

"I didn't know this. How awful."

Tears began to seep from Adalet's eyes, sliding down her face like a sudden spring shower. Mark wiped them away with his hand.

"I'm so ashamed. All of this has been my fault."

Mark moved his chair closer and wrapped one arm around Adalet while stroking her face with the other. "No, Adalet. All of this was not your fault. If Yasar hadn't been having an affair, you wouldn't have sensed his distance. That's most likely why you didn't tell him. And unfortunately for everyone, an earthquake in Turkey is hardy unusual. You aren't responsible for your parents' deaths."

Adalet leaned into Mark's embrace, tears still sneaking down her cheeks. "If only I'd been honest; if only I'd been more patient," Adalet insisted.

"If only," Mark repeated. "We can all say that about so many things." Mark took a handkerchief from his pocket and dried the last of Adalet's tears. "What a dreadful time you've had." He kissed each of her eyes softly, and then her lips. Adalet drew back, remembering where she was.

"Can we go?" Adalet asked, squeezing Mark's hand to let him know that she wasn't pushing him away but was uncomfortable showing intimacy in public, even though as she surveyed the room, no one was paying any attention to them. The room had filled somewhat, but all eyes were focused on the menu or one another.

At first he'd been startled by Adalet's reaction, but now Mark smiled. "Yes, I'll just pay the bill. We can have coffee at my place."

Adalet laughed aloud when Mark stopped at a white five-story building she'd passed so many times on her way to walk along the Bosphorus. Adalet had noticed it because of the stone leaf and flower decorations along the tiny iron railed balconies. She'd thought many times that the building looked like a wedding cake, even when laundry items on the various balcony railings kept the icing-like sugared ornaments hidden from view. She liked to pretend they were candles. "You're kidding," Adalet paused behind him. "I walk by your building at least several times a week. It reminds me of a cake. This is how I like to go down to the water."

Mark smiled as he inserted a key in the front door. "I bet I can even show you a shortcut by some great pastries."

"The little Greek shop down the alleyway?" Adalet asked, following Mark through a second door and into a small lobby.

"That's the one. Such a clever girl. You know it already." He pushed the button on an elevator that looked even smaller that the one in Adalet's building. She must have been mistaken about his reaction the first time he'd visited her and Meryem. She'd thought he might have been nervous about riding in it. Hmmm, she thought. Maybe he was nervous because of me. She touched his hand lightly.

The elevator shook its way down to them, making a great deal of noise as the cage banged threateningly against the sides. "Her bark is much worse than her bite," Mark reassured her. He held the door open for her while she entered and pushing the button for the 5th floor when she was safely inside.

"All the way to the top?" Adalet asked.

"Yes, and I have a surprise for you there. Something you can't see from the street."

When the doors opened again, Adalet could see there was only one apartment on the fifth floor. The entrance was just across from the elevator. When Mark unlocked the heavy wooden door, it opened into a large space filled with light from skylights and wall-to-wall windows. Two of these windows reached down to the floor almost up to the ceiling, and Adalet could see they led out onto a roof greenhouse garden. "Oh, Mark, this is beautiful. I never expected anything like this."

"Have a look around if you like," he said. "I'm going to put on some coffee."

The space was wide open with a modern kitchen that spread across one length of the room. The appliances looked brand new. Different patterns and colors of carpets were splashed as if tossed by a child across the heavily polished hardwood floors. Several antique couches were placed around and under those hanging on the walls. A small dining area was sectioned off within the kitchen space with an old large square wooden table and six matching chairs. A blue silk hereke rug lay on the table, graced by a painted ceramic bowl covered with painted birds and flowers. None of this looked at all like Mark's office at the university.

Adalet wondered where Mark slept and where the bathroom was until she noticed that the wall on the far side was a sliding wooden door on a track. She gave the wall a push and it slid easily, opening into a room the same size as the one she was standing in. In fact, the skylights and windows were identical with two more large ones opening onto the roof. The floor was the same but the carpet in this room was quite large and very old. It looked like it might have once been a wedding carpet that had made it through more than a few generations. Some of the vegetable dye had faded perhaps from the sun or much wear, but it still held its elegance like a worn diva just making her entrance onto a concert stage.

A large, heavy four-poster wooden bed sat on this carpet, covered by another carpet, a little less ancient, with a set of camel bags at one end. Adalet wondered if he used these for pillows, thinking they'd be awfully scratchy and uncomfortable. She hoped not. Two large armoires stood side by side across from it. Another sliding wooden door divided this room from a remaining third room that Adalet discovered. When she gave this door a push, it opened into an amber glass and marble bathroom. It was as modern as the kitchen. How could a visiting professor possibly afford this? Yasar's parents could live here and be happy. Adalet was dismayed by all of this. What was the professor hiding from her?

Mark called from the other room. "Coffee will be ready in a few minutes. We can take it out onto the roof. Would you like to see the greenhouse while we wait?"

Adalet walked back into the main room where Mark was unlocking and opening the doors to the roof. "I'd love to see it," she said.

They stepped out onto what seemed more like a large veranda than a roof. Walls hid the garden from the street, but they weren't too tall to look down over and spy on the activity below. There was an outdoor dining table and chairs. She was pleased to see a clothesline strung from one end of the roof to another. He must not have a dryer. She hadn't noticed one, but she hadn't looked so closely.

The greenhouse was what she'd expected, warm and wet with a small but impressive collection of exotic plants and flowers. "Do you take care of all of this?" Adalet asked.

"Of course not," Mark said, running the tip of his finger over the edge of a white rose. "A woman who used to live on the second floor had always wanted a greenhouse, and so my grandfather gave her permission to put it here. Now her daughter lives there and cares for it. She and her husband also look after this apartment when no one is living here."

"This belongs to your family?"

"Yes, but it's a long story, so let's get our coffee and sit out here where we can watch the night light up around us."

When they were first seated with their coffee, Mark remained silent. Some stars could be seen dotting the sky here and there, but an earlier rain in the day had left many clouds lingering. Mark sipped the thick Turkish brew he'd served in the small special cups designed for this blend of coffee. Adalet tasted hers and sighed. "Such wonderful coffee prepared by a New York Jew."

"It won't seem quite so strange to you after I tell you my family story—at least the family on my father's side."

Adalet leaned forward. "Please tell me." After her confession at dinner and in her subsequent surprise at Mark's lifestyle, she realized that she'd completely forgotten to tell him about Meryem. And now she was glad she hadn't. It would be Meryem's place to tell him, if she ever did.

CHAPTER 23

Mark took a last sip of coffee and set his cup back in the saucer. He leaned back in his chair and gazed off into a clouded Istanbul night sky, as if the clouds were pages he could turn back to the past.

'My great grandfather's name was Hermann. He was born in Germany in September of 1914, just after his father was sent to fight in the war. Exactly how and when it happened, we don't know, but his father was killed in combat before he and Hermann ever met. His mother was young and pretty and married a German man at the end of the war in 1918. Hermann was just four years old and had never known a different father."

Adalet took the light sweater she'd taken with her to dinner and put it around her shoulders. The night air was cool but not unpleasant.

"Would you like to go inside?" Mark asked.

"Not yet. It's lovely up here. I'll let you know if it gets too chilly."

Mark moved his chair closer to hers and put an arm around her shoulders. "And I'll help to keep you warm," he said.

"And so, by the end of the war, Hermann was living in an essentially German household. The wedding had not been a religious one, as neither his mother nor his new stepfather attended any synagogue or church. According to the story, as it was passed down, Hermann's biological father had little interest in religion and only followed some tradition to keep his parents happy. Hermann's mother didn't care to pass on the traditions to her son, and so though he was exposed to religion through extended family and friends, Hermann considered himself a German first, and secondly a secular Jew."

"I never thought about Jews not practicing their religion until I met you," Adalet admitted. "I guess I never thought much about it at all. But how did he end up in Turkey?" She moved away from Mark's embrace long enough to slide her arms into her sweater but then slid back against him.

"Hermann never made it to Turkey. He was murdered in Poland with his wife, but he managed to get his son out first by sending him away. Hermann had become a fairly wealthy banker. Apparently, he'd seen the writing on the wall and had saved cash in a secret hiding place. He'd saved a good bit more than he was able to hide, but the Nazis got hold of the rest of it before he could hide any more. He'd been too afraid to go to his hiding place and be followed and caught, so he only went the one time after he'd hidden it. At least that's how the story goes. There was only enough money to send his son, Jacob, my grandfather, out of the country. Jacob was his only child. I don't know why. Maybe they died before they could have more children or maybe they didn't think it wise due to the terrible situation in Germany. The Germans kept good records and my grandfather discovered much later that neither of his parents had survived. Hermann died of typhus in Treblinka and my great grandmother had been gassed long before that in Auschwitz. Jacob made it to Istanbul with a Jewish woman who raised him as if he were her own child. She'd worked for Hermann in the bank and had promised to take care of him. I think Hermann must have paid for her passage as well. He wouldn't have been parted from his wife. So many parents did this, sent off their children and stayed behind. It's hard for me to imagine; I can't imagine being sent off to a foreign country with a stranger, having no knowledge of the language or the customs." Mark's voice quivered; he hesitated for a moment and took a deep breath to get control over his emotions.

"Let's go inside now," Adalet whispered. " This story is too sad to be passed on to the wind." Mark turned to face her and saw that her eyes were filled with tears.

"You're crying." Mark touched her face and wiped away a tear.

"I can't imagine it, to have to send your own child away to another country on his own. How could they have known what would happen to him?"

"They couldn't."

Mark helped Adalet up from her chair. She reached out to pick up the dirty cups, but Mark stopped her hand with his. "Leave them. I'll get them later." Adalet was grateful. She didn't want him to stop talking, and she was afraid that washing cups would break the mood. She was pleased but nervous when he led her into the bedroom, took the camel bags and tossed them on the floor, revealing two soft pillows underneath. "Do you mind if we lie down here while I tell you the rest? It's not an easy story to tell."

"No, it feels right." She took off her shoes and lay down beside him in the crook of his arm. But her heart began beating so loudly that she was afraid Mark could hear. It had been a long time since she had lain on a bed with a man. But there was no time to think because Mark picked up the story where he'd left off.

"Apparently, Jacob, just like his father, also did very well as a banker in Istanbul. He was a secular Jew like his father, but he was also a leader in a somewhat diminished Jewish community. When Turkey became a Republic after the First World War, the Jews didn't do as well as they had under the Ottomans. They became minority citizens, along with the Greeks and the Armenians."

"But that was done to protect them, Adalet protested. "In the new Republic, only Turks could be full citizens. There was a new sense of Turkish pride, of building a new Turkey that would be secular. No more Arabic alphabet or veiled women. Ataturk wanted to move the country out of superstition and backward beliefs into the 20th century, into competition with the West." Adalet felt her body tense. Her impulse was to pull away from Mark. Was he saying that the Ottoman Empire was better than the New Republic? Who could say such a thing?

Mark leaned toward her and looked into her eyes. He smiled. "Ah, I'm up against the Turkish pride thing and undying loyalty to Ataturk. This isn't a personal attack on Ataturk. This is what happened to Grandpa Jacob. Remember? This is my story?"

Adalet sighed. "Yes, I'm sorry. And there is always another side to every story. It's difficult for me to hear it, but I will. Please, go on."

"Are you sure you want me to?" Mark was still leaning over her and peering into her eyes.

"Yes, yes, okay." Adalet gently pushed him back down and leaned into him. She turned to him and forced a smile. "Sometimes I have to listen even if I don't like what I hear. Ataturk is every Turk's hero, not just mine."

"I know that. But I will tread onward, carefully, of course. So Grandpa owned a few buildings. Owning property always seemed the safest way to invest his money. Or at least that is how the story went. Since the way the minority law was written, foundations, religious groups, could not own property, Jacob owned the building that housed the synagogue. The synagogue rented from him, and he was the sole owner of the building."

"He did this for the Jewish community?" Adalet interrupted.

"Well, yes and no. It was a good investment for him. My Dad always saw his father as a practical man. He was a businessman first, a Jew second. And the building was not known as a synagogue. Jacob lived in the upper three floors of the building with his family, and the synagogue was on the first two floors. Well, actually the rabbi and his wife and two children lived on the second floor, and the first floor was the synagogue. Grandpa Jacob had renters and the rabbi had the same small group of worshippers on the Sabbath and holidays. It worked well until it didn't."

"What happened?"

"It leaked that there was a synagogue operating there, and so the government seized that property as well as his others. Simple as that."

Adalet sat up abruptly, unaware that she was even doing so. It was as if the bed itself had startled her into an upright position through no will of her own. "But that's not possible. How could that be? He paid for it, no? He bought it. It was his house. He had papers to prove it, didn't he?"

"He had minority citizenship. What might have been done to genuinely protect him ended up being his ruin. He'd spent his own money to turn the first floor into a synagogue with the arrangement that the rent would be somewhat higher until the synagogue could pay him back. I think he also did some work on the rabbi's living quarters. He lost a lot of money, to say nothing of losing his home."

"That's terrible. Didn't the government pay him anything?" Adalet lay back down on one elbow, facing Mark. She suddenly felt cold and visibly started to shiver.

"You really don't know anything about this, do you?" Mark pulled the cover up and around Adalet's shoulders.

"How could I know about your family?"

"It didn't just happen to my family, Adalet. Many people lost their property. Not just foundations or religious establishments, but families, too. Over time, people left."

"Where did they go? What could they do with no money?" Adalet slipped off her elbow, tired now from leaning on it, and snuggled back into Mark.

"They went where they could. Jacob initially took his family to Israel. His wife, a Turkish Jew descended from a prominent family during Ottoman times, hated Israel. Her family had always been secular. They could trace themselves back to the Spanish Inquisition. She didn't know any Hebrew and didn't want to learn. She said the language was ugly and she refused to speak it. She became bitter and angry and isolated. She wanted to go to America."

"Poor Jacob," Adalet found it hard to be sympathetic to Mark's complaining Grandmother.

Mark laughed. "Poor Jacob embezzled money from the Israeli bank he managed, and got his family to America before Rebecca, my grandmother, could run away without him. She was a beautiful woman, magnificent really, and Jacob couldn't bear the thought of losing her. Again," —and now he smiled with a questioning quiver of one side of his mouth—"that's how the story went. My father eventually managed to get the house back."

Mark rolled over on top of Adalet. He pushed her dark hair back from her face. He bent to kiss her, but she reached out and held her hand over his lips.

"Is that it? Isn't there more?"

Mark gently moved her hand away. "Much more. Later." And he kissed her until she found herself melting into him, becoming him, moving into the rhythms of his body, as if she'd been waiting to give herself over to this all her life.

CHAPTER 24

Adalet is floating in a sea of warm water. She's weightless. She looks down at her body and sees that she is completely naked. The scars on her legs are outlined in dark blue ink, as if they've been tattooed there. She feels a hand reach for her leg, and she's sure that it is Mark's. But the hand that grabs her leg is bloated and the body that surfaces next to hers is covered in blood. She tries to pull away, but the hand that is now gripping her leg is clamped down onto it like a vice. She struggles as it pulls her under the water. Her arms flail as she fights to raise her head above the water to breathe.

"Hey, what's wrong? You just smacked me across the face. And I thought we were doing so well." Mark leaned over to look at Adalet. He was touching his face where she'd struck him. She had to sit up to force herself out of her dream and into reality.

"Oh, I'm so sorry. I had a weird dream. It started out as a dream, but then it turned into a nightmare. I don't know. I thought it was you and then it was a bloated, bloody monster." Adalet hugged her shoulders and shivered. Mark sat up and pulled the blanket around her. Adalet stared at him. "It wasn't you, though."

Mark laughed. "I'm so glad to hear it." And then he became quiet, serious. "I do believe that dreams have something to tell us. This one seems painfully clear to me."

"But I don't have any idea what it could mean. What are you thinking? Please tell me."

"I promise to tell you over coffee. By the way, does Meryem know where you are?"

"Oh, no. She must be so worried. I'd better call her right now."

Adalet stared as Mark rose from the bed naked. Even in her agitation from the jarring dream, she was distracted by his body, muscular and strong for a man who appeared so slight in clothing. Observing her look, Mark grinned and tossed her a bathrobe that lay hanging over a chair near the bed. "I'll be in the kitchen," he said," pulling on a pair of last night's jeans as he headed out the door, but he returned quickly as Adalet was fastening the robe, her legs dangling over the side of the bed.

"Good morning," Mark said as he bent down to kiss her. She kissed him back.

"Do you remember where I left my bag? My cell phone is in it."

Mark leaned over the other side of the chair, raised Adalet's bag and handed it to her.

"Thank you. I'll just be a minute."

Mark's brows furrowed quizzically. "A minute? Explaining all of this to Meryem?" He shook his head and mumbled "Good luck."

When he was gone, Adalet reached into her bag for her phone. She'd shut it off in the restaurant and hadn't turned it on since. She waited for it to light up and was surprised to see that there was only one message from Meryem.

"Sleep tight." And then there was the sound of a kiss. Would Meryem ever cease to surprise her? Adalet wished she could have been as wise at Meryem's age. She dialed her number, shaking her head and smiling as she did. She got voicemail.

"You got me. Leave a message." So Meryem.

Adalet waited for the beep. "Thanks for your sweet message, Meryem. I guess you're off doing something since it's Saturday. Hope you're having fun. See you sometime later. Let me know when you're going to be home, okay? Not like I didn't." She ended the call but left the phone on in case Meryem should call her back. She took it into the kitchen with her.

Mark was just pouring boiling water into a French press. "That was quick."

"She didn't pick up. I left a message."

"Had she called?" Mark reached for two cups while the grounds cooked in the press.

"She called."

"What did she say?" He reached across the counter for the sugar and then into the refrigerator for the cream. "Come on," he teased, "tell me."

" 'Sweet dreams', and she blew me a kiss."

"She sure is something, our Meryem." Mark pushed down the press and poured the coffee. He remembered to put cream and sugar into Adalet's. He left his own black. He carried the cups to the small wooden table in the kitchen, set them down and pulled out a chair for Adalet. Once he was seated, they both sipped quietly. Mark reached across the table and took Adalet's hand. It reminded her of the dream.

"Tell me now about the dream. What do you think it meant?" she asked, resisting the impulse to pull her hand away.

Mark stroked Adalet's hand before he withdrew his, as if he'd understood. "I don't know if you'll like what I'm about to say."

"Say it anyway. Please."

"I think you're conflicted about me, Adalet. One minute you're floating in warm, calm water, and the next minute you're being drowned by a monster. I don't think it's terrible. I just think you're afraid. From what you've shared with me about your marriage, I get it. I understand. I think you're afraid I'll hurt you."

Adalet sat very still. She picked up her cup, took a sip and placed it back on the saucer. "That's some dream interpretation. Where did you learn to do that?"

"In my psychoanalysis."

"Oh?"

"Everyone in New York goes into psychoanalysis." He grinned a bit foolishly. "Well, not everyone, but it's a pretty popular thing to do. Especially for artists who don't think they're good enough to make art."

"Ah, I see. Did it help?"

"Yes. I stopped fooling myself and became a teacher. Art history is a safe place for me, and I do enjoy it. When I get a student like Meryem, it feels like a calling."

"A calling?" Adalet looked confused.

"Something that I'm meant to do." Mark looked away at the window.

"Won't you ever make art again?" Adalet asked. She leaned forward and touched his face.

"I don't know," he said, turning back to face her. "But you do have a knack for changing the subject."

Adalet stood up and walked over to the window. It was the only window that had no view except for the side of another building. Laundry hung from a balcony across the way.

"I don't think you'd mean to hurt me. I think you're a good man, Mark. And last night was so loving. I didn't think I'd ever feel so perfect with anyone. It's life that is so difficult to predict." She turned back to face him. "I wish I could know the future, but the one thing the earthquake taught me is that I can't. We can do all the planning we like, but nature, God, whatever you wish to believe, can shift it all in a heartbeat."

Mark rose and came behind her, putting his arms around her waist.

"I think I love you, Adalet. No, that's not true. I know I love you. Whatever comes."

"I love you, too, Mark." Adalet turned into his arms. "But I've given this a lot of thought. I live in Turkey and you live in the United States. You'll go back to New York when you're time here is up. It's okay. I accept this. But this is what it is."

"Why do you think like that?" Mark stroked her hair. "Why does it have to be impossible? There are all kinds of ways to settle this. We can marry and live here or there, or we can live in both places. We can do whatever we want. I can stay on until Meryem graduates and then we can decide what to do."

Tears began to roll softly down Adalet's cheeks. She turned away from him and began to sob.

"What's wrong? Adalet, please tell me what's wrong."

Mark tried to pull her back but she shook him away. "You know I can't marry again."

"What are you talking about? Are Muslims like Catholics, not allowed to marry after a divorce?"

"I can't have children—ever again! You know this. I've told you." Adalet was surprised to hear the finality in her voice.

"Is that what all this is about? Adalet, I don't care if you can't have children. I never really wanted to have children anyway."

Adalet could not believe what she was hearing. "How could you not want children? What kind of man doesn't want to have children? You wouldn't want me to have a baby?"

Mark reached out for her hand again, and this time she didn't pull away. "Adalet, my dear, not every man wants babies. Maybe this is true in Turkey, and maybe not, I don't know. But no, I don't want to have any babies. Please come and sit with me. Let's just talk."

"Do you have some *çay*?" Adalet asked. "I really prefer tea. I can make it."

"You are a true Turk. *Çay* in the morning; Turkish coffee after dinner. Sorry, I should have asked." He coaxed her back into her chair. "I'll get it for you. It's nice to have someone to wait on here. I've never had anyone here before."

"Why not?" Adalet rose and took a Kleenex from the counter and walked away to blow her nose. She went to the sink to wash her hands and settled back into her chair. She wondered if Mark was aware of this Turkish disdain for blowing one's nose at the table, but he made no comment. He may not have even noticed.

"I've never been in love," he said. "This place is special to me, almost sacred in an odd way. My family went through hell and back over it. It's hard to explain."

Adalet felt her stomach lurch, but she could not yet address the word "love." Instead she said, "I think I know how you feel. My parents' house was like that for me. When I lost them, and the house was destroyed—she broke off and sighed deeply. "It's still hard for me."

Mark brought a glass of Turkish tea to the table. Adalet was smiling at him again.

"You didn't think I'd serve you English Breakfast Tea, did you?"

Adalet blushed. "Well, maybe." She folded her fingers around the hot tea. "A glass of tea is nice. It calms me, refreshes me. Mark, do you really believe what you say about us? Do you believe we could be together?" She wanted to be sure that he wasn't just motivated by the moment, by the night of intimacy, by something less than real. And whatever he said, how could she know? Only time. She'd have to face it. That was all there was.

"I want to marry you, Adalet. This I know. And if we both want this, we'll figure out a way."

And even though he looked into her eyes as he said the words, and she believed in that moment he meant them, Adalet felt eerily as if she were an actor in her dream, that she was not really Adalet and that Mark wasn't really Mark.

PART III

BETWEEN WORLDS

CHAPTER 25

Adalet sat on the camel pillows in the shrinking afternoon sunlight and folded the letter from Fatma's lawyer. She placed it back into its official-looking envelope. Yetim yawned from her favorite spot on the window ledge by the balcony. Older and fatter, Yetim lorded her position over the hordes of street cats wandering below. Sometimes Adalet imagined that Yetim longed to be free among them, but then Yetim would come into her lap and rub and purr against her body, and it made Adalet sad that she couldn't bring all of those homeless cats inside. Some of them were as small as Yetim when Adalet had first found her under the bushes in Avanos. Adalet played with the envelope, a bit catlike herself, lacing it back and forth between her fingers.

In the four years she'd been living in Istanbul, she'd visited Fatma exactly four times with Meryem, and always for Bayram. Fatma had made two visits to Istanbul, was satisfied with what she'd seen and vowed not to return. The trips were too hard on her, the streets too steep for her to walk very far, and the broken cobblestones posed a constant threat to her balance. The risks were hardly worth it, Adalet thought, and she knew that Fatma trusted her and that Fatma had even begun to trust Meryem. Adalet missed Fatma and was looking forward to the upcoming Bayram. Ramadan would begin in a week, so the holiday wasn't that far off. Adalet had become so busy with work that it was harder for her to get away. There were always more families with deaf children on the wait list to see her.

Adalet had been surprised but relieved at Fatma's reaction to Meryem's disclosure that she was gay. "Ach, no more babies to worry me. It's a good thing." She'd smiled at Isha, Meryem's exotic East Indian girl friend, another painter Meryem had met in her third year at Mimar Sinan and who Meryem had brought along to meet Fatma that year at Bayram. Adalet had been staring down at her feet during this expected traumatic event, waiting for Fatma to ask her where Adalet had gotten to while all of this was going on. Adalet had suddenly looked up and caught the mischievous glance exchanged by Meryem and Isha.

"See, I told you the only thing she was ever worried about was me having a baby. My *anneanne* doesn't know that lesbian couples can have children." Meryem had winked at Isha while tossing back her long, dark hair.

"And just how would they manage to do that?" Fatma asked, eyeing her granddaughter's beautiful lover in a completely new light with this most recent revelation. Isha's ebony eyes were almost large enough to be Turkish but her nose was too short and too flat. Her hair was longer and thicker than Meryem's and curled in all directions, much like a poodle in dire need of grooming. Isha was even more slender than Meryem, something Fatma would not have believed possible. Later when Fatma and Adalet had been alone, Fatma asked Adalet if she should worry. "Aren't they too thin? Do I need to worry about that skinny disease?"

"Do you mean anorexia? Adalet asked.

"Yes, that one."

"That's how young women like to look. Meryem and I wear the same size. Why don't you ask me if I'm anorectic?"

Fatma laughed one of her heartier laughs. "Because I see you eat! They eat like tiny little birds, a few pecks and they're done." Fatma waved her hand in a motion that seemed to be intended for shooing away persistent little birds or even a pesky Yetim.

"You wouldn't say that if you ever watched the two of them de-
vour a pizza."

"Ach," Fatma made a fake spitting motion, "that isn't food. And
tell me please, how could Meryem and Isha have a baby?"

Adalet thought it was interesting and endearing how Fatma in-
cluded her in these conversations, made her a fellow conspirator in
her worries. Adalet mused that these were not so much worries.
This was a way for Fatma to discuss her granddaughter with
someone who might have some insight that she herself, now past
80, might miss and even find comforting. Fatma treated Adalet as if
she were many years older and wiser than Meryem, even though
there were only six years between them. Fatma still didn't seem to
recognize how sensible and accomplished her granddaughter had
become. Or maybe she saw more than she shared with Adalet and
simply wanted confirmation—or even just conversation.

And Isha. She'd been living with them for the past year. Isha was
kind and considerate, loving, witty and also very talented. Recently
Meryem and Isha had created some paintings in collaboration. They
were planning a show of these works. There didn't seem to be a
competitive bone between the two of them, although they both
assumed a fighting stance with the outside art world.

Often Adalet wished she could be as confident and spontaneous
as Meryem. Although Adalet felt she'd grown in a number of ways
since returning to Istanbul, she still felt herself shy and cautious
around intimacy. Her work at the school for the deaf had grown into
a four day a week job, and she no longer had to accept money from
Yasar's family. Although she knew she was liked and respected at the
Yeditepe School for the Deaf, she hadn't made any close friends
there.

Adalet was truly grateful for the once or twice a month she was
able to meet with Nuray since she'd run into her in the marketplace.
What was disappointing to Adalet was that they didn't seem to have
that much in common anymore. Since Nuray's mother had passed
away a couple of years ago, Nuray began writing and editing for a
new women's magazine that was still struggling to advance from a

crawling stage to a teetering walk. Nuray was also involved in an
nascent women's movement growing from the magazine. Produc-
tion and meetings took up much of her time and made her often less
available than Adalet.

Adalet enjoyed doing things with Meryem and Isha, and sometimes wished she might be gay herself. It often appeared to be
easier. But Adalet was not sexually attracted to women. In any
event, she recognized from being around Meryem and Isha's gay
friends that not all gay relationships were as harmonious as Meryem
and Isha's, and that Meryem and Isha were fortunate to have found
one another.

At 32 years of age, Adalet had still not allowed herself to marry
Mark. His 38th birthday was tomorrow, September 12th. She
thought he might propose again and wondered if she should just say
yes. Adalet worried that Mark didn't know his own mind. The
doubt persisted and nagged her that one day Mark would want to
have a child or even children, and that he would then come to
resent her because she couldn't. At times she recognized how
foolish this was in light of Mark's loving loyalty and persistence.
And when she was momentarily clear about this, she knew that it
was her own past chasing her, and that her misgivings had nothing
to do with Mark.

Yetim, always tuned into Adalet's moods, jumped down from the
balcony ledge where she'd been meowing in concert with a band of
local feral cats. She climbed into Adalet's lap. It was one of the
several hours of the day prior to garbage pickup, and the street was
alive with the sounds of the cats' pleasure and hoarding of their not
so meager banquet. Adalet ventured to guess that they probably ate
better than most of the people living in Istanbul's streets.

Yetim placed a tentative paw on the edge of the envelope, re-
minding Adalet that it was still there, still to be dealt with, this
unexpected legal document from Fatma's lawyer. If she'd read it
correctly, it said that Adalet would inherit this building in Beyoğlu
in the event of Fatma's death. It was incredibly confusing. In the
first place, Adalet had always thought that Fatma's son, Ahmet,

owned the building or that he at least owned it with Fatma. And even if Fatma did in fact own the building, why wouldn't she leave it to Meryem or Ahmet and his brother? Why would she choose to leave it to Adalet, and how was Meryem going to feel about all of this?

And why was Fatma doing this now? Adalet fought against a strong urge to pick up the phone immediately to call Fatma to make sure she wasn't dying. Adalet and Meryem had already scheduled their visit to Fatma at Bayram. And Meryem and Isha were planning to stop in Avanos to check in on her this weekend while they were in Cappadocia for a short holiday. No, she should show the letter to Meryem first. She should wait for Meryem to get back. If Fatma were so ill that she was afraid she might be dying, surely Meryem would let Adalet know. But the scenes playing out in her mind pursued her relentlessly, giving her no relief.

Adalet scooped Yetim from her lap in order to get up to retrieve her phone. Yetim screeched with displeasure. "Sorry Yetim, dear girl." But Yetim was already distracted by the bread man's calls as he proceeded down the steep cobblestones chanting, "Fresh bread! Good fresh bread. Bread! Bread!" And as if this didn't happen every day, several times a day, Yetim sprinted onto the balcony to see what the fuss was about. Adalet wished that her own attention could be so easily diverted.

Adalet found her phone on the table and pressed Mark's number. Three times she pushed the disconnect button before she finally allowed the call to go through. She got his voicemail.

"Hello, this is Dr. Aronson. I am unable to answer your call at this time. Please leave your name and phone number, and I will return your call as soon as possible. Thank you."

Adalet hung up at the beep and slid the phone back onto the table. She'd be seeing him in a few hours. She briefly thought about trying to reach Meryem by cell phone but then decided that wasn't a good idea. If Meryem was going to be upset about this, there was no reason to ruin the holiday weekend for her and Isha. Adalet slid the letter out of the envelope to read it again. Maybe she'd misread or misunderstood something due to the stiffly worded nature of the language. But no, it was exactly as she'd understood it the first time.

Through the open balcony door, Adalet could hear the fellow from Crimea berating the young Russian woman who worked for him in his café. Adalet could only guess what it was this time. He always criticized her in Russian. A neighborhood that had once been only Turkish had become a Tower of Babel. The Crimean always seemed to be angry with the girl about something. Adalet could never hear her replies, not that she would've understood them anyway. A passing vehicle obliterated the harsh sound of the Russian words with blaring Turkish music. By the time the vehicle made its way along the cobbled street, the scolding voice had stopped.

Adalet adored this dirty, noisy, cranky street with its dank and decaying stench wafting its way up from the Bosphorus and down from Taksim Square. The old buildings and even older cobble-stones, uneven and elevated out of place, their cracks filled with centuries of accumulated refuse and dirt, provided Adalet with a certain sense of stability. She loved that she could always count on the old house wares shop owner from across the way to sweep this impossible street several times a day. Adalet didn't think he'd changed his jacket once in all the time she'd lived here. He'd never smiled or said good morning or acknowledged in any way that they were neighbors or that she was even alive and had purchased several items in his store. But he was always there, someone she could depend on. And thus was the neighborhood.

Every morning the old Kurdish lady (whom Adalet had never actually seen) lowered her wicker basket from her third-floor apartment, and pulled it up after the grocer's helper had fulfilled her requests.

Each evening the butcher tossed his scraps out onto the street for the feral cats who claimed his territory. There would be a fairly long and sometimes bloody establishment of dominance before the lineup for dinner could begin.

There were so many scenes like this that Adalet expected in each of her days that it was like the recorded sounds of the Imam calling the people to prayer five times a day, like the knowledge that there would be a 12:00am and a 12:00pm.

When Adalet had been a child, the predictable scenes and sounds were of her family; her father washing for prayer in the morning, her mother rolling out the dough for the bread and the hissing of water for the morning tea. The earthquake and the breakup of her marriage to Yasar had destroyed this sense of predictability, and now Adalet was feeling that this new life had given her back something of her sense of security.

This was one of Adalet's obstacles to life with Mark. He didn't live so far from here, but his neighborhood's silence reminded Adalet too much of the area where she'd lived with Yasar. Adalet had learned to sleep through a background of noise that often sounded like a street fair or a holiday celebration. What might seem like a ruckus to some people was the music of life to Adalet. She didn't sleep as well at Mark's.

Mark. What would he think of this inheritance? He loved Istanbul, but he had family back in New York. As much strength as Adalet had gathered in the years since she'd moved to Avanos and then Istanbul, she feared meeting Mark's mother. There might be Turkish blood in Mark's paternal family, but the maternal family was pure Ashkenazi, without a single drop of Sephardic blood, even by way of marriage. They had fled Russia in 1903. They were fairly affluent and they'd had several relatives already living in New York. These early immigrants had had enough sense to get out during the first wave of pogroms, knowing that this did not predict a positive future for Jews in that part of the world. Adalet had found it strange that a people who'd been so persecuted could have prejudices among their own people, but the Ashkenazi, according to Mark, were considered a superior race of Jews. He'd known nothing of his great grandfather or his grandfather's time in Turkey. He was always told they were all from Germany. To this day, he'd told Adalet, his mother refused to confess that she'd ever known differently. Mark thought she didn't want to be the first to tarnish the family bloodline, even or especially through marriage.

The ring of the phone broke Adalet's reverie. She rose quickly to retrieve the it, but in her haste neglected to indentify who was calling.

"Hi Mark," she breathed into the phone.

"It's Meryem." She sounded sick, out of breath. "Adalet, are you there?"

"Yes, I'm here." Adalet felt a sharp pain stab in her chest, something like gas, but she knew it wasn't.

"It's Fatma, Adalet. She was just sitting in her chair, like she always does—." Her voice broke and she started to wail. Adalet could hear the phone crash and then someone pick it up.

"Adalet, it's Ahmet. Fatma's gone. She simply slumped over in her chair. The doctor just left. He said her heart gave out. Can you come right away?"

"Of course, I can. I will fly to Ankara and rent a car. I don't know if I can get there tonight, but I will be there tomorrow. Please put Meryem back on, if she can speak to me." Adalet could hear the phone being passed again.

"Hello Adalet." Meryem's voice was a shaking whisper.

"I'll be there as soon as I can get a flight out. I love you, Meryem."

"I love you, too, Adalet." The line went dead.

CHAPTER 26

Adalet didn't allow a tear to drop until she'd booked the 8:00 pm flight to Ankara. She rented a car, booked a hotel for one night, arranged for a car to drive her to the airport and plotted her drive from Ankara to Avanos. Quickly she ran downstairs to ask the neighbor, Seyma, to come in to feed Yetim, and then she collapsed in the middle of the living room floor in a sea of tears.

So many regrets, she thought. Always more regrets. Is this what life is for me? First my parents, then my baby and my marriage. Now Fatma. Why didn't I visit her more often? Why? Adalet scolded herself for the weekends she'd been too busy or too tired. Was she selfish? It was certainly a question she felt she had to ask herself. But then again, it had always seemed that there would be enough time later.

Adalet rolled into a ball, hugging herself, choking on her sobs. Finally, she got up and blew her nose into a tissue she had in her pocket, and then reached for another from the box sitting on an end table. The screech of the doorbell overwhelmed the silent room. What an awful racket, she thought. I must change that bell. It must be Mark. I'd completely forgotten about him.

Adalet straightened her clothes and her hair and pushed the buzzer for the door. She didn't bother to ask who it was. The sound of the footsteps, confident and evenly spaced, firm but not heavy, confirmed that it was Mark. She knew those footsteps well by now. But somehow they seemed to move more slowly today, or was that her projection? Adalet could see him now rounding the curve on the stairway. He looked up at her. "Adalet," he said, pausing on a stair to say her name and then continuing up.

"Is something wrong, Mark? What's happened?"

Mark went past her into the apartment, removed his jacket and his shoes, and took her in his arms, holding her very close.

"How did you find out about Fatma? Did Meryem call you?" Adalet could feel more tears pushing their way forward.

"Fatma?" Mark pulled back from Adalet, still holding her hands so that he could see her face. "What's happened to Fatma?"

Adalet burst into tears. "She's gone. She had a heart attack this afternoon sitting in her favorite chair. If it hadn't been so sudden they might have thought she'd fallen asleep."

Mark pulled her close to him again. "My God, I'm so sorry, sweetheart. Strange that it would happen today. At least she'll never know. She was spared that."

"Spared what?" Adalet had no idea what Mark was talking about.

"You don't know. You haven't had the television on at all?"

"No, of course not. After I got the call, I was busy making arrangements to go to Ankara this evening. Do you think you could go with me? I could call now and see if I can get you on the same flight. I rented a car from there to drive to Avanos." Mark looked blank, as if he hadn't processed a word Adalet had said.

"Please sit down, my dear. I have some terrible news." He led Adalet to the couch and sat with her. He took both of her hands in his. "Something terrible has happened in New York."

"What, Mark? Is your family okay?"

"I don't know yet. The phones aren't working and I can't get through. I can't even get through to my mother. Some terrorists hijacked planes and drove them into the World Trade Center buildings. It was horrible. I saw it on the screen. It was just before 9:00am in the morning there. People had just gotten to work. Oh,

God, David, my cousin, David! He works in the North Tower. I must try to call again. Please turn on the television."

"Planes drove into the World Trade Center? It can't be." Adalet lifted the remote from the camel bags next to the couch and pushed the on button. Explosions and people were erupting from the buildings and into the streets. This pandemonium was being broadcast on every channel. But she knew that Mark would never understand the Turkish at such a rapid pace, so she turned to World CNN and lowered the sound in case any of Mark's calls went through.

Mark was pacing the floor and pushing buttons on his cell phone. "Damn, all I get are busy signals. Wait, now there's an announcement—all the lines are down." He shut off the cell phone and put it back in his pocket. "I tried to book a flight right away, but all the airports are closed. I can't even get there." Mark put his head in his hands. His frustration filled the room. Adalet could feel the weight of it.

Mark took his hands away from his face and turned to look at Adalet. "Come with me," he said. "As soon as the airports are open, come with me."

"How can I go now? I must be there for Fatma's funeral. Why don't you come with me, and then we'll see when the airports are open again. I have appointments at the school that I'd have to postpone. I don't think I can just run off to America without giving anyone notice."

"But Adalet, the airports could reopen at any time. I don't really know. Nothing like this has ever happened. Suppose we're in Avanos and the airports open? I don't even know if my family is alive. My mother often goes to meet David at his office—but wait— no, that would be for lunch. It was too early. But David—Oh, God, I just don't know." Mark took out his cell phone and then, as if he'd forgotten and then remembered that the lines were down, he stuck it back into his pocket. "Let's see what they're saying on the TV. Can you turn up the sound?"

They sat down together on the couch facing the television screen. Yetim sensed that something serious was taking place and jumped between them. She rested her small head on Adalet's thigh, and let her tail graze Mark's leg. The newscaster was repeating the same segment that Adalet had seen when she first turned on the television, the buildings collapsing over and over again. Underneath, the scrolling read that no one yet had claimed responsibility for the attacks, but the FBI and CIA had confirmed it was a terrorist attack. People were believed to still be trapped inside. Hospitals were on the alert and emergency services were standing by to receive the wounded. Police and firemen had rushed to the site. Even those who weren't on duty were going anyway. The news anchor once again showed a film of people running through the streets and the towers collapsing. He warned against going near the area unless you were a first responder.

Adalet looked at her watch. It was almost 6:00. She would need to leave in a few minutes in order to meet the car downstairs that she'd called to drive her to the airport. Mark seemed to be hypnotized by the television. She wondered if he'd forgotten Fatma's death. Just when she needed him, he was already miles away. The same film flickered across the screen again and again, interrupted by the intermittent comments of the reporters and the anchor. A plane seemed to almost glide into a building that then collapsed, erupting and sending people running through billowing smoke into the streets.

Adalet squeezed Mark's hand. "I'm going to have to leave soon." She didn't like the sound of her voice, as if she were pleading with Mark to leave this horrible vision that seemed to have possessed him. She consciously changed her tone and said, "I must go to the funeral, Mark."

Mark started, as if her voice had interrupted a trance. "Fatma's funeral, of course you have to go." He stroked her hand for a moment before releasing it. "I'm so sorry, Adalet, but I can't go with you. I have to be on the first flight out of here, or at least the first flight that I can find a seat on to New York. I hope you can understand."

And Adalet could understand. Of course he'd want to get to his family as soon as possible. But Fatma was her family. And Meryem was her family. How could she run off with Mark at this time? It was out of the question.

Mark seemed to read her mind. "I know that you can't come with me now, but if you can, join me later. We'll stay in contact by phone; the signals can't be shut down forever. I'll take my laptop with me as well, so we can email. I wish I could be with you now, my sweetheart, but please say you'll try to come as soon as possible."

"I don't even have a visa," Adalet shook her head. "I don't know if I can get one. It's not so easy here. Lots of red tape. It's a problem."

"I'll figure that out somehow with the university. You'll be my research assistant or something. Or we could just go get married. What do you think?"

"Even if we wanted to get married now, there's no time." Adalet wondered why she felt relieved by this unfortunate fact. She leaned over and kissed him. "I'll see what I can do if you can figure out a way for me to get the visa. I can promise you that much. I must be sure that Meryem is okay before I do anything, though." She rose from the couch to gather her suitcase and jacket and to put on her shoes by the door. Yetim followed her, appraising her filled food dish in the kitchen as well as the suitcase. "It's okay darling, your friend Seyma will come to see you."

Mark flicked the remote to off and stood up. "I'll go down with you. I have numbers at home that I don't keep in my phone. I want to try everything I possibly can to get through to someone who might know anything."

The car was waiting for Adalet. The driver jumped out to put her suitcase in the trunk. "We'd better go, there's traffic."

They kissed on both cheeks like family or good friends, and then Mark helped Adalet into the car. She squeezed his hand. "You have all our numbers," she whispered, and he nodded and closed the car door. She'd wanted to add an I love you, but before she could even mouth the words through the window glass, the driver pulled away from the curb and Mark was just a shadow on the darkening street.

CHAPTER 27

It was just after 2:00am when Adalet pulled up in front of her home in Avanos. For reasons she could not even fathom, Yasar's family had never reclaimed the house. Adalet still possessed it without any papers to prove it so, but if Yasar had ever told them she was in Istanbul, they'd made no sign of it. She'd been thinking about that during a good bit of the drive.

Adalet hadn't considered the fact that Fatma would have to be buried in the morning according to Muslim tradition when she'd booked the room in Ankara. She'd called Ahmet after she picked up the rental car and realized from their conversation that staying overnight in Ankara would not be possible.

"Her body has already been washed and shrouded by the women from the mosque," Ahmet told her. "The burial will begin at 9:00 tomorrow morning. It will take you four to five hours to drive here." He sounded tired and slightly annoyed, forgetting or perhaps not even having paid attention to what Adalet had told him her plans were earlier.

"Okay," Adalet told him, "I'll cancel the room and come immediately. Where should I come? Should I meet you at the cemetery?

"You could, but Fatma considered you her daughter. If you like, please walk with us to the cemetery. We'll leave from the shop at 8:30

196

and carry the body there. You won't be able to walk with us, but you can walk behind with Meryem. You do know that women are not allowed to carry the body or to be in the front of the procession."

Adalet hesitated. She really didn't know. She'd never thought about it. She still suffered from the torment of having been much too ill to attend to her parents' burials. Her burns from the earth-quake were just too severe. And she'd been much too young to remember the specifics of her grandparents' funerals, or if she'd even been allowed to attend. She didn't think she had.

"I've never attended a funeral, Ahmet. This will be my first."

"Sorry, Adalet. I'm very tired. It was so sudden. My brother and I were not prepared." For a moment he paused and then added, as if it were an afterthought, "Oh, Adalet, please don't wear black. Even though we all consider you part of our family, tradition calls for only blood descendents to wear mourning clothing."

Adalet hesitated, not knowing what to say. Family that wasn't really family. It made her think of Yasar's family, and how she'd always felt like an outsider. In fact, she hadn't even brought black clothing. She'd pulled out a blue suit Yasar's mother had picked out for her, something she never wore but that had seemed appropriate in her haste to pack.

"Adalet, are you there?" Ahmet's voice interrupted her reverie.

"Yes, Ahmet. I admit I hadn't thought of it, but I brought a blue suit." She wondered if he would ask the length of the skirt, as if she knew nothing at all of being a Muslim woman.

"I'm sure it will be fine," he said. He'd sounded relieved, as if he thought she might decide to challenge him. There were many customs that she loved about her religion, but she had also learned to resent some of them at times. It was hard for her to believe that Allah considered her to be less than the men who ran her religion and her country. She hadn't questioned these things until she'd attended the university and met women who did. She still felt confused by the way men treated women. Even though she had doubts that Allah would have conceived of things in this way, and was fairly convinced it was the men who'd come up with all of these restrictions, her father had always been in charge of their family. Her mother had respected and accepted this. Mark behaved as if he and Adalet were equals.

"Okay then," she told Ahmet. "I will see you tomorrow."

"Be careful on the road. Even though the highway will not be busy at this time of night, there are the trucks and the people who don't seem to think they need headlights."

"I will be careful," Adalet had promised, but she had to wonder at how Ahmet instructed that she not present herself as one of Fatma's family and yet treated her like a younger sister. She'd never spent much time with either of the brothers, Ahmet or Bekri. She thought again about the building in Istanbul and the letter from Fatma's attorney. She hoped there would not be any trouble. She'd decided that she would give up the building if there were any bad feelings.

Now Adalet set the parking brakes, got out and pulled her bag from the trunk. The night air was chilly. She pulled a small flashlight out of her bag to see her way to the front courtyard door. The light revealed that the courtyard had been swept. She had no doubt that Temel and Ermine had taken good care of the house. In the four years she'd been in Istanbul, the house was always clean and cared for when she returned. Adalet smiled as she looked at the trimmed bush under which she'd discovered Yetim, five years ago now. Yetim had become such an integral part of their lives, hers, Meryem's and now Isha's. Why hadn't she thought to ask Meryem and Isha to stay with her here? She couldn't imagine them staying as a couple with Ahmet or Bekri. It had taken some time for her to get used to Meryem being gay, although she had nothing against homosexuality. But Ahmet and Bekri? Their families and friends? These thoughts were going through her mind as she struggled with the key in the lock. A light went on inside and before Adalet could get the key to turn, the door opened. Meryem stood in the doorway and put her finger to her lips to silence Adalet. Meryem whispered, "Shush, Isha is sound asleep. Oh, God, Adalet, I'm so glad you're here." She pulled Adalet inside and then saw her suitcase sitting on the ground. In her bare feet and pajamas, she stepped onto the cold stones to get it.

"But you don't have any shoes on," Adalet protested.

"This isn't Istanbul," Meryem smiled. "I'm not likely to step on anything gross." She set the suitcase down and pulled Adalet onto the couch beside her. "We have to whisper," Meryem reminded her. "Isha isn't having an easy time of it without Fatma to protect her here. Ahmet started in immediately with something like, I hope you don't plan to introduce her as your lover or partner or whatever it is you call each other. For the sake of Fatma's dignity, can't you just say she's a friend from school?"

Adalet burst into tears. She tried not to make too much noise, but when Meryem put her arms around her, she could not control herself. "Nothing will be the same without her," Adalet sobbed. "She protected us all. Poor Isha. She adored Fatma, and Fatma couldn't take her eyes off her. She thought Isha was the most beautiful woman she'd ever seen."

"Did she really?" Isha's voice startled Adalet. She leaned away from Meryem and saw her standing in the doorway to the living room, also barefoot and in pajamas.

"Oh, I'm so sorry, Isha. Meryem warned me not to wake you. Everything just hit me all at once. And yes, Fatma did think you were the most beautiful woman she'd ever seen. She once told me that was the other reason she was able to accept Meryem being gay, aside from the fact that she was relieved that there would be no more babies she might have to care for. And she didn't think Meryem would ever find a man as attractive, especially after her friend the pimply boy."

The three women looked at each other and burst out laughing.

"He was pretty ugly," Meryem agreed, "and his motorcycle wasn't much better. That was all I liked about him anyway." They laughed until Adalet once again felt the tears cascading down her cheeks. When she looked up again, Meryem and Isha were both in tears. "We're all going to miss her so much." Adalet said, motioning to Isha to come and sit with them. They sat with their arms wrapped around each other, almost as if they were posing for a picture.

"At least we're all here together," Meryem said. She rose from the couch. "You must be exhausted, Adalet. Do you want to get some sleep for a few hours? Isha and I are camping out in my studio. Uncle Ahmet didn't even try to get us to come to his house. He's so embarrassed with the gay thing. Does he really think I'm going to announce that I'm gay at Fatma's funeral? What an idiot. Since Isha truly is far too gorgeous to go unnoticed, we'll say we paint together and let them draw their own conclusions. By the way, I know it's ridiculous, but we have to wear headscarves. I knew Ahmet would be afraid to tell you, so we brought you one."

"He certainly didn't mind telling me why I mustn't wear black. Why would he be afraid of mentioning a headscarf? "

" You're asking me?" Meryem pulled Isha up from the couch. "In any event, it seems to be what Ahmet is asking us to do. So we're going to make him happy and not do anything to upset him at his mother's funeral."

"When did you become so mature, Meryem? And me sounding like an offended child. Of course we'll do as he asks." She kissed Meryem and Isha on both cheeks, picked up her suitcase and started to make her way to the bedroom.

"I learned a lot from Isha," Meryem called after her. "If you think Turkish families are challenging, you should trying living in an Indian family for a week or two. I'll wake you in the morning. I hope that blue silk will match whatever color you're wearing."

"Perfectly," Adalet called back to her, and shut the bedroom door behind her.

CHAPTER 28

The scarf didn't exactly match the blue of her suit perfectly, but Adalet accepted it in good spirits. And it wasn't Istanbul. No one, except maybe Meryem and Isha, would notice what she wore anyway. Other than wearing black or being inappropriate, she couldn't imagine drawing negative attention. Isha had been to visit Fatma on several occasions, and no one had gossiped or it would have gotten back to Fatma. People assumed she was a good friend of Meryem's. Ahmet was overreacting and didn't know Meryem very well if he thought she would come out to the community at Fatma's funeral. Adalet could not even imagine such a thing. Adalet certainly would not have announced that she was sleeping with Mark if he'd come. Let them think what they would. No one would have the audacity to ask.

After she'd gone to her bedroom the night before, Adalet realized that she hadn't seen another car in the driveway. She asked Meryem and Isha about it in the morning.

"We left the rental car at the pottery shop because Ahmet didn't want us to drive over here at night," Isha told her.

"He was afraid of us going to the house alone because it's been sitting here empty," Meryem chimed in. "Ahmet seems afraid of everything. He said to call him in the morning and he'd send someone to pick us up. They'll be reading the Koran by Fatma's body until we go to the cemetery. Let's get dressed and do the headscarves, and maybe we'll have time to stop in the village and see if the bakery is open. There will be lots of food after the service, but I'm starving and there's nothing here." They agreed to hurry, as they all thought some *çay* and a pastry would be a good idea. Meryem said she would call Ahmet and let him know that she and Isha would not need a ride, even though he might have reasoned that himself, if he'd had any time to think.

Adalet stood in front of the mirror in her bedroom to assess her appearance. It was a bit odd, she thought. The suit was very modern, a silk affair with a fitted jacket and round buttons covered in the same blue silk. The skirt was long and had an A-line flair that moved easily with her body. Her head was covered in typical Turkish style with the blue silk scarf from Meryem that somehow managed, in spite of both being blue, to clash with her suit. But she was pleased with how well she'd managed the two tucks on each side; from the neck up, she looked very Turkish. From the neck down, she could have been attending a dressy occasion just about anywhere in the world. Or so she thought. Simple black flats covered her feet.

When she stepped into the living room, Meryem was tying Isha's headscarf. Meryem turned to look at Adalet. "Oh, dear, the scarf doesn't match at all, does it? I must wear black, but maybe you and Isha can switch?" She unraveled the scarf she'd been tying on Isha, a silk medley of colors and held it next to Adalet's suit.

"That is so much better," Isha agreed. Adalet undid her headscarf and held it next to Isha's light gray suit, a simple but elegant jacket and pants, similar to the black suit that Meryem wore, but Meryem's suit had a long, straight skirt, not too fitted.

Meryem clapped her hands. "It is perfect. Just as you said, Adalet. Now go tie that on your head and I'll fix Isha's so we can grab something to eat." Adalet stood there and just stared at Meryem. "Well, what are you looking at?" Meryem demanded.

"The only time I ever saw you in a head scarf was years ago when we went to the Blue Mosque. Do you remember? You were just a girl then, but now you look like a real Turkish woman."

Meryem laughed. "A real Turkish woman is exactly what I am."

"Hurry, the two of you, or we won't get a thing to eat." Isha sat back against the chair again so that Meryem could complete the procedure that was alien to Isha, who could have shaved her head and still made heads turn.

The three women piled into Adalet's rental car. The car looked much like the one Meryem had once painted but a newer and cleaner version. The old painted Fiat was parked at Temel's house. He used it to carry his tools and supplies to work and maintained it while Adalet was in Istanbul. She'd told him many times that it was his now, but he seemed to prefer to think he was keeping it for her.

It wasn't until she'd backed out of the driveway that Adalet turned to ask Meryem the question that had been on her mind. "Does it really seem to you that Ahmet is afraid of everything?"

Meryem was sitting next to Adalet in the passenger seat. She turned to look at her. "I guess I was never really around Ahmet enough to know him very well. He was always in the shop, working, or running errands for Fatma. Even though I stayed with his family, I spent most of my time in the shop with Fatma. I don't really know his wife either. She was kind to me and to her children, and it seemed, to Ahmet as well. I don't know if he's afraid of everything, but it seems to me that he's afraid of making mistakes now that he thinks would upset Fatma. If that makes any sense."

"Yes, it does. It makes a lot of sense. Fatma was the matriarch of the family for so many years, and now Ahmet's become the patriarch. Even though he ran the shop, he never ran Fatma. It must be hard for him to be in charge of her funeral."

The car behind them sped up close to their rear bumper and honked their horn. A car coming in the other direction prevented the impatient driver from passing. Isha, in the back seat, turned to look at him. "He means business," Isha warned. "You'd better pull over and let him pass."

"There's a place where you can pull over coming up," Meryem offered when the driver leaned on his horn without a pause.

As Adalet pulled to the side, the angry driver, an older man, sped by them, disappearing in a puffy cloud of dust. Isha muttered,

"You'll be going to a funeral soon yourself, mister, if you don't slow down. And it will be your own." Isha had told Adalet on many occasions how much she hated the driving in Turkey and would not get behind a wheel. Meryem had confided to Adalet that Isha also felt the same way about driving in Mumbai, where she was from.

Fortunately, the small adobe brick bakery was only a few moments farther and the open sign was hanging in the window. The sign read *Mohammed's Wife's Pastries and Çay.* "I wonder if Mohammed's wife has a name," Isha giggled.

"This is great," Adalet said, as she pulled up to park right in front of the door. Her cell phone started to play Turkish music, indicating that she had a call. She got out of the car and pulled it from her purse. Meryem and Isha stepped out with her and headed into the bakery. "I'll be right there," Adalet called after them. She checked to see who was calling. The name Mark Aronson displayed on her screen. She touched the on signal.

"Hi Mark. Did you find anything out yet?"

"My mother is okay but pretty badly shaken. No one has heard from my cousin, David. There are search teams down there looking for survivors. The planes still aren't flying. I think it's going to be a few days. Would you like me to come up there?"

Yes, Adalet thought. Yes, I'd love it if you did. Into the phone she said, "I do appreciate that you would come, my dear man, but there is just too much going on for you right now. I'm okay, really I am. Meryem and Isha are with me."

"You're sure? I could fly to New York from Ankara."

"It's so kind of you, sweetheart, but the funeral is in 45 minutes. And you would have to meet all of these people under these sad circumstances. Just let me know when you're leaving."

"Of course I will."

Adalet couldn't tell if Mark was disappointed or relieved from his tone. Perhaps neither, she thought. He's probably been up all night staring at the television. "Have you slept?" she asked.

"Very little. I dozed off here and there in front of the television." So she'd been right.

"I've got to go, Mark. Meryem and Isha are waiting for me to get a bite to eat before the funeral. I'll call you later. I love you."

"I love you, too, sweetheart. Bye, bye."

"Bye."

Adalet saw that a message was blinking on her phone. It was from Nuray. Adalet had completely forgotten to cancel lunch today with her. She looked at her phone with dismay. She had to go inside. She walked into the shop and saw that Meryem and Isha were the only ones there, sitting at a small table in the back.

"Please order for yourselves and get me a *çay* and a pastry. Any kind will do. I have another call to make," Adalet told them and dashed back outside. She pressed "return call" before even stopping to listen to the message. Nuray answered on the second ring. "It's me," Adalet said.

"I was so shocked. I had to call you. How is Mark?"

"He's fine, Nuray. Thank you for calling. I'm in Avanos now. I found out yesterday that Fatma had passed away from a heart attack. This all happened so quickly. I came right away. I'm so sorry, but I won't be able to meet you for lunch today."

"Oh, my goodness, Adalet. That is the least of it. Do you want me to come up there?"

"Thank you, Nuray, but I think I'm going to head back right after the funeral. I might be able to see Mark before he leaves."

"Oh, God. Is Mark going back there?"

"He has to. His mother's okay, but they can't locate his cousin, David. He worked in one of those buildings. No one's heard from him. Listen, Nuray, let me call you after the funeral. We don't have much time now, and Meryem and Isha are waiting for me."

"Okay, my dear friend, let me know if there is anything I can do for you."

Maybe Nuray was a better friend than Adalet had thought. Human behavior was a constant surprise to her. She realized that she didn't understand people all that well. Meryem teased her on this issue constantly. She shut down her phone and ran into the bakery. A hot *çay* and an apple pastry were sitting on the table at an empty place between Meryem and Isha. Adalet immediately sat and took a sip of the *çay*. "Mmm," she mumbled as she bit into the gooey honey-coated pastry.

"What was all that about?" Meryem asked.

"Yes, who called?" Isha inquired, taking the last bit of pastry from her plate and putting it delicately into her mouth.

"It was Mark. And then I called Nuray. She'd left me a message. I completely forgot that I was supposed to have lunch with her today."

"So how come Mark didn't come with you?" Meryem, as always, sticking to the main point.

"He's going to head back to New York as soon as he can get a flight." Adalet sipped deliberately at her *çay*, as if this would be enough information to satisfy Meryem.

"And you're not going with him? Why?" Meryem looked Adalet directly in the eyes.

"I couldn't miss this funeral for myself, and then I had to see you and find out how you were doing. He asked me to go, but it's not so easy. I told him I'd think about joining him later, but I'll need a visa."

Meryem glared at her. "Honestly, Adalet, you used me as an excuse? That's pathetic. Do I seem in need to you? Yes, it's great that you're here and Isha and I—

"Don't get me involved in this, Meryem." Isha pushed her chair back, as if to separate herself from the developing disagreement.

"But you are involved, Isha, and that's the point I was trying to make. I'm a grown woman now, and you are my life partner. We take care of each other. And it's not that we don't take care of you, too, Adalet, or that you don't take care of us, but can't you see that it's different now? You need to be with Mark. He is your life part-ner—or isn't he?"

The direct gaze and the strength of Meryem's words were a slap across the face to Adalet. She hunched forward, put her face in her hands and rubbed them, as if soothing a wound; then Adalet abruptly moved her chair back from the table. "Where's the waiter? We need to pay and get to the shop. We'll be late."

CHAPTER 29

Adalet was more moved by the funeral than she'd expected. She realized that the telephone conversation with Ahmet about what she should wear and where she should stand through the ceremonies had not set well. His words had left a sour taste in her mouth that dissipated as the day wore on.

It looked to Adalet as if the entire village had turned out for the march to the cemetery. Several of the village elders, along with Ahmet and Bekri, served as pallbearers and carried the body the entire way. Fatma had insisted on a traditional Muslim funeral, and so she had requested to be buried without a coffin in order that her body be returned to the earth as soon as possible. She had been wrapped in white cotton sheets after the traditional washing of the body. The walk seemed to take forever, but in reality, Adalet remembered it to be about a ten to fifteen- minute walk from the pottery shop.

The morning air was as crisp as fresh fall apples but not yet cold. The sun was blindingly bright, as if it had been misinformed as to the solemnity of the occasion. Adalet and Meryem walked just behind the last of the men who consisted of Temel and several of the workers employed in the pottery shop. Knowing how Fatma felt about Temel, Adalet had to wonder what she would have thought about that. Ahmet and Bekri's wives walked behind Adalet and Meryem, and Isha walked behind the two wives. Ahmet's children were not present. A flurry of women from the village trailed behind. Adalet recognized a few of them from the shops she'd gone to while living in Avanos. One of them Adalet recognized as a cheerful woman who sometimes visited Fatma in the pottery shop. She nodded to Adalet and Adalet nodded back. Emine was there, and she had also not brought her children. It was a silent march, and Adalet did not turn around again. A couple of times, either Adalet or Meryem would grasp the other's hand for a quick squeeze of reassurance. It felt odd to Adalet to be here without Fatma. It was hard to imagine that it was her body wrapped in those sheets and carried by her sons and the other designated pallbearers. And since Adalet had lost sight of the body being carried ahead of her, it was not so difficult to imagine that Fatma was walking somewhere behind them, or perhaps sitting in her chair in the pottery shop, waiting for all of this ceremony to end.

When they reached the cemetery, the line of people circled around the burial site. The gravesite had already been dug, and soil was piled around it. A shovel was stuck into the accumulated soil. Several bricks lay at the bottom of the grave to support Fatma's head. The bricks were arranged so that Fatma's head would be facing east. The men praised Allah and then gently began to ease the body into the grave. As they lowered the body, they recited "In the name of Allah and with Allah, and according to the sunnah of the messenger of Allah upon whom be the blessings and peace of Allah." Several boards were placed over the body to cover the shroud. Ahmet grasped the shovel and poured the first of the dirt into the grave. When he finished, he handed the shovel to Bekri, who then passed the shovel to the man next to him.

When Adalet first witnessed the pouring of the dirt into the grave, she clasped Meryem's arm and both women wept. Isha must have had her eye on Meryem because she left her place in the gathering to join and comfort them. This was not noticed, as people were no longer in a specific line or place, other than the men being in the front and the women in the back. Adalet felt a rush of relief to have Isha close by, no longer separated from what had become Isha's only family in Turkey.

When all the men who wished to do so had flung dirt into the grave and some individual prayers had been offered, the remainder of the dirt was left to the two gravediggers who stood by for that purpose. The procession then made it's way from the cemetery back to the pottery shop where several of the women had stayed behind to set several tables that were now laden with food prepared by most of the women in the village. Since many of the villagers thought of the pottery shop as Fatma's home, Ahmet and Bekri had decided to hold the gathering there. They'd moved the pottery and furniture out of the way and set up three large tables with folding chairs in a circle around them for the people who wished to sit. Adalet was impressed with the care that everyone had taken. She thought Fatma would have been touched by both the adherence to her wishes for a simple Moslem funeral and by the abundance and delicacy of the dishes that had been prepared.

"They'll be bringing food for a week," Meryem turned and whispered to Isha. "We never eat better than when someone dies. Even weddings don't compare."

"Believe it or not," Adalet confided to them, "this is my first funeral. I was too ill to bury my parents."

"I wasn't allowed to go to my mother's funeral," Meryem said with a tone of sadness in her voice. "My father thought I was too young. But I do remember the huge amounts of food people brought to Fatma's house."

"Then your mother is buried here?" Adalet asked.

"Of course," Meryem sighed. "Do you think Fatma would've permitted my father to bury her in a Christian cemetery? She would've followed him to hell and back."

"Meryem, you always make Fatma sound so mean. She really wasn't," Isha countered. "I don't know why you do that."

"You didn't live with her. I did," Meryem retorted. "And she wasn't mean; she was just Fatma. And you have to admit she was in a category of her own. I bet your aunties are nothing like her."

Before Isha could respond, Adalet felt a hand on her shoulder. She turned around to look at the lovely young woman in a beaded shawl who was interrupting this discourse. Emine threw her arms around Adalet, and Adalet embraced her warmly. "I'm so glad to see you, Emine. Thank you for coming. Have you met Isha, Meryem's schoolmate?"

"My painting partner," Meryem clarified under her breath.

"So nice to meet you, Isha."

"And you, Emine." The women kissed each other lightly on both cheeks.

"Do you really paint together?" Emine asked.

Adalet was again distracted by a light tap on her arm. She turned to face Ahmet. "How are you doing?" he asked.

"It was a beautiful ceremony, Ahmet. Fatma would have been very proud."

A single tear ran down Ahmet's cheek. "Sometimes she annoyed me so much, but I miss her already. Who will boss me around now? Who will check the food and criticize everything? Not Meryem, surely. You will have to step up, Adalet."

They both smiled. "Leave it to your wife, Ahmet. It's about time she got to be in charge. Will you say a prayer for the food? I think people are ready to eat."

"There you go. I knew you could do it."

"Oh, Ahmet, I'm so sorry. I didn't mean—."

"Don't be silly, Adalet. I'm only teasing. But you are right. It's time to say a prayer and let people eat. Oh, can you stay one more night here? I don't know your plans. Tomorrow morning we will be reading Fatma's will, and we'd like you and Meryem to be here."

"Yes, I can stay," Adalet told him. She had planned to leave early in the morning to catch Mark before he left, but perhaps there wouldn't be any flights going to New York yet. Thinking back on the lawyer's letter, Adalet knew she would have to be present at the reading of the will. How was she going to handle the family when they found out about the apartment building? Even if she immediately relinquished all claims, how would the family feel about her?

Oh Fatma, she thought, I wish you hadn't done this. You and Meryem and Isha have been my only family. Well, whatever their reactions might be, better that she be present in Avanos than in Istanbul or New York, although New York was hardly possible. She would call Mark that evening and discuss it with him. He knew nothing of the building and Fatma's wishes.

Ahmet called everyone's attention and he and Bekri said the prayer before the meal. The married women first brought plates of food to their husbands before they took their own. Adalet was hungry, but she waited until the flurry around the tables was finished before she attempted to make her own plate.

There was an assortment of hot *bulgur* dishes and cold *bulgur* salads. These were Adalet's favorites and she took small samples of several. She skipped over the variety of chicken, fish and lamb dishes, not wanting anything as heavy as meat, but she stopped to take a small bowl of red lentil, *bulgur* and mint soup. The scintillating smell of paprika and Turkish red pepper mixed with onion, garlic, olive oil and mint drifted up in the steam from the bowl to Adalet's nostrils. It made her feel too hungry as she made her way on to the cheese and spinach *borek*, meat *borek*, plain pita and pita topped with tomato and cheese, so she piled on a spinach and cheese *borek* and a plain pita. She took a bottle of water from the drink table and searched for Meryem and Isha and Emine and Temel. The four of them had grabbed some chairs and were sitting together next to the table of desserts. There was an empty chair for Adalet in between Meryem and Emine.

"This is a dangerous place to sit," Adalet said as she settled into her chair with her food. "Near all the desserts."

"Fatma's favorites," Temel grinned. "Too bad she's not here to join us."

"I've had that feeling all day," Adalet told them, dunking a piece of pita bread into the soup. "I keep looking for her everywhere. It's the oddest feeling being here without her."

"Did Ahmet speak to you, Adalet?" Meryem whispered to Adalet.

"Yes, I'm staying tonight. Can you?" Adalet murmured in response.

"Yes, but we'll have to leave right after the will is read."

"Me, too. I want to try to see Mark before he goes to New York."

"Why don't you just go with him?" Meryem said a bit too loudly.

"What are the two of you talking about?" Isha turned her attention from Emine.

"Nothing," Adalet said at the same time as Meryem said, "Mark."

"Who is Mark?" Emine wanted to know.

"Adalet!" Meryem exclaimed. "You haven't said anything to Emine about Mark in all of this time? I can't believe you. You act like you're still married to Yasar and having an affair with Mark. What's wrong with you?"

All the eyes in this circle were now focused on Meryem and Adalet, going from one to the other, waiting for one of them to speak.

"Actually," Adalet finally said, "we were talking about the reading of the will. We'll be staying for that tomorrow morning, and then we will have to get back to Istanbul."

Meryem shook her head and just looked at Adalet. "Excuse me," she said. "I think I need something sweet after all of that food." Meryem got up and crossed to the other side of the dessert table.

CHAPTER 30

The reading of the will was so quick and simple that it left Adalet in a state of shock. It had never occurred to her that Fatma would have discussed leaving the building to her with everyone in her family prior to making her will, and that they would have agreed that this was the best and the right thing for Fatma to do. She was even more nonplussed when Ahmet took her aside and told her that he would be happy to continue to administer the maintenance of the building until she became familiar enough with the contractors he used that she felt comfortable doing it on her own. What made it easier for Adalet to accept all of this was that she learned from the reading of the will that Fatma had been quite wealthy, and Meryem and Ahmet and Bekri were well taken care of with assets, investments and the pottery shop.

Adalet wondered now how she would broach the subject with Mark. His whole heart and soul seemed to already be in New York, although he hadn't been able to leave Istanbul yet. They'd spoken on the phone in the evening after the funeral, and he was adamant about leaving as soon as possible.

"Aren't you worried that something might happen again?" Adalet had asked, revealing some of her own fears about traveling to New York now.

"Nothing will happen now. It's probably as safe now as it will ever be." Mark sounded confident.

"Why do you say that? How could you possibly know?" Adalet was beginning to realize that it wasn't only the visa that held her back.

"It's not likely that another massive attack like that could happen so quickly. And my mother tells me that New York looks like a city under siege. There are cops everywhere and security is on the highest alert. She told me I should prepare to be searched at the airport. I don't have a lot of choice, Adalet, I must go, and I wouldn't ask you to come if I didn't think it was safe. When will you be back in Istanbul?"

"I'm leaving as soon as the will is read tomorrow morning. There are so many flights from Ankara to Istanbul that I'll just go straight from the car rental to the airport. Once I know what flight I'm on, I'll call the car service. Shall I come to your flat or will you meet me at mine?"

"Are Meryem and Isha coming back now?"

"Yes, also after the reading of the will. They're driving the whole trip, though, so I don't think they'll be back until the next day."

"Yes, do come here anyway. If the airports open up again, and there's some talk that they will, I'll want to leave right away."

It was a short conversation, but Mark only asked about the funeral in what seemed to Adalet to be an afterthought.

"Oh, how was the funeral? How is Meryem?"

"The funeral was moving. Ahmet did a good job arranging for everything. Fatma would have loved it all."

"And Meryem?"

"She's doing well. Isha has made a big difference in her life. She's all grown up."

"Good, then she won't need you so much. I've spoken with my Department about getting a visa for you as my assistant. I think it can be done. See you tomorrow then." And that had been the gist of the conversation. He hadn't asked about New York again and she hadn't answered.

Meryem had spoken sternly to her last night, "You knew this time would come eventually. Even without this tragedy in New York, did you think he'd stay forever? Did you think that he'd never want to go home and take you with him? Honestly, Adalet. Sometimes I do wonder about you."

Had she thought about this moment? Only in the abstract. In the very beginning of her relationship with Mark, she'd had fantasies of traveling to New York with him. She'd gone online and studied the city. Mark was to be the prince who would take her away from her life in Turkey. But now her life in Turkey was better than she ever could have envisioned. Unless something unforeseen and unimaginable happened—and life had certainly taught her that it could—she felt secure and independent for the first time in her life. What a gift Fatma and her family had given her. She could never have imagined that she would stand where she now stood five years ago.

And she could not have dreamt that her position at the Yeditepe School for the Deaf would become so important to her and that she would feel so valued there. After speaking with Nuray, she also considered that the reason she hadn't made any close friends at Yeditepe might have been her own doing. She'd lost so much trust in people after her divorce. And she'd lost so much faith in life after the earthquake and the deaths of her parents and her unborn child. She never would have imagined that she meant so much to Fatma and her family; that they truly loved her for her belief in and support of Meryem. Perhaps they even loved her for herself. She'd lost two families, her own and Yasar's, but now she'd been favored enough to acquire a third. Besides, Mark had never mentioned moving back to New York, in spite of what Meryem had said.

Adalet felt as if she were the rope in a tug of war, prying her away from one direction and pulling her towards the other. A sharp shooting pain traveled from her gut to her heart and kept repeating itself off and on the whole way back to the rental car company. At one point, she'd had to pull the car over to the side of the road in order to breathe. It was a relief to return the car and get on the plane in Ankara.

When the driver finally pulled up in front of Mark's building at 9:30 pm, a wave of exhaustion overcame her, and she almost asked the driver to take her home. Meryem had been asking her whatever did she think she was doing, and now for the seemingly one hundredth time on this trip, Adalet asked herself the same question.

She paid the driver at the front door, where he'd deposited her suitcase. Adalet debated ringing up and then decided to use her key. It would give her just a few more minutes to try to think. By the time she turned the key in the door, Mark was opening it from the other side.

"I was watching for you from the window," he said, taking her in his arms and holding her close in the doorway. He pushed her hair aside and kissed the back of her neck softly several times. Then Mark took her suitcase from the threshold where Adalet had dropped it to embrace him and ushered them both inside, kicking the door closed behind him.

"I couldn't wait to see you. The airports will open tomorrow. I'm on a 12:30 flight." He set the suitcase down and took her coat, a smart black leather one that Yasar had once insisted on buying for her. It did occur to her at one point during the funeral that with the exception of her shoes, she was completely decked out in clothing purchased either by Yasar or his family.

"Have you eaten?" Mark asked.

"Not a thing all day. Just a cup of *çay* on the plane."

"Good. I made dinner for us. I'll put your bag in the bedroom and then pour us each a glass of wine." He disappeared down the hallway and Adalet felt the pain in her gut again. Soon they were both sitting at the dining room table with a bottle of Sancerre, a case of which Mark had arranged to be shipped from France. He could not get used to Turkish wine, although he did drink it when that was all there was to be had. He'd baked a large, red snapper, head still attached. This he removed before setting it on a bed of *pilav* with vegetables. He'd baked the fish in lemon juice and surrounded it with lemons. It was seasoned with Turkish pepper. He served a plate for Adalet and then himself. His attending to her brought Adalet back to the scene after the funeral where the women had filled the plates for the men. "This is lovely, Mark. Thank you." And without another word, Adalet began to eat. She hadn't realized how hungry she was. They ate in silence, but began to talk after Mark poured them a second glass of wine.

"This was so kind of you to make this meal when you've had so much on your mind," Adalet told Mark, lifting her glass and taking a sip. "This wine is lovely. I wasn't able to relax at all on the way home. I had this horrid cramping in my stomach and now I think it might have just been hunger."

"I have good news," Mark set his wine glass down on the table and took her hand. "I think we'll have a visa for you within a couple of weeks. It could take a bit longer due to the attacks. If I hadn't done it through the university, we probably would have been denied. The restrictions will continue to tighten up now. But that will give you time to catch up on your appointments at Yeditepe and let them know you're going to be away."

"Where will I stay?" Adalet asked him, the fact that she was actually going to go slowly sinking in.

"We'll stay with my mother, of course. She has a two-bedroom apartment. It's very nice. My tenant is still in mine, so we can't stay there."

"We're going to sleep in the same bedroom at your mother's? What will she think of me?" Adalet withdrew her hand from Mark and waved both of hers in the air. "A divorced woman coming to New York to stay with her son in the same bedroom with him in her apartment?"

"Meryem and Isha live together in your apartment," Mark countered.

"That's not the same thing at all."

"My mother knows you're joining me and she'd be hurt if you didn't stay with her. Trust me. She's very modern." Mark smiled at her, as if this would be a simple relief to Adalet.

"I don't know if I can do that, Mark. I really don't. I guess I'm the one who isn't so modern. I've never even met your mother. It doesn't feel right to me. We're not married." Adalet was immediately sorry she said that, as it was through no fault of Mark's that they weren't.

"Okay," Mark grumbled. "We'll get you a room in a hotel nearby. If I don't stay with my mother, she'll be terribly offended." His voice lightened. "Will you be okay staying on your own?"

"Sure. Thank you, sweetheart. I don't want to start off my relationship with her in the wrong way. I hope you can understand."

"I'm trying," Mark muttered. "I never thought my girl friend would have a more restrictive sense of morality than my mother. She knows we sleep at each other's apartments all the time."

"Yes, but not in her apartment."

"Technically speaking—." Mark started to say.

"Yes, but she doesn't live in this apartment." Adalet was shaking her head in some annoyance now.

"Okay, okay, I'll make a reservation for you. The university will contact you when the visa's ready. They'll contact me as well, so I'll take care of the tickets and the hotel then. I'm so glad you're coming, even if it isn't the best of times. We're still searching for David. No word yet."

"You see. That's another reason for me not to burden your mother right now. She must be frantic." As she said this, Adalet realized that she was afraid that Mark's mother might not like her and that she might not like Mark's mother. She knew that she could be polite no matter what happened as long as she had a room of her own to come back to. No matter what Mark said, she knew that Mrs. Aronson would have to suffer some feelings about the fact that Adalet was Turkish and Moslem. Moslems had attacked New York City, and as open-minded as she might be, Mrs. Aronson might be less inclined to embrace Adalet at this point in time. It was now Adalet's turn to hold her face in her hands.

Mark rose from the table and pulled her into his arms. "You could never be a burden to me or my mother, silly woman. And yes, we're both frantic about David. But you are my family and my mother will adore you no matter what. She's just so happy that I've found someone I love. I will always try to respect your wishes, and so we'll do things your way. I want you to be comfortable."

"Thank you, Mark." Adalet allowed herself to surrender to Mark's caresses, even though there were still so many questions on her mind. He'd have to leave first thing in the morning and there would be plenty of time to address some of her doubts at a later date and time.

CHAPTER 31

Rain pounded on the New York City streets and a thick blanket of gray clouds hung outside of Adalet's hotel room window. The desk clerk told her that she had a view of Central Park from her room, but he must have been mistaken. Perhaps he was used to some embellishment, like the tourist hotels in Turkey. All she could make out was a fairly steady stream of lights chasing each other up Madison Avenue.

Airport security had been a nightmare at JFK. Mark had hired a car to pick Adalet up and take her to the Hotel Wales, but her entry through customs and the meticulous search of her luggage delayed her so long that she'd had to call Mark to hire another car. The customs officer had unceremoniously pulled open the zipper to her plastic bag of Tampons and glared at her until she'd blushed. In all of this confusion, the first driver left the airport. Adalet had to wait another hour and a half because, Mark told her, it's impossible to get a taxi or hire a car when it rains in New York. Mark had a driver's license but he'd never actually owned a car. "Who needs a car in Manhattan?" he laughed. "Or in Istanbul for that matter?"

Now Adalet was cold and hungry but wanted a hot shower more than she wanted food or even sleep. It had taken a month for her visa to come through and it was now the end of October in a wet and cold New York City.

Via the red blinking light on the phone next to her bed, Adalet discovered that Mark and his mother had gone down to the Red Cross and FEMA services on the Pier for more information about Mark's cousin, David. They'd received a call that some of David's remains might have been found. Mark said they would come to the hotel later when they were finished and take her to dinner.

Adalet stripped off the clothing she'd been in since leaving her apartment in Beyoglu, Istanbul, just 24 hours ago, and stepped into the sizable hotel shower. Beads of hot water cascaded over her head and onto her body. Other than the language, the height of the buildings and the width of the shower, she could have been in Istanbul. No, Adalet reminded herself; I'm not in Istanbul. I can't just walk into the next room and find Meryem and Isha there. It's so gloomy here.

Stop this at once, she demanded, lathering her hair a bit fiercely with the thick, silky hotel shampoo. The shampoo and the conditioner smelled just like the lavender that grew outside her house in Avanos. She was homesick already and she hadn't actually walked on the streets of the city other than out of the taxi and into the hotel. The clerk had asked her if she was with the Red Cross. When she said no and turned over her passport for his inspection, he seemed at first disappointed and then a bit leery.

"We've got some Red Cross from out of town staying here," he'd said, as if she might find that a higher recommendation than the four stars the hotel boasted.

Adalet stood under the pulsing water and rinsed her hair. Stop being afraid and sad. You're going to meet your boy friend's—fiancée's—mother. She hardly knew how to refer to Mark anymore. Mark had asked his mother to resize his grandmother's diamond engagement ring for Adalet. This much she knew. But since she kept evading the marriage question, she didn't know what his thoughts were now, or her own, for that matter. Would he expect her to live here?

Adalet turned off the water and stepped into the fluffy white bath towel that might have held two of her. Would it be so bad to live here if all the towels were this soft? A thick, white terry robe hung on a hook on the back of the bathroom door. She exchanged her towel for it, wrapping it once and a half around her before she tied the belt and stretched out on the king-sized bed. Not so bad, she thought and instantly fell asleep.

A tall, slim, elegantly dressed woman sat facing her in the armchair across from her bed. The woman was staring critically at Adalet's form as she slept. Mark stood behind her. She didn't even dress for dinner, Mark's mother was saying. She's not for you, Mark. And no grandchildren? Turkish? Muslim? What were you thinking? Take me home now. I want nothing to do with her.

Adalet sat up and shook herself awake. There was no red button flashing on the phone to indicate a message. It was an awful dream and it had seemed so real. The clock on the nightstand said 8:00pm. Had they been here and left? She had no idea.

Adalet dressed hurriedly in the same blue pantsuit she'd worn to Fatma's funeral. She applied her makeup carefully in the magnified mirror in the bathroom, brushed her hair, and was debating whether or not to order room service when the phone finally rang. She said hello in English.

"Adalet, it's me. It's been a dreadful day. They've identified David. His head—this is so horrible. I can't talk about it yet. My mother is in pieces. She and my father raised David, and he was a second son to her. I'm going to get her home in a taxi, put her to bed and come to the hotel. We'll go have something to eat." Adalet could hear sobbing in the background.

"Where are you?" she asked.

"The morgue," he whispered into the phone. "I'll call you from my mother's once I've gotten her settled down. I love you, Adalet."

Before she could respond in kind, the phone clicked and the dial tone was ringing in her ear. Adalet pushed the hang-up button and picked up the room service menu from the writing desk. She rarely ate meat, but the idea of a hamburger and French fries on her first night in New York seemed very American. She called the kitchen, ordered and waited until her food arrived to change back into the hotel bathrobe. She was too hungry to postpone eating until Mark got his mother home and "settled down," whatever that might mean.

Adalet didn't feel angry or even annoyed. She was simply hungry. She'd eaten nothing since her breakfast on the plane. Of course Mark needed to take care of his mother, and Adalet was relieved not have to meet her in her current state of grief. Adalet believed that grief was a private affair and other than the silent tears she'd shed when the dirt was first shoveled into Fatma's grave, she had not cried in public. Even after the earthquake, when the Israeli nurse had notified her of her parents' death and the death of her baby, she'd waited until the nurse had left before sobbing into her pillow. From what she'd seen on television and in movies, Americans seemed looser with their expressions of any kinds of emotions. She didn't know what she could expect from Mrs. Aronson.

Adalet curled up in bed and turned on CNN. A month after the fact, the rubble at the site of the World Trade Center was still being excavated. She took a bite of her hamburger and then set it down to listen to what the newscaster was saying.

Volunteer crews continue to dig at Ground Zero. Now they are only looking for body parts and items that might help to identify the victims. The Medical examiner's Office has been working overtime to close the many unresolved cases that continue to be listed as missing. Families gather and still hold out hope that their loved ones might have wandered off and still be lost out there due to head injuries, but it's become pretty clear over the last few weeks that there were very few survivors. The difficulty now is that body parts were so scattered and destroyed that identification is a long and arduous process.

Adalet switched the channels for something less oppressing and immediate. After making the rounds, she happily settled on an old John Wayne film, *The Searchers.* This felt so right, the perfect choice of movie to go along with her hamburger, coke and French fries. As a child growing up in a small village in Turkey, Adalet had watched American Westerns with her father. This had been her image of America until she was in her teens, when her vision was expanded through American sitcoms, crime shows and more current American films.

Adalet curled up inside the hotel comforter with her tray of food balanced on the bed. She set the largest Coke she'd ever seen on the nightstand where she could easily reach it. Then she settled back against the propped pillows and allowed herself to become lost in the cinematic world of John Ford.

Adalet could not help comparing the hatred Ethan (John Wayne) had for the Comanche with the disgust and revulsion that some Turks had for the Kurds who'd settled in Turkey, some of whom had been there long before Adalet was born. Like the Native Americans who were displaced from their ways of life, their tribal rituals and economies, many Kurds had abandoned mountain lands to come to Istanbul where they had hoped to educate their children and improve their lives. The Turkish government had encouraged this migration in order to quell the rebellions in Eastern Turkey where the Kurdish population was the largest. The Turkish government had both rejected and even outlawed their language and customs, calling them Mountain Turks, as if they belonged to no other cultural identity.

The Kurds that Adalet knew personally dressed like everyone else in Istanbul and were intelligent and educated. They were young people who had assimilated. If they even owned any native dress, she'd never seen them wearing any. Adalet didn't understand the elaborate feathers or the painted faces of the Native Americans, but she had to admit that Scar, the Native villain in the film, was actually quite attractive. She fancied that if he hadn't had all those other wives, there could have been worse things than being kidnapped by him.

Adalet couldn't understand why Ethan would want to kill his niece. It hadn't been her fault that she was captured. And what else could she have done? She'd heard stories of Muslim girls who'd been raped or even had consensual relations who'd been killed by their fathers or brothers. She was relieved when Ethan embraced his niece and brought her back to their family. But the film ended with the doors to the house being shut and Ethan walking off into the sunset. Adalet found herself in tears, weeping for the lonely man who was never to know a lasting love. Ethan hadn't returned home after the civil war and his brother had married the woman Ethan loved. The film made it clear that his brother's wife was still in love with Ethan. What a crazy world.

Adalet set the empty dishes onto the tray and deposited it just outside her door. The clock on the nightstand read 9:30pm. Just as she was about to curl back up in the comforter, there was a tentative tap on the door. "Yes?" she called out from the edge of the bed.

"Adalet, it's Mark."

Adalet rose from the bed to open the door. Mark rushed in, took her in his arms and held her close. "This has truly been one of the worst days of my life," he muttered. "Thank God you're here." He held onto her for several minutes without uttering another word. Finally he let go, and they sat on the bed together.

"I'm glad you went ahead and got something to eat. I saw the tray outside. You must have been starving. I finally had to call my doctor friend to write a prescription for my mother. I don't remember ever seeing her like this, even when my father died."

"Is she okay now?" Adalet asked, her voice filled with concern.

"Well, she took the Ativan I gave her and she's asleep now. I don't know what it will be like when she wakes up. I'm so sorry, sweetheart. I didn't imagine that things would go this way."

"Don't be silly, Mark. I'm fine. I had a real American hamburger and French fries while I watched *The Searchers*. It was very interesting."

Mark chuckled, looking more like the Mark she'd known before the Towers went down. "You watched a John Wayne Western? "In America, you're considered in the East right now."

"I know. But I used to watch Westerns with my father and it made me feel at home. Besides, I think the Indians and the Kurds have some things in common."

"Do you want to get dressed and tell me about that over dinner?"

"I don't think so. You should get something to eat to take back to your mother's and spend the night there. Suppose she wakes up and she's all alone?" Adalet remembered waking up in the hospital tent structure after the earthquake with no one to hold her or comfort her. She didn't want Mrs. Aronson to have that experience.

"Are you sure?" Mark asked, looking deeply into her eyes as if to make certain she was being honest with him. "You just got here and I've seen you for about ten minutes."

"After the earthquake, I woke up alone. A complete stranger told me that both of my parents were dead and I'd lost my baby. She was very kind, but she was a stranger. I don't want your mother to be alone when she wakes up."

Mark pressed her close and held her again. "Thank you, dearest Adalet She loved David as if he were her own child. He never gave her worries in the ways that I did."

"Go," Adalet urged him. "Call me in the morning and let me know how she's doing. If I'm not here, don't worry. I might go to breakfast and explore the neighborhood if it's not pouring rain."

"Thank you my sweet love. I'll come and get you as soon as I can."

"And you, Mark? You've just lost a cousin who was more like a brother."

"In some ways he was; in some ways he wasn't. To be honest, we all knew he was dead. Funny, I was always a bit jealous of David. My mother always expected so much from me and David almost always fulfilled her wishes. I think he was afraid of losing her love in a way that I never was. She was his aunt and my mother. He was ten when his parents were killed in the car crash, and he was too old to call her 'Mom.' She was always Aunt Esther. I admired David and loved him, but I was grateful when he did something she didn't like."

"And what was that?"

"He married an African-American girl he met in college."

"David was married? You never mentioned."

"Yes, and he has a little boy, too, Jacob. His wife converted to Judaism and my mother loves her and Jacob dearly, but it took some time. They're in California now staying with her parents. David's disappearance was a great shock to her. I think she was pretty sure that David was dead because she couldn't imagine that he wouldn't have come home by now. She cried when we called, but she also seemed relieved that he'd been found. I think it was much worse for her not knowing what had happened to him."

"Will she stay in California now?" Adalet asked.

"I don't know. I don't think she knows. And Mom misses seeing Jacob, too. She looked after him when he was little and they were very close."

"And you?"

"I've been away so much. I hate to admit it, but I barely know them. I came back for two days to be David's best man but left to go back to Europe just afterwards. We met in Florence during their honeymoon in Italy, but I didn't see them again until Jacob was almost three years old. David actually turned out to be the better son, as I was always off in pursuit of art. David was happy to be living in New York. I don't think he would have even traveled at all had it not been for Tricia."

"Is that her name? Tricia?"

"Well, it's Patricia, but everyone always calls her Tricia."

"I like her name," Adalet smiled. "Will she come back for the burial?"

"Of course. Mom and I will make the arrangements tomorrow." Mark didn't say anymore about the condition of David's body and Adalet did not ask.

"I'll call you in the morning," Mark repeated after he kissed Adalet good-bye and headed out the door. Adalet had to keep herself from asking him to stay. She knew it was the right thing, but how long had it been since they'd made love? Was it the night she came home from Fatma's funeral or the night before he left? She could hardly remember now. Adalet asked herself the question she'd been dreading; did she even want to make love with Mark anymore?

Adalet stood in the doorway in the hotel robe and watched him heading towards the elevator, now a shrinking figure in the long hallway of doors. So many good-byes in such a short time, Adalet thought as she shut the door. She sat back down on the bed and wondered how many more good-byes she would have to say in her lifetime. She pulled out her cell phone to call Meryem and Nuray which she was supposed to have done when she first arrived. They would be waiting to hear from her, but she was too tired for any details. As luck would have it, she got only voicemail. *Arrived safely,* she told them both. *More to come tomorrow after I've rested. All is well. Love, Adalet.*

CHAPTER 32

Esther Aronson was not at all what or whom Adalet had expected. She was about 5'2, slightly chubby and clearly not in the habit of trying to conceal her age. Plump cheeked with short salt and pepper hair, Adalet guessed her to be somewhere in her late sixties, early seventies. She was dressed in an unflattering but nice enough looking sweat suit of a soft blue velour that looked warm but not meant to leave the house. She embraced Adalet as if she'd known her for many years.

"Come in, come in. I'm so glad to meet you at last, Adalet. Please call me Esther. My goodness, you are beautiful. Mark, you didn't exaggerate the least bit."

"I'm sure he did." Adalet could not help breaking out into a big smile, but then she quickly corrected herself, remembering what Esther Aronson had just been through.

"No, the smile does me good," Esther Aronson told Adalet, as if she could read her mind. "Please come in and sit down. We'll have a nice New York breakfast together. It was a rough night for me, but it wasn't unexpected. We all knew David would've come home if he were alive."

"I'm so sorry for your loss," Adalet told her, squeezing the hand that Mrs. Aronson offered to her.

Esther Aronson handed Adalet's coat to Mark and ushered her into a small dining area just off the kitchen. "I'll show you the rest of the apartment after breakfast," she said, ushering Adalet towards a chair at the glass and chrome dining table. "There's not much to see, but it's perfect for me at this time in my life. I don't need a lot of space anymore."

"Can I help you with anything?" Adalet asked.

"No, please. There's nothing for you to do but sit and relax," Esther assured her.

Adalet sat back in a white and gold French provincial style chair with a light green tapestry cushion. The wallpaper in the dining area was similar to the chair cushions with dancing French bourgeois along side stripes in green and gold. It was a bit fussy but elegant. It didn't look at all like Esther.

The table had been set for three. There was a white tablecloth with gold trim and braided gold design throughout, white China with a black trim, exquisite gold-trimmed water glasses filled with artistically arranged cloth napkins that matched the tablecloth. The silver was ornate and clearly real. Adalet gasped, "What a beautiful table setting!"

"Thank you," Esther smiled. "I know it looks like it's set for dinner rather than breakfast. The food is simple, catered in from Zabar's—Mark will have to take you there. When my husband was alive, he liked everything to be simple. He felt like a bull in a China shop with these sorts of things. After he passed, I sold the brownstone we'd lived in and bought this apartment. I decorated it exactly the way I wanted. The only things I didn't change were our carpets."

Adalet looked around. "Oh, but they're Turkish, aren't they?"

"Yes, all of them. But of course you would recognize the patterns. My husband's family was from Turkey, you know. Not originally, but they emigrated during the war. They were German Jews. My family was all from Russia."

"I think my family is Turkish only, but I don't know that for certain. I only knew my mother's parents. They lived in a home attached to ours in Duzçe, so I grew up with them. Neither of my parents had siblings and I was also an only child, so I have no family anymore other than the one I've created."

"And I'm sorry for your loss," Esther sat beside Adalet and patted her hand. "Mark told me about Fatma. You must be very sad to lose her." Adalet suddenly felt tears forming but controlled them. Fortunately, Mark came bustling to the table with a large basket of sliced bagels in one hand and assorted cheeses in the other. These he set on the table with a flourishing gesture that a waiter in an upscale restaurant might make. He disappeared back into the kitchen and returned with two more platters.

"Here are the lox and whitefish salads," he announced while placing one platter on the table. "And here are the egg and tuna salads," he said, setting the second platter down. "Mom, would you like some coffee? I made *çay* for you, Adalet."

"Yes, Mark, some coffee, please. But do bring Adalet her tea first."

Adalet's impulse was to jump up from the table and to help Mark with the coffee and *çay* at least, but as she began to inch her chair forward to rise, Esther patted her hand again saying, "No, Adalet, just enjoy being my guest."

Adalet allowed herself to remain seated, but she felt a lump forming at the base of her throat. Yes, she thought, I suppose I am a guest to her and she's just trying to be hospitable and polite, but this seems so strange in light of how upset she was last night. And the elaborate table? I don't know what to say to her. I wish she'd let me help Mark. Esther was saying something about the carpets.

"My husband became adept at the bargaining system in Turkey. He used to say he didn't like it; that it felt like begging, but he was able to talk salesmen down to one third of the price they were asking. I imagine it's different nowadays."

"Not so different," Adalet told her. "Sometimes they will tell foreigners today that they will not bargain, but that is also part of the bargaining. If they can get the customer to believe that they are only bargaining for them, they can get more for whatever they're selling. It is quite an art form. I learned a good deal from watching Fatma's sons."

"Do the Turkish bargain amongst themselves or just with the foreigners?" Esther took the coffee that Mark was now handing to her. "Thank you, Mark, for taking such good care of us." Mark also carried a cup of tea that he handed to Adalet. "I'll be back in a minute, my darlings, I have to get my coffee." He bent over each of them and kissed them in turn on their foreheads. This was a side of Mark Adalet hadn't seen.

"The Turkish are born to bargain," Adalet smiled at Esther. It's in the blood."

Mark brought his coffee in and sat across from Adalet and his mother. He handed the bagels to his mother and the lox and whitefish plate to Adalet. "Try everything," he said. "It's all incredibly good. There is no whitefish salad anywhere that can match Zabar's."

Adalet put small amounts of everything on her plate and then watched as Mark and Esther spread the cheeses and other spreads onto their bagels. She followed suit. It was delicious. The plate with the egg salad and tuna also had freshly sliced tomatoes and onions. Adalet took a couple of slices of tomato but passed on the onions. Too much raw onion upset her stomach. Mark and Esther both heaped the onions on the top of everything. Adalet was pleased that Esther didn't comment on what or how much she was eating. Adalet loved the whitefish salad and the egg salad and took seconds of each. The tomatoes didn't taste like tomatoes in Turkey. Not as good, Adalet thought. Some of the cream cheeses had scallions or salmon or vegetables in them. Adalet tried all three and decided she liked the vegetable one the best. There seemed to be enough food for ten people, and Mark and Esther continued to eat while Adalet sipped her tea. All Esther said was, "You're so tiny. Of course you don't eat much." Adalet guessed that she wasn't the typical Jewish mother that Mark had described, until Mark set his fork down on the plate.

"Have more, Mark. It won't be so good tomorrow." Esther passed the bagels to him. When he didn't reach out to take the basket from her, she dangled it in front of him.

Mark patted his stomach. "I can't, Mom. I've had two and a half bagels already. Maybe later." Adalet was relieved that Esther set the bagels back down on the table and didn't continue to press Mark to eat. Perhaps some Turkish mothers were more aggressive than Jewish mothers. Adalet's mother always told her how slender and beautiful she was and then pressured her to eat, eat, eat. How did her mother think she stayed as slender as she did?

Mark rose from the table and began to clear the dishes. "Let me help you," Adalet said, pushing her chair out and starting to rise.

Adalet was shocked to feel Esther's hand on her arm, gently but firmly pushing her back into her chair. "Please just sit, Adalet. You've come such a long way. Mark and I will clear up in no time at all." She started to move her chair.

" Don't get up, Mom. Stay and talk with Adalet. I can easily get this."

"Thank you, dear. Could I just have a drop more coffee while you're up? " She handed her cup and saucer to Mark.

"More tea, sweetheart?" Mark asked, taking her cup and saucer as well. "No, thank you," Adalet said, not especially caring for the way Mark was jumping up and down and waiting on them, or how he kept disappearing into the kitchen, leaving her alone with Esther. Adalet suddenly felt tired and tongue-tied. Was this jet lag or anxiety she was feeling? She couldn't be sure. Adalet had never traveled so far until yesterday—or was it the day before? And all the tanks and soldiers everywhere, in the airport and on the streets. It all felt so alien, so strange.

Mark came back into the room with his mother's coffee. "Are you okay, Adalet?" he asked.

"I don't know," she said honestly, "I'm feeling so tired."

"You see, I knew it," Esther exclaimed. She stood up and took Adalet's hand. "Come lie down in the guest room. This is all too much at once."

"Thank you, Esther," Adalet was grateful. "I think I will lie down for a bit." She got up and followed Esther down the hallway to a room just off the living room. Adalet spotted Mark's suitcase sitting in a corner out of the way. Mark had made the bed, if he'd even slept in it, and Esther took the decorative pillows off and threw them onto a rocking chair in the corner. She turned down the bedspread. "Come, dear. Have a nap. We have many arrangements to make for David's funeral, so rest as long as you like."

Esther left the room and Adalet was alone. She took off her shoes and lay down on the bed in her clothing, on top of the crisp sheets but under the warm blanket. She also felt chilled and began to shiver. Sobs began to shake her as well. She wanted to stop them. Adalet had no idea where they'd come from. She muffled her cries into the pillows until she finally exhausted herself into sleep.

Adalet awoke in a cold sweat. Everything was fuzzy and she wasn't sure where she was. Hands were feeling her forehead. "She's burning up," a familiar voice said from somewhere above her. "I'm going to call my doctor right now," another voice said. Adalet tried to get words out of her mouth, where am I; what's happening to me; but her lips felt locked together as if glued shut. Where am I, where am I, she kept trying to say.

"Don't try to talk, sweetheart. We're getting the doctor. We may have to take you to the emergency room. Just rest. I'm here with you." Is it my father speaking to me? Adalet wondered. Where is my mother? *Anne, Anne,* she tried to call and then before she could know if any of the words she tried to utter had made themselves audible, everything was dark once again.

When Adalet opened her eyes, she was in a dry nightgown in fresh sheets. Mark was sitting in the rocking chair but once he saw that Adalet was awake, he got up and sat next to her on the bed.

"How are you feeling?" Mark asked, running his fingers across her forehead to push a few stray hairs away from her eyes.

"What happened?" Adalet asked. "Did I pass out? I don't remember."

"Mom's doctor actually came over to save us from having to go to the emergency room. He said you were dehydrated and thinks you had a panic attack. I told him I'd never known you to have any but I wasn't sure. Do you have panic attacks, sweetheart?

Adalet took Mark's hand away from her forehead and held it in her own. "I did have something after the earthquake, but nothing like this. Then I thought it was just severe anxiety and would go away with time. My heart would race and I would feel like I wanted to jump out of my skin, but I know it was never as bad as this. I'm so ashamed. Your poor mother."

"Don't be silly. She was concerned enough to get her doctor here and that was a good thing."

"But there's absolutely nothing wrong with me," Adalet attempted to sit up but felt woozy. "The doctor must have been upset to come all this way and discover that I was anxious. I am so sorry, Mark."

"There isn't any need to be sorry, please. The doctor was quite sympathetic. When I told him what you'd been through, he said something like, oh, of course. He thought that coming here at this time, right after the explosions, could have triggered the panic attack. And thank goodness you are okay. I thought you might have gotten sick from the hamburger."

"So what did the doctor do?"

"He gave you a shot of something to calm you and gave me a prescription for you. My mother has the same pills and says she doesn't need them anymore, although the doctor said we should fill the prescription anyway in case the funeral sets her off again. So I went downstairs to the Duane Reade and had it filled for you."

Adalet forced herself into a sitting position, threw off the blanket and swung her legs over the side of the bed.

"Where are you going?" Mark asked.

"First to the bathroom and then to apologize to your mother."

"Let me help you walk to the bathroom, but as for apologizing to my mother—-."

"I must, Mark. My behavior has been rude." But Adalet took the arm that Mark offered to her, not because she wanted to admit to any weakness on her part but because she was afraid she might pass out and cause another scene. And if that happened, she didn't know if she would ever be able to face Esther Aronson again.

CHAPTER 33

Adalet allowed Esther and Mark to discourage her from attending David's funeral. Even though she was feeling better, she didn't know their customs and she was feeling insecure in the bustling of all of these arrangements. Adalet had spent two day and two nights at Esther's and she wanted to go back to the hotel for a change of clothing. Mark looked like he could have used a nap after having spent two nights on the couch. Esther had been adamant that Adalet remain with them until they left for the services in the morning. Then she could return to her hotel by taxi, rest and shower, and come back to Esther's whenever she felt ready.

Since Adalet hadn't known David or his family, Esther's doctor had advised against it when Esther called to ask him about the wisdom of Adalet accompanying them to the funeral. "It may trigger something," he warned. "She can be there at the *shiva* if you'd like, but the funeral isn't a good idea. Especially since she's just buried someone very like a mother to her."

"What is a *shiva*?" Adalet had asked.

"Well," Mark tried to explain, "Shiva means seven. It's the week of Jewish mourning for immediate family. We call it 'sitting *shiva*.' Technically, David doesn't qualify, but he has no one to sit *shiva* for him. He had so many friends though that they'll want to come and pay their respects. We won't do it for the whole week, as an Ortho-dox *shiva* would be—just this evening after the funeral and the following day. My mother's rabbi is Conservative and flexible. He'll come tonight and say some prayers. David attended services with my mother, so there will be a *minyan*. Oh, I'm sorry, Adalet. That means there will be at least ten males there, enough to say prayers."

"Don't be sorry, Mark. You don't have to explain everything to me. I'm really okay now."

"But I am truly so sorry, Adalet. The timing of all of this is so bad. I wish I could see you back to the hotel. I wish I could show you around New York. There's just been no time and you've needed to rest. The other thing is that we have to bury our dead very quickly according to Jewish custom. We would have done every-thing a day earlier but Tricia couldn't get a flight from California that would arrive in New York early enough. Her flight didn't get in until late in the evening."

"Of course I understand," Adalet told him. "It is the same for Muslims."

"We would have done it all a day earlier if Tricia could have got-ten a flight."

Adalet was relieved at the thought of returning to the hotel on her own. There was something about Esther's way of doing things and her way of directing everyone that Adalet found disturbing. Yes, Fatma had certainly directed everyone around her, but it was in complete confidence and expected of her. Fatma always knew exactly what to do, at least when it came to these sorts of things. Adalet had heard Esther on the phone making arrangements. Esther had turned to ask Mark about every decision; then she would ask whoever was on the other end of the line what they thought. Esther would tell Mark what they'd said, and then Esther would come up with an answer that seemed to pop into her head out of nowhere and seemed unrelated to any of the opinions she'd heard. Some of what Adalet heard went like this:

Esther: "Mark, did you look at David's clothing to see what we should bury him in?"

Mark: "I thought we were doing a shroud."

Esther to the phone: "What do you think, Mr. Weiss?" Mr. Weiss is the funeral director. Esther hands the phone to Mark. "You talk to him." Mark listens and nods his head.

Mark to Esther: "It's a closed casket anyway, Mom. You know there isn't enough of him to dress, really. Mr. Weiss thinks the shroud is best."

Esther: "Okay, whatever you think."

Mark to the telephone: "Okay, Mr. Wise, we're going to go with the shroud."

Esther: "No, no wait. I think he should be in the suit he wore when he married Tricia. Do you know where it is, Mark? You'll have to go get it from their apartment in Soho. Yes, that's it, Mark. We want to bury him in that suit."

Adalet didn't like the way Esther didn't seem to have all that much regard for Mark or awareness of what she was putting him through. Adalet felt like an afterthought, in the way, an unnecessary inconvenience, a small child to be checked on every once in a while.

Esther ran off lists of things for Mark to do. Go pick up the clothing. Call a caterer. It has to be kosher, just in case. Write up something for the Rabbi. Go meet with the Rabbi. Yes, she'd gotten the doctor. Don't forget we'll need drinks. My friend downstairs has a large coffee pot we can borrow. I'll call her and send you down to get it. Oh, yes, we'll need cream for the coffee. She made no list that Mark could have followed, and he made no suggestion that she do so. So they both ran around like two houseflies, buzzing irritatingly with no specific destination in mind.

And why was she sending Mark all the way to David's apartment for a suit that might not be found or could possibly be covered in dust. Tricia had taken Jacob out of the apartment to her parents' home in Los Angeles because of all the dust and debris. Adalet had attempted to see if there was anything she could do to be helpful, but Esther and Mark both motioned her back to the guest room to rest. Adalet complied only to be out of their way.

Adalet had been lying down when Mark left to go to Soho. "I'll be back as soon as I can," Mark reassured her. "I'll pick up some dinner on the way. I have to take the suit to the funeral home so they can dress him."

"But Mark, I thought there wasn't enough of him to dress."

"My mother knows that but doesn't want it to be real. So getting the suit means to her that there's enough of him left to bury him in it. It doesn't matter. It's a closed coffin and Mr. Weiss will put the suit in with his remains. I actually think it will make Tricia happy. I know it will make my mother happy. My mother's not in the least bit religious but when it comes to tradition, everything has to be just right. Jews are supposed to go into the ground exactly as they were born, no tattoos and all body parts. Don't expect anything my mother does right now to make much sense."

Adalet waved him off and went back to sleep. Between the jet lag and the emotion of the panic attack, she was still quite tired. By the time Mark finally arrived with the suit and Chinese take-out, Adalet had made herself a cup of tea and gone back to sleep. When she woke and walked out to see if he was back yet, it was 10:30pm and Mark and Esther were sitting at the table with chopsticks and half-eaten paper cartons of food.

"How are you feeling, dear?" Esther asked.

"Much better, thank you. I think I can go back to the hotel now and let Mark have the bed back."

"No, dear, it's too late," Esther shook her head in the negative. "Why don't you stay here tonight and go back in the morning when we go to the services. We'd worry about you, wouldn't we, Mark?"

"Yes, we would, although if you really would be more comfort-able—."

"Nonsense. I think you ought to be supervised for one more night at least. Mark doesn't mind sleeping on the couch, do you, dear?"

"It's fine, Mom. Adalet, do you want some Chinese food?"

Adalet saw that they'd been eating straight out of the cartons and felt slightly nauseous. Esther took a mouthful of something and a couple of noodles fell from her chopsticks into the carton. Adalet pushed politeness into her voice. Suddenly she felt angry. Why hadn't Mark set some food aside for her?

"No, thank you. I'm not really hungry. I think I'll go back and lie down, if you don't mind."

"I'll come and tuck you in," Mark got up from his chair and put both of his hands on Adalet's shoulders, steering her to the guest room.

"Are you sure you don't want anything to eat? I set aside some food for you if you change your mind. It's in the refrigerator and I can throw it into the microwave."

"Oh." Adalet sighed, feeling foolish. Mark would never have been so inconsiderate. "I thought—I didn't know that you'd saved me some." Adalet could not summon the words to tell Mark how uncomfortable she'd felt and that if she were going to eat anything, she'd have to eat alone in her room. "No, that's okay," she said instead. "I'm feeling much better but I'm not hungry. I'll just go to sleep."

"Okay. If you change your mind, there are two cartons in the fridge, one with Chinese mixed vegetables and another with rice. I also got you some sesame noodles to try. I think you'll like them."

Adalet slid under the covers and Mark sat on the edge of her bed. "Thank you for bringing back food for me, sweetheart. I'll try some later."

"Is something else troubling you?" Mark asked, taking her hand in his.

"I don't really know. There's so much going on. And I haven't even adjusted to the time yet. I'll be fine tomorrow."

Adalet had lain in bed awake until she heard Mark saying good-night to Esther and hearing her bedroom door close. Then she waited until Mark had turned off the lights and she heard light snoring. She got out of bed and tiptoed out of the guest room and into the kitchen. She opened the refrigerator and found the sesame noodles and a fork. She quietly crept back into the guest room and quickly ate the carton of noodles. They were good and she was starving. She set the empty carton and fork on the nightstand and climbed back into bed. Why was she behaving so strangely? She didn't know. She didn't understand.

Adalet slept soundly after eating the noodles. She couldn't remember any dreams, although she had a sense of Fatma when she woke; that she and Fatma had been doing something together and that Fatma was much younger, maybe even Adalet's age or just a bit older. Fatma. How she missed knowing that Fatma was in the world. Even if her visits hadn't been as frequent as she would have liked and Fatma would have wanted, just knowing that she was there was enough. Tears instantly filled her eyes. Adalet hurriedly rubbed them away, hearing voices in the living room. She got out of bed and slipped on the robe Esther had given her to wear. It was a bulky powder blue terry, comfortable and quite large for Adalet.

In the living room, Esther was rummaging through a drawer to find a *yarmulke* for Mark. Adalet had never seen Mark in a suit. "You look so handsome," she whispered, running her fingers along his sleeve.

"Thank you, sweetheart. How are you feeling today?"

"So much better," and as she said it, Adalet felt that it was true. The dreadful fatigue she'd been feeling was gone. "I feel rested. Are you two all set to go?"

"Almost. Mom is trying to find David's *bar mitzvah yarmulke* for me to wear."

"What is that?" Adalet asked.

"It's the skull cap, prayer cap, that we wear in the synagogue."

Esther was throwing little caps onto the dining table from a drawer in her workstation. "Ah," she held one up in triumph, "this is their wedding *yarmulke*, even better. Oh, good morning, Adalet." Esther handed the blue velvet *yarmulke* to Mark and watched while he placed it on his head.

"Perfect," Esther said, "just perfect."

"You don't think it's morbid?" Mark asked her.

"Definitely not. It's sentimental and it speaks of paying attention to detail."

Mark took the *yarmulke* off and placed it in the inside pocket of his jacket. "Are we ready now?"

"Yes, I suppose we are." Esther placed a black felt hat on her head. It was bowl-shaped with decorative flowers on one side.

Adalet thought the hat was attractive, and that Esther actually looked quite nice in a black silk suit with an old-fashioned off-white silk blouse that boasted pearl buttons. She wore small pearls in her ears, her hair was neatly smoothed back, and she looked more the part of Mark's mother than she had since Adalet met her. "You look lovely, Esther," Adalet said, and gave her a little hug.

Esther smiled. "Why thank you, Adalet. Do you need anything before we leave?"

"No thank you. I'll be fine. I'm going to go back to the hotel and rest and shower and I'll be back here for the *sheeva*?"

"*Shiva*, darling." Mark took her into his arms and gave her a loving kiss and meaningful hug. "See you later. Make sure you eat something, although there will be so much food at the *shiva*."

"Just like at Fatma's funeral," Adalet stood back and eyed them both. "But you look more fabulous than anyone did at Fatma's."

"It's New York," Esther retorted with a smirk, "we're supposed to look fabulous. It's respect for the dead."

Mark tilted his head and rolled his eyes behind his mother's back as they exited the door. Adalet closed the door behind them and laughed. Esther was a character, and she seemed to be straight out of a British comedy, minus the accent. Adalet had loved British theater, as much as she could get of it through television, film and bad Turkish performances.

Unfortunately, though, Adalet didn't think she liked Esther very much. Perhaps it was the circumstances and the behavior was unusual for Esther, or could it be that she was always like this? Being her daughter-in-law would be weighty, cumbersome, filled with rules and regulations that Adalet could not begin to understand.

Adalet wandered back into the guest room and sat down on the bed with her cell phone. She would try to call Meryem. It was still early enough if Meryem hadn't gone out to dinner. But it was Isha who answered.

"Adalet, thank goodness. Meryem will be so sorry she missed you. She went out to buy some paint and she hasn't come back yet."

"Okay, just a minute. It's a bad connection, Isha. I can hardly understand what you're saying. Let me call you back." Adalet clicked the call-ended button without knowing for certain that Isha had heard her. She dialed all the numbers once again.

"Adalet, is that you? Say something so I know if I can hear you now."

"I'm here, Isha. Can you hear me?"

"Yes, it's much better. Meryem said she's tried to call you but you haven't called her back. Is everything okay there?"

"I wasn't feeling too well after I arrived. I guess it was a combination of jet lag and the fact that it's now definite that Mark's first cousin is dead."

"David? The one he grew up with?"

"Yes."

"How awful. Is it terrible there now? The pictures on television are horrible."

"I don't know, really. I'm not staying in that neighborhood. And because I wasn't feeling well and David's death, I haven't been out anywhere other than my hotel and Mark's mother's apartment."

"What's she like? Is she nice? Poor thing must be in a terrible state."

"She's nice enough," Adalet told her. "She's not at all what I expected. I can't tell if she's just overwhelmed by David's death, or that she is normally this—this—I'm not sure of the right word—maybe fussy." Adalet looked around at the furnishings, the frilly pillows and bed cover and the French provincial furniture. "Yes, maybe that's it. Fussy."

"What do you mean?" Isha sounded puzzled.

"I don't know. She gets a notion about something and doesn't rest until it's done exactly as she wants it. And it doesn't seem that Mark really notices."

"Oh, Adalet, you need to meet my family, especially my mother."

"Funny, that's exactly what Meryem says."

"She criticizes everything and everyone and she looks so sweet and harmless that if you look at her while she's saying these things, you can't even be angry with her."

"Well," Adalet paused, "it's not quite the same thing. She's very polite and nice to me. But at the same time, it's as if I don't exist."

Isha laughed. "Maybe you should be thankful for that."

"Maybe." A sob tore lose from Adalet's throat.

"I'm sorry, Adalet. I didn't realize how upset you were."

Adalet burst into tears. "I want to come home. I don't belong here."

"Then come home, dear. You don't have to stay if you don't want to."

"But I would feel bad about leaving Mark. Meryem always says how unfairly I treat him." Adalet took a tissue from the nightstand and wiped her eyes and blew her nose.

"Meryem? You are getting relationship advice from Meryem?" Isha asked with a tone of irony. "Meryem is the last person to give relationship advice to anyone. Yes, she has grown and changed, but if not for my patience with her, she wouldn't be in a relationship. Meryem feels so strongly about everything. It's all black and white. Yes, she's wonderful and I love her more than anyone I've ever known, except that the truth is that she can be very selfish and when it comes to Mark, she only sees things one way. Mark encourages her so much with her art. He believes in her talent. She worships him. That's no reason for you to love his mother."

"Oh, Isha, if it were only his mother. It's how he is with his mother. He treats her like she is a queen."

"Sounds a lot like Ahmet and Fatma."

"I thought so too, at first, but it's not like that. It's so complicated. I'm not even sure I understand it myself. I don't. Please don't tell Meryem I'm so confused."

"Adalet," Isha said in a gentle voice, "Meryem isn't what is important here. These decisions are yours. You must follow your heart and do what is best for you. It's not up to Meryem, or me for that matter."

"You're right, Isha, but I don't like to let people down."

"Not 'people.' It's Meryem you don't want to let down. You are too concerned with what Meryem thinks and feels. Meryem is busy living her life and you must do the same. Meryem will continue to love you whether you are here or over there or you marry Mark or you don't. We will both love you always."

"Thank you, Isha. I know in my heart that it's true, but my head doesn't always agree with my heart." Adalet shook her head back and forth, closed her eyes and sighed.

"Then listen to your heart and forget your head. What is it that you want, Adalet? Look at who you've become. You don't have to run away anymore. You can do whatever you like."

"No wonder Meryem loves you so much. I bet you tell her off when she's selfish." Adalet smiled for the first time in their conversation.

"Yes, I do tell her off. And she doesn't always listen either."

"That I can believe. Thank you, thank you, Isha. Please just tell Meryem that I called to say everything is fine here and I will be in touch."

"You are very welcome, my dear friend. Now go take a shower and do something in New York!"

"Yes, I think I will. *Maşallah*, Isha.

"*Maşallah*," Isha said, and she was gone.

CHAPTER 34

Once Adalet had showered and dressed back in her hotel room, she knew exactly what she wanted to do that day. It was just about noon when she took the elevator down to the lobby. The fellow at the main desk who'd asked her if she was with the Red Cross was chatting with an older woman and a police officer.

"My daughter will be down in just a few minutes," she was telling them. "It's so kind of you to take us."

The police officer shook his head and replied, "It's no trouble at all. When Lisa grabbed me and told me your story, I was more than happy to come."

The fellow behind the desk noticed Adalet. "Can I help you?" he asked.

"I don't know," Adalet said. " I don't know if it's even possible, but I want to see the wreckage of the World Trade Center buildings. Is there any way I can do that?"

"Where are you from?" the policeman asked.

"I am from Turkey," Adalet told him. "I'm here visiting my boyfriend whose cousin was killed there. They were like brothers. I want to see where it happened."

The older woman spoke. "My son was killed there, too. He worked for Cantor Fitzgerald."

"Why that is where David worked, too." Adalet exclaimed.

"My daughter and I came from Boston to visit the site. This nice policeman and a woman from the Red Cross are going to take us there. We're waiting for my daughter to come down from our room, and the Red Cross volunteer went into the bathroom. She'll be right back. Maybe you could come with us?" She looked at the police officer.

"Well, I don't know," he said. It's only for family viewing. Let's see what Lisa says when she comes back. Lisa is the Red Cross volunteer," he told Adalet.

"I won't be any trouble, and this will most likely be my only chance. I'll be going home soon." Adalet smiled at the older woman. "It's very kind of you to suggest this."

"I'm not sure that I'm authorized to suggest it and perhaps I spoke out of turn, but let's do ask Lisa. I don't see why she'd mind. Ah, here comes my daughter now. Bianca, this is – what's your name?"

"I'm Adalet," Adalet said, taking the woman's outstretched hand.

"I'm Daphne Biaggi, and this is my daughter, Bianca."

"Hello Bianca, it's nice to meet all of you." Adalet now shook the hand of the daughter who looked to be about Adalet's age. She was slender and blonde like her mother must have been at one time. Mrs. Biaggi reminded Adalet physically of Esther, only taller.

"And I'm Officer Gould," the policeman said. "Actually, everyone calls me Artie."

"Are you also Turkish?" Adalet asked the officer.

"No," Artie smiled. "I'm Jewish."

"Ah," Adalet smiled back at him, "so is my boyfriend."

A wisp of a dark-haired young woman dressed in a bulky gray down coat and hiking boots approached the group at the desk. "Okay, I'm ready to go," she said, not noticing Adalet.

"Lisa," Artie spoke up, "this is Adalet. She also lost someone in the Towers and Mrs. Biaggi thought she might come along with us. Can we squeeze another body in? Mrs. Biaggi can ride up front with me and the three of you can sit in the back."

"I don't see why not," Lisa said.

"How are we going there?" Adalet asked.

"My squad car," Artie replied with a grin. "Have you ever ridden in a police car?"

"No, I haven't, either here or in Turkey. This will be my first time."

"You are Turkish?" Lisa asked. "I've always wanted to travel to Turkey."

"Why don't you come then?" Adalet asked, relieved that Lisa didn't say she'd better stay behind because she was Turkish or Moslem or even ask any of those kinds of questions.

The four women waited in front of the hotel while Artie went to get his squad car. Mother and daughter were pretty quiet while Lisa grilled Adalet on what life was like for young people in Istanbul. Adalet instantly took a liking to Lisa. She enjoyed talking about her home. It made her feel less fragile and more comfortable.

"What's it like for young women there? Can you date? Do women have sex before marriage? Are you even allowed out of the house alone?" Lisa was quite direct, and it surprised Adalet. She liked how honest Lisa was, no hemming and hawing or beating around the bush.

"In Istanbul life is not so different. We do what we like there. Of course, the rules can change with the leaders in the government. I come from a village and life is different there, not so modern. My mother walked me to school and I didn't go out on my own. To be honest, I don't know if I was allowed or not. It's just the way it was; then I went to the university and lived away from my family."

"Did the other kids make fun of you when your mother walked you to school?" Lisa asked.

"No, not at all. I didn't have any sisters or brothers to walk with me, so it was accepted. I never thought about it one way or the other."

"Do you discuss politics?"

"Yes, like young people all over the world, we talk a lot about politics, but we are careful about where and with whom."

Adalet answered the questions she chose and before too much more could be said, Artie pulled up in front of the hotel and they piled into the car, Mrs. Biaggi in front and Bianca behind her mother, Adalet in the middle and Lisa on the opposite end. It was no longer raining, and there was enough sun at last for Adalet to notice the red and yellow colors of the autumn leaves. She could see how the city could be quite beautiful.

Lisa didn't stop asking questions about Turkey for most of the drive. She would hesitate, perhaps thinking about Adalet's answers, and then plunge into more questions. Mrs. Biaggi talked with Artie about her son, and Bianca was fairly quiet, making a comment here and there to add to what someone else was saying.

As they entered the area near the World Trade Center, everyone stopped talking. There were roadblocks and rubble everywhere. The air was heavy with dust. When Artie lowered his window to consult one of the many police on foot patrol as to how he could get through, a pungent odor filled the car, like the smell after a building fire, wet ashes and burnt flesh. Adalet took a deep breath and started to cough.

"Are you okay?" Lisa asked her. "The air is still pretty bad down here."

Something got into Adalet's throat and she was unable to control her coughing. That smell. She'd smelled it before. Yes, in the infirmary tent after the earthquake. It was the odor of death and decay, the disintegration of everything that had been. Her mother. Her father. The baby. All of those people. All of these people. Oh, God. The choking sensation would not stop.

Bianca reached into her bag and pulled out a cough drop that she handed to Adalet. "Here you go. This will help. They taste awful, though."

Adalet accepted the menthol drop gratefully. "Thank you," she said, breaking into another fit. Adalet hacked and wheezed through the directions that the police officer was giving to Artie in order to get to the site. Finally, the medication did its work and she was able to quell the coughing spell. The area looked like pictures Adalet had seen of war zones after bombings. Why had she come? Why would she ever want to put herself through this?

In another couple of blocks, there was another police officer and another roadblock. This time it was a woman. She came over to Artie's open window. "Where are you headed?" she asked.

"I've got some family here of victims who want to see where it happened."

"Well, the family viewing area is right over there." She gestured in the direction of upturned sidewalk. I can let you through this roadblock and it's over on the right-hand side just a couple of blocks from here."

"Thanks," Artie told her. "It keeps changing down here so quickly that I wasn't sure where to go in. These roadblocks are new since last week, aren't they?"

"Yes. Curiosity seekers want to come through, and it's dangerous, the air alone. It's pretty torn up around here due to the subway explosion. Be careful where you walk and don't let these folks breathe this air too long."

"I won't," Artie assured her. The female officer removed the barricade and then replaced it after Artie drove through. Adalet turned around to watch. She had some idea of what the area had looked like before this destruction through pictures and film, but there was nothing now that was recognizable. She flashed back to her family home and digging through the debris to find anything that might have remained. The wedding dress was the only thing she'd taken. The huge pot that had burned her was lying among upturned floor tile.

Two police officers stood beside another roadblock and Artie pulled off to the side of the road near them. "The viewing area is behind them," he said. "We'll get out here. Bianca, take your mother's arm and everyone be careful. Lisa, show them your Red Cross identification."

Adalet watched Lisa walk over to the officers and show them her badge. Adalet had asked to see Lisa's identification card in the car. It had Lisa's picture and name and the dates she was volunteering, along with the words, *Ground Zero Accessible*. The police motioned them through. They walked up some wooden planks that had been placed there in order to create a makeshift stairway. At the top of this was a small platform surrounded by more planks placed loosely together for walls.

There was no roof to cover the platform other than the open sky. Pictures of victims lined the crude wooden walls. Memorial books sat on boxes for visitors to sign and express their feelings of loss. Relatives and friends had left candles and personal items near the photos of their loved ones. Off to the side and not too far from the viewing area stood the remnants of one tower. It loomed sideways and upward like some alien skeleton. Below was various excavation equipment and men with hard hats and digging gear. A couple of cranes were poised near the alien remnant steel. Adalet gulped, unprepared for the storm breaking loose in her. She wanted to cry but no tears came. Her heart was racing and she was afraid she'd have another panic attack. She'd left her pills in the hotel room. Mother and daughter stood near her weeping. Lisa stood back with Artie.

For the first time since she'd awakened after the earthquake, the enormity of her losses swept over her. She dropped to her knees. Why would human beings do such a thing to each other when nature was destructive enough? She didn't understand anything anymore. When Adalet looked up, she was staring into the memorial picture of a fireman. He looked like someone she might have known. He was young enough to have been an older brother. His smile was wide and warm. It was a handsome face. She leaned in closer to see what was written there. He had rushed into the second tower to save lives and had lost his own.

Adalet burst into tears unlike any she had shed in her life. They poured from a place she hadn't known existed until this moment. Sobs erupted from the bottom of her belly. She heard a strange wail emerging from her throat. What was this? What was happening to her? Adalet covered her face and in the darkness she could see everything, the rows of tents, the bloody bandages, her parents' kitchen, the damaged wedding dress, the baby she had never seen, the Yasar she had first known, herself and Nuray as young girls new to university, and Fatma, Fatma who had truly loved her. She could see the people jumping from the burning buildings. Worlds crashing down. If only Adalet had known then what she knew now. If only she could have seen and accepted the love that others had wanted so badly to give to her. If only she'd been wiser sooner.

"Are you alright?" Artie was kneeling down beside her and rested one hand on her back. The other women were looking at Adalet with concern. Artie grabbed the crook of her arm and helped her to her feet. Adalet took a few deep breaths and blew her nose into the handkerchief Artie handed to her.

"You have a great deal of grief in you," Lisa said, stepping up to take Adalet's arm. "Do you want to go back to the car now?"

"No," Adalet said in a determined tone of voice. "This is good for me. It feels so important."

"I have an idea," Artie said, letting his arm drop from Adalet's shoulder now that Lisa had hold of her and Adalet had quieted down. "I know the fellows at a blockade at the actual site. If you want to do it, and it's completely up to all of you, I can take you there. I'm pretty sure they will let us walk in there, if we're very careful."

Mrs. Biaggi shook her head. "I don't think so," she said. "This is hard enough."

"I would like to go, Mom. You could wait in the car for us." Bianca took her mother's hand and looked into her eyes.

"That would be okay, Artie, if you want to take Bianca."

"I want to go with you," Adalet heard herself saying. She hadn't known she was going to speak. "If that's okay," she added. "I can't explain this, but I would really like to go."

Artie looked at Lisa and the Biaggis. No one spoke. Lisa finally did. "I think it will be okay," she said. "Artie?"

"Sure. Let's head back to the car and we'll drive to the opening. It's not far from here but the sidewalks and streets are all torn up. It's better if we stay on the cleared portion of the streets."

No one spoke until Artie pulled his squad car up to a barricade and turned the engine off. Two officers stood nearby. "Hey, Artie. What's up?" the older of the two asked.

"Got some family here," Artie said. "Okay if we come in? One of these ladies wants to stay behind."

"I'll stay with Mrs. Biaggi," Lisa offered.

"No, dear," Mrs. Biaggi said. She opened the car door and began to step out. "I've changed my mind. "I think I'll regret it if I don't come along. There's not going to ever be a burial and this may be the closest we get to a cemetery for him." She walked around the car to Bianca and took her hand. "I'm ready," she said.

The smell of decay was even stronger now; Adalet could feel the stench permeate her nostrils. Dry dust blew around their shoes as they made their way beyond the barricade. No one said a word. Adalet could hear the crunch of their feet penetrating through the top layer of dirt and debris. She hoped they weren't stepping on any bones. This is what it must have been like after the earthquake, she thought. If I could have walked there, this is what it must have felt like. She could feel her heart pounding, but she leaned over to run her fingers through the soil.

Now the little group stood facing the steel façade once again. It struck Adalet that the force that had taken these buildings, those people, their lives had been torn apart by something so much more evil than the earthquake that had taken her parents and her child. Nature had taken her family. The evil plotting of human beings had taken the Biaggi's son and David, and so, so many more. Adalet reached over and took hold of Mrs. Biaggi's other hand. The three women stood there together, silently, each in her private place of grief. Lisa and Artie stood behind them, quietly and patiently waiting for them to be ready to leave.

Adalet squeezed Mrs. Biaggi's hand and then dropped it, leaving mother and daughter to stand alone. Adalet walked over to Lisa and Artie. "We're standing on hallowed ground," she said and walked by herself back to the car.

Adalet got into the back seat and closed her eyes. Something in her had changed. She felt that her anger and grief had all come pouring out and that her heart felt cleansed in some new way. If only, if only, she thought. If only Mrs. Biaggi's son had been sick that day. If only her parents had agreed to come to Istanbul to visit her and she hadn't been there to stay with them. She could think *if only* until she died, and it wouldn't change a single thing.

Adalet heard the others approaching, but she didn't open her eyes again until they were back at the hotel. They all thanked Artie and Lisa and waved good-bye as he drove off to take Lisa back to the Pier where she was working.

Adalet hugged Bianca and then Mrs. Biaggi. "Thank you so much for this," Adalet told them. "I can't even explain how important it was for me."

"You must have loved him very much," Bianca said as they entered the lobby.

"Who?" Adalet asked.

"Your boyfriend's cousin," Bianca replied.

"I never met him," Adalet admitted, "but I lost both of my parents in an earthquake. There is always something of the past we have left to mourn."

CHAPTER 35

Adalet had no idea of the time when she opened her hotel room door and glanced at the clock. It was now after 4:00 in the afternoon, and she'd said good-bye to Mark and Esther at 10:30 in the morning. Sure enough, the red light was blinking on the hotel phone. She sat on the edge of her bed to retrieve the messages.

Message 1: *Hi Adalet. We're back at my mother's apartment. It's about 2:00 or a little after. So just come whenever you want to.*

Message 2: *Adalet, it's Mark again. It's a little before 4:00 and I'm a bit worried since I haven't heard from you. Please call me at Mom's or on my cell. I hope everything is okay.*

Adalet shook her head and immediately began to dial Mark's cell. How selfish she'd been not to let him know where she was and that she was fine after all that had happened. And how many times had she scolded Meryem for behaving exactly as she had today?

Mark answered his cell phone instantly. "Adalet, is that you? We've been so worried."

"I'm sorry, Mark. It was thoughtless of me. I should have known you and Esther would worry. I'm fine. I'm going to change quickly and take a taxi over. I'll tell you about it when I get there."

"Okay. Are you sure you don't want me to come and get you?"

"No, I'm really good. Better than I've been in some time. I'll be there as soon as I can. Please tell Esther that I'm sorry I worried her."

Adalet took a quick shower to rid her senses of the dust that had penetrated her skin. She dressed quickly in the outfit she'd worn to Fatma's funeral, adding a sweater over her blouse and under her jacket for warmth. A taxi happened to be sitting in front of the hotel waiting for a fare. The concierge opened its door for Adalet as she stepped out of the revolving hotel exit.

"Taxi Miss?"

"Yes, thank you." Adalet climbed inside and gave the dark-skinned man in the turban Esther's address. East Indian music came through the speakers. The driver didn't respond to Adalet, but she was happy to see that the street numbers decreased and they were heading in the right direction. The driver also didn't respond when they were stopped in front of Esther's building and Adalet handed him the fare plus tip. She wondered briefly if she'd given him enough but then decided his silence might have had to do with the fact that she was a woman.

When Adalet stepped out of the elevator, she was surprised to see that Esther's door was wide open. She could hear many voices and the clatter of dishes and glasses and silverware. Adalet could smell a strong odor of roasted coffee beans and something she was unable to identify. She hesitated in the hallway. Adalet had never liked meeting a group of strangers all at once, and especially not now, after this extraordinary day. She took several deep breaths and stepped inside the apartment.

The dining room table was covered with bagels, lox, a variety of cream cheeses, whitefish salad, tuna fish, egg salad, sliced tomatoes and onions. It was much like Adalet's first New York breakfast only more of it. There was a large fruit salad in a glass crystal bowl and a smaller table had been set up with coffee and tea and several plates of desserts.

Adalet spotted Mark in the midst of a group of young people. He wasn't facing the door, and so he didn't see Adalet come into the apartment. She made her way over to him and tapped him lightly on the shoulder. He turned around and immediately embraced her.

"Adalet! Everyone, this is Adalet, my fiancée. This is Robert, Angela, Melanie and Tina. They all worked with David. Angela and Melanie were out sick that day. Tina had gone to run an errand and Robert called in to say he'd be late. His little boy was sick and Robert had to take him to the babysitter. If not for these miracles, none of them would be standing here."

"It's so nice to meet you all," Adalet said. If not for miracles, Adalet thought. There are those words again, *if not for* the whims of chance. And now Mark has introduced me as his fiancée. What do I do with that?

Before Adalet could say anything, Esther came over to give her a hug. "So glad you're here, darling. We've been waiting for you. Mark wants to introduce you to everyone and wants me to announce your engagement."

Adalet could not help the shocked expression that spread across her face.

Esther took a half-step back and shook her head, as if not quite understanding. "Well, I know it's not exactly the right time, but David would have been so happy for you and Mark."

Adalet walked over and put her arm through Mark's, pulling him slightly away from the group. "Mark, we have to talk. Now isn't the right time for this. We have too much to discuss. Please don't let Esther do this now."

Mark had been flushed with excitement. Now he turned pale. "Okay. I was afraid it wasn't the right time. I got carried away when my mother suggested it. We can announce it another time."

"Mark," Adalet said a bit too loudly but only to make sure he was listening. "I'm not sure I can marry you now."

A hush fell over the group. Esther stopped in her tracks. Fortunately, of the thirty or so people in the apartment, only Esther and the small group of people Adalet had just met heard her words.

Esther immediately turned to Adalet and intervened. "Whatever do you mean, Adalet?"

"I'm sorry, Esther, but this is just between the two of us. We need some time to talk."

"Of course you do," Esther responded, waving a half-emptied wine glass in the direction of the guest room. "Go talk. Everyone is so busy eating and chatting anyway."

Mark led Adalet into the guest bedroom where they both sat on the bed.

"What's going on, Addie? Are you angry with me? If you are, I can understand. This has all been so different from what I'd planned and what you expected." He set his glass of wine on the nightstand and took her hands into his. "When I told Mom I wanted to take the diamond from her and give it to you, she sort of ran with it. I didn't want her to announce it today or for her to announce it at all for that matter, but it was the first time I'd seen my mother smile since David disappeared."

Adalet frowned. Whatever was going on with this new nick-name? "You've never called me Addie before."

"Mom came up with it. I kind of liked it."

"I don't like it, Mark. Please don't call me that anymore."

"Okay, I won't. What's going on? You seem so different."

"And you seem so different to me. Ever since I got here, your mother has completely taken over. I've never seen you like this."

"My mother is hardly herself, Adalet. I will admit that she wants things to be her way and that she is a force, but she's not thinking clearly. I'm sorry you had to meet her under these circumstances."

"It's not just your mother, Mark. I wish it were that simple. It's so hard for me to explain."

"Please, try." Mark squeezed her hands. "Whatever it is, you can tell me."

"When I got on the plane to come here, I was in so much confu-sion. Meryem so wanted me to come. I didn't want to disappoint her or you. Fatma, Meryem and Isha and you have been my only family for so long. I feel so selfish, Mark."

"Adalet, my sweetheart, what do you mean? There isn't a selfish bone in your body."

"I didn't want to come to New York now. I wanted to stay in the safety of my home. I didn't even want you to go. I wanted you to be with me at Fatma's funeral. I know it was selfish, but I did. I felt abandoned. I wanted you to stay in Turkey."

"Oh, Adalet, when I offered to go with you to the funeral, I meant what I said. You have to learn to trust me. I could have taken a later flight. I thought you wanted me to come here."

" I did want you to come here, but can't you understand that I also wanted you to stay?"

Mark was silent. Finally, slowly, he said, "Yes, I can understand. But you must take me at my word. And you must be honest with me. Trust is so important between us."

"Trust isn't so easy for me. Oh, Mark, when I turned up on Fatma's doorstep seven years ago to look at the pottery, I felt that my life was over. Any chance I'd had at happiness was gone. In one awful moment I'd lost my parents and my baby and my woman-hood. In the next moment, I lost my husband."

Mark shook his head back and forth and squeezed Adalet's hands again. "I do know how difficult everything has been for you, sweetheart."

"There's so much I didn't understand about myself until today," Adalet told him, all the anger gone from her voice now. She wanted to express herself to Mark in a way that she'd never been able to do with Yasar. She felt compelled to do so, or there would be no hope for them. "Avanos is a beautiful place but I felt that I'd been ban-ished there, which truthfully was the case. I thought of myself as so badly damaged, that the best thing I could ever do would be to hide away with my ugly scars until I was old and no one would care anymore."

Tears came into Mark's eyes.

"But my story isn't sad anymore, Mark. Fatma and Meryem gave me a new life. And then you and Isha came along. And my work has given me a sense of pride and confidence that I had never known."

Mark nodded. "I know. I've watched you grow."

"As much as Fatma's death was a terrible blow to me," Adalet continued, "her will hit me even harder. I always doubted that she really thought of me as family. I knew she appreciated me and loved me in her own way, but never did I realize how much she valued me or what I meant to her."

"You want to go back to Turkey," Mark said softly.

"It is where I belong, Mark."

"Let's not talk about this anymore today. The rabbi will be here soon to say the prayers. Let's talk more tomorrow. After we've had a chance to speak, you can make whatever arrangements you wish, but at least hear me out. You're absolutely right; this just isn't the right time or place for this discussion. My mother was wrong to corner both of us this way. Do you want to stay for the service or go back to the hotel now?"

"Do you think it's wise for me to stay after all of this?" Adalet asked. "Won't your mother—"

Mark smiled what Adalet liked to think of as his smile of complete confidence. He looked her directly in the eyes. "I'll handle my mother. I would like it very much if you would stay. I won't let you just walk out of the door or my life this way."

"I'll stay then." Adalet rose and Mark followed. They stopped short before the door and embraced.

"Let them think what they want," Mark said. "It's not like they've never had any problems in their relationships. Some of them are having a pretty tough time right now. They've lost friends and colleagues and are struggling with survivor's guilt. They have more on their minds than us."

Mark opened the door and they walked back into the living room arm in arm.

Esther turned to look at them. "I told you," she said to the woman standing next to her, "just a little misunderstanding. They're fine now."

Mark smiled at Adalet and grabbed his mother by the hand. "Come, Mom, now it's our turn to have a little talk. Everyone, this is Adalet. Introduce yourselves." And Mark led Esther back down the hallway.

CHAPTER 36

Mark arrived before breakfast the next morning. Adalet answered the door in the hotel bathrobe that Mark quickly removed: he picked her up and carried her off to the king-sized bed. They made love for the first time in what seemed to Adalet to have been months, although it had only been weeks. Afterwards, they held each other close, passion sated and intimacy restored.

"Now," Mark said, stroking her hair as she lay with her head on his chest, "what's this all about that you can't marry me now? Haven't I suffered long enough?"

"I went to Ground Zero yesterday."

"You went there by yourself?" Mark lifted her head and turned her face toward him so that he could see into her eyes. Adalet realized how much she'd missed Mark's touch. At that moment, she could not have wished herself anywhere else.

Adalet turned and put her head back on Mark's chest. "Please don't stop. I love it when you play with my hair."

Mark placed his hand back on her head and asked, "How did you get there?"

" It was just by chance that I met some people in the hotel lobby who were going. They agreed to take me with them. They'd lost a son at Cantor Fitzgerald, where David worked."

"Oh, my God. You went there after you had that panic attack?" Mark sat up, bringing Adalet with him. "Sorry, darling." He lay back down. "Please go on."

"It wasn't at all like that. It was healing. We stood in that dust and dirt, that rubble, and I was finally able to grieve. I cried for everything I'd ever lost, my burned body, my lost baby, and all the babies I'll never have, for my parents, that they left me too soon, for Yasar and the way we didn't take good care of our marriage. I cried for the loss of Fatma. I cried for all of the people in the planes and the Towers. Then I thought about us, Mark, and I cried for us, too."

"But why, Adalet? Why did you cry for us?"

"Istanbul is my only home now, Mark. Even if Meryem and Isha leave and travel or go to live somewhere else, Istanbul is still my home and my heart is there. It's been so long since I've taken a day and really thought about what I want."

"Do you know what you want now, Adalet?"

"I wish I could say that I know. All my life I've lived to please other people. Then I've resented them for it and acted selfishly. I resented that Yasar left to travel for his work and never took me with him. I never asked him to take me. I was afraid. And I should have told him I was pregnant and not run off to tell my parents first. I hadn't grown up myself and I was so quick to criticize Meryem."

"But what does all of this have to do with us? I'm happy to live in Istanbul."

"Mark, do you really think you could? Your mother is still young and healthy. She just lost David."

"You have the wrong impression of my relationship with my mother. She's trying to recreate with me what she had with David. It's something I didn't anticipate so I haven't known how to react to her. I've played along to make her happy for now. I guess I even took on some of David's role without realizing that's what I was doing. She knows I don't plan to stay. And I'd like to know, if it ever came to that, why we couldn't live in both places?"

"I did think of that. But we are so different. Your world is so different from mine in every way. Yes, funerals might look alike and our customs might cross over but we are not the same. You don't observe your religion, just on special occasions. I do believe in my religion and will always read the Koran and pray. It is how I was raised. Oh, how can I ever explain?"

"I would expect you to be just the same as I've always known you. I don't expect you to be anyone other than my dear Adalet. It's the only way I would want you, Adalet. Is this why you've always hesitated? Or is it because you thought I would want children?"

"That is part of it and the other part is that we come from two such different worlds. You mean so much to me, Mark. You've been there while I regained my sense of myself, and that's the only way I know how to express this. You will always be in my heart, but I can't marry you to please Meryem or your mother, or even just to please you, for that matter. I must be sure that I'm not marrying you because I'm afraid to be on my own."

"But don't you want us to be together always? You know that's what I want."

"Yes, Mark, I do want to be with you, but I want us to be as we were in Istanbul. Something hit me while I stood weeping at Ground Zero. What if I were standing in all of that destruction in Istanbul? What if this terrible thing had happened there? Suppose I'd lost Meryem and Isha and our home together? What if The Yeditepe School for the Deaf was nothing but a pile of rubble? I knew for certain when I stood in that horrid place that I love my home and could not bear to leave to live anywhere else. And yet I know if this means losing you, I would regret it for the rest of my life."

"You don't have to lose me, sweetheart. We've both just been through a trying experience. My mother isn't behaving like my mother and New York isn't at all like New York. We're all traumatized. How could we possibly be ourselves in all of this?"

"It's brave of you to offer to live in Istanbul, and I will never forget that you were willing. Istanbul has been exciting for you, but what about in the future? What about living with a government that can change according to religious beliefs? Jews are only minority citizens there. What will that feel like for you?"

"German Jews thought they were equal citizens until they weren't. No one can predict the future. I only know that there is no one or nothing more important in this life for me. This isn't temporary. I'm a grown man. I know exactly what I want."

"But what if you feel differently in a few years?"

"What makes you think I could?"

Adalet sat up and back against her pillow. "I don't want to resent anyone again, and I don't want anyone to resent me. I don't know if I can marry you. I do enjoy my freedom to come and go as I please. I never had this before in my life."

"Have I ever tried to stop you from anything you've wanted?"

"You know, I was terrified to mail that letter to Yasar's family, telling them I was independent. I wasn't sure that I would be able to take care of myself. And I'm still not completely sure, but I am positive that I want to try. I want to know that I'm able to live on my own before living with anyone else."

"I still don't see why you and your independence can't live with me and mine?

"I just get so afraid, Mark, that you'll change your mind."

"I'm not Yasar. Please don't ever confuse us. I will not leave you like he did. It's time for you to believe me."

Adalet leaned forward and put her face in her hands. "I want to, Mark. I really do want to believe you."

"Look at me, Adalet." She did. He kissed her softly on the lips. "My love for you is not going to change. Ever. If anything, it will only get stronger."

"How can you possibly know that?"

Mark laughed. "You are the most stubborn woman I've known and the only woman I want to know. How can anyone be sure of anything? Life will take its course, but I know I want to run that course with you, wherever it takes me. Why don't we book a flight to Istanbul for both of us right now? Let's get back to Istanbul and then we'll talk more about everything. I think I can get you to see more reason on your own turf."

Adalet looked deeply into Mark's eyes. She would tell him what she felt; she would be completely honest this time. "I would love that, Mark, but I can wait a little longer. Spend some time with your mother, and then join me. I do mean what I'm saying, no hidden surprises."

Mark smiled. "Well, I won't give you too much time to think. Even a day seems dangerous."

"Take a few," Adalet told him, kissing him tenderly. "I promise I'll still be there."

"Now that is music to my ears. We'll book a flight for you tomorrow. I'll rent a car and take you to the airport. Right now, let's order up some breakfast. You'll need to eat something before you get more foolish ideas in your head." Mark slipped out of bed and picked up the menu from the dresser.

Adalet hesitated for a moment. She asked herself if it would have made a difference if Mark had picked her up from the airport himself. Would it have made a difference if Esther had not been so controlling? She couldn't answer either question. Suddenly a flash of memory struck her. It was Mark standing on the sidewalk in front of his building in Istanbul, fading into the shadows. She had to hold herself back from jumping into his arms and telling him that her doubts were all a foolish mistake. Of course she would stay as long as he wanted. But then why was she doing this in the first place?

Instead, Adalet curled up next to Mark who was scanning the menu. "I want a stack of pancakes, two scrambled eggs and a toasted bagel with cream cheese," Adalet told him.

"Now that's my girl," he said.

CHAPTER 37

Adalet placed her carryon above her seat, sat down by the window and buckled her seatbelt. Ironically, she'd flown in on American Airlines but was flying home on Turkish Air. As it happened, this was only for convenience, but Adalet could not help but note it anyway. A tall dark-skinned man and a much shorter light-skinned woman approached the empty seats next to her. The woman smiled at Adalet and sat down next to her while the man placed a couple of bags in the luggage compartment near Adalet's. They spoke to each other in a language Adalet couldn't identify. She thought they might be African.

Adalet pulled her handbag out from underneath her seat and decided to take one of the anxiety pills she had gotten for her panic attack. The past week had been emotionally draining, and she wanted to sleep during the trip home. Mark had driven her to the airport and seen her off as far as he was allowed. The security at Kennedy was as tight or even tighter than it had been just one week ago.

Mark had kissed her goodbye at the security gate. He'd smiled and said, "I won't be here much longer. I can't afford to lose my job in Istanbul now. In fact, I must try for something more permanent. Call me when you get to the apartment so I'll know you've arrived safely. We'll talk about everything when I get there."

"Okay," Adalet had told him. "Until then. Be safe."

"You too, sweetheart," Mark said as he kissed her lightly again and walked away. Then he'd turned around, walked back and kissed her again.

Now Adalet rang for the stewardess to ask for a cup of water to take her pill. After she took it, she made sure her seat was in the upright position for takeoff and closed her eyes.

Adalet was standing in front of a mirror in her mother's damaged wedding dress. But as she stared in the mirror, the dress began to repair itself. The color became as pure a white as it had been on her parents' wedding day. The torn lace stitched itself back into place. In one glance, her face became her mother's as a young woman. In the next, the face she saw was her own. Someone was tapping her on the arm—-.

It was the woman in the seat next to her. The stewardess was standing with a dinner tray in her hand. "Would you care for something to eat?" she asked.

"Thank you," Adalet managed. As she was taking the tray she asked the stewardess for a glass of wine. "A *pinot noir* if you have it," she said.

Adalet tried to eat, but thinking about her dream had her staring out the window into a black night sky. All she could see were the lights on the wing of the plane. She couldn't have said exactly what the dream meant, if someone had asked her to explain, but the feeling she had now was one of contentment. Her *anne* would always be with her, as long as Adalet lived and breathed. Something from the smell of the food in her tray brought her back to her *anne's* dumplings. A soft smile crept across her face. Adalet took a sip of wine, then another, and set her glass down on the tray. She closed her eyes and was fast asleep again, having dreams she could not remember.

"Seat backs up all the way. Fasten your seat belts. We'll be landing in Istanbul in about 20 minutes."

Adalet looked at the customs declaration card on her lap and laughed. She hadn't bought a single item while she'd been to New

York. How disappointed Meryem and Isha would be. She smiled at how surprised they'd be to see her so soon. She hadn't let them know she was coming back. She would have to deal with Meryem's unhappiness about her early return and the fact that she'd left Mark behind, but she was sure she could do that now. And it would be funny to see Meryem's face when she told her she hadn't done anything while she was there or bought a single gift. Well, she had gone to Ground Zero.

The couple next to her were smiling and holding hands. Adalet wondered if they were newlyweds or just a happy couple on vacation. As the plane began its descent, the couple squeezed each other's hands tightly. For just a moment, Adalet felt saddened. It could have been Mark's hand she might have gripped if she'd stayed. But this had been her choice, and Mark had respected and supported her decision.

Perhaps he really could let her be independent.

The airport was not terribly crowded, and Adalet was able to recover her bag and go through customs without too much trouble. It was certainly quicker than it had been at Kennedy International. She was waved through with her bags unopened and unchecked. Once outside, the line for taxis was not too long. She was third in line and was motioned into a taxi in less than five minutes. It was the middle of the day on a Thursday, and the traffic was bumper to bumper. It was unseasonably warm for October in Istanbul. Adalet smiled remembering the bright red and yellow leaves on Madison Avenue.

A melody of car horns played a welcome home serenade. Exhaust fumes filled the air and entered the taxi through open vents. Istanbul, Adalet thought, I'm home. New York hadn't felt to her at all like Istanbul. Maybe it would to the untrained eye, ear and nose. New York didn't smell like lamb or fish or the smoky smell of vendor corn, but she certainly had caught New York at its very worst. Perhaps she might give it another chance at some future time.

When the driver pulled up in front of Adalet's building, he smiled when he told her the fare in Turkish, her own language. The smile was probably for the tip he hoped for and did receive, but

Adalet didn't mind. It was still, after all, a friendly face. That wasn't quite fair, she thought, the Americans she'd met at the hotel were lovely people. She'd even exchanged email information with the Red Cross worker, Lisa, who'd promised to visit.

The taxi left Adalet standing in front of her door with her suitcase. She decided to let herself in and not to buzz Meryem or Isha. Just as she entered her key in the lock, the call to prayer started. She stopped and listened and waited until it was over. How she'd missed that sound! It vibrated inside her flesh and filled her with joy.

Adalet dragged her suitcase up the winding staircase to the second floor. She stood in the hallway for a moment, listening to the laughter of Meryem and Isha inside. Tears of happiness filled her eyes. She wiped them away and put the key into the lock. When she opened the door, Adalet saw clothing tossed into piles everywhere. What was this? She looked into the surprised faces of Meryem and Isha.

"Adalet, you're back! This is unbelievable. We were hoping to surprise you in New York! Come in, don't just stand in the hallway." Meryem hugged and pulled her into the apartment, suitcase and all. Isha didn't seem quite so surprised, but she hugged Adalet tightly once Meryem finally let go of her.

"What is all this?" Adalet asked. "Are you giving all your clothing to charity? Why is it all piled up here?" Yetim stuck her head out from under a pile of pants. "Oh, Yetim, I've missed you so!"

Meryem grabbed Adalet's hand and squeezed it tightly. "Isha got a job in New York!" She began to jump up and down like a small child. "We're going to New York for a year." She looked at Adalet and seemed to regain her senses. "Oh, Adalet, I thought you'd be so happy. We didn't know you were coming home and thought we'd just show up. We're leaving in a couple of weeks. Isha will be teaching at New York University, NYU; isn't that exciting?"

"It is very exciting." Adalet turned to Isha. "Congratulations, Isha. That's wonderful news. But what will you do there, Meryem? And where were you going to leave Yetim?" Adalet pulled a dining room chair around some clothing and sat down. Yetim jumped into her lap. Life was certainly filled with surprises.

"Nuray was going to come and stay with her until you got back. What will I do in New York? I'll study and paint. Oh, Adalet, it's the opportunity of a lifetime. Will you come with us? Will you go back to Mark? Tell us."

"Let me put my suitcase away and get something to drink first. It's a long trip, as you will see." Adalet headed for her bedroom, opened the door, and found it to be the only space that wasn't covered with clothing. Thank goodness, she thought, setting her suitcase down. She lay down on the bed. Yetim followed, curling up next to her. Soon Yetim was asleep, her purring turned to a light snore.

So there were to be more goodbyes, Adalet thought. Would they come back to live in Istanbul? Would she visit them in New York with Mark? Perhaps. She would go to see them if they stayed on, but this was her home. She knew that now.

Adalet jumped off the bed and went back to where Meryem and Isha were discussing jackets. "It rains a lot in New York, doesn't it?" Isha asked Adalet.

"It was raining when I arrived and looked like it was about to rain when I left, if that answers your question."

"You see," Isha affirmed her position, "we'll definitely need rain-coats and jackets."

"We'll wear them on the plane under our coats. They take up too much room."

"We'll look like bag ladies," Isha cried. "We need more luggage."

Adalet sat back down after she'd gotten a cold bottle of water from the refrigerator. For a time, she just watched the two young women sorting and making piles, forgetting which were piles to be packed and which were to be left behind. Adalet smiled at the complete disorganization.

"Why don't you put the to-go pile in the living room and the stay-behind pile in the dining room," Adalet suggested.

"Oh, Adalet, it's so good to have you home," Meryem laughed and hugged Adalet as she sat in the chair. "Will you come with us, please?"

"Yes," Isha joined in, "please come, Adalet. It would be so much fun."

Adalet smiled at the two of them. "No, I can't go with you," she said. "If you stay on longer than a year, I may have to come to visit. I may even visit before then. But what I learned in New York is that my life is here in Istanbul. My work is here, my building is here, and my home is here. I don't wish to live anywhere else."

"What happened with Mark?" Meryem immediately wanted to know.

"Nothing happened with Mark." Adalet took a long drink of water. "He and I will get together when he gets back to Istanbul. I think he will come soon. But a good deal has happened with me."

"What? Please tell us!"

Meryem's enthusiasm was so compelling that Adalet had to resist the impulse to grab onto her and hold her forever close. "All this time I've been telling you to grow up, Meryem, and I needed to grow up myself. I was turning to everyone else to help me to live, and now I want to try living on my own. I think your going to New York is a good thing for both of us, for all three of us, no, all four of us. It's timely."

"And what does Mark say about all of this?" Meryem looked straight into Adalet's eyes.

Adalet looked back without a blink. "That is between me and Mark."

Meryem smiled. "Okay, I can see that it is. Good girl, Addie. Why, I don't think I've ever called you that before."

"No," Adalet smiled back, "I don't think you ever have. I kind of like it, coming from you."

"Me, too," Isha added. "Addie's got a mind of her own. Maybe living with two lesbian feminists has rubbed off on you."

"I don't know about that, but watching your relationship grow has helped me a lot. I've learned so much from both of you. Now I want to spend some time discovering who I am."

"But how will you ever do that without us?" Meryem asked, half jokingly.

"It won't be easy," Adalet said seriously, "but I do want to try. I went from my parents to Yasar to Fatma and then to you, Meryem, and then there was Mark. Now I've realized that I wasn't such a giving person. I've been selfish. I used you, Meryem, to get out of Avanos. I used Fatma as well."

"But we're all selfish and we all use the people we love, Adalet. Meryem is using me right now to get to New York." Isha was so kind and dear. Adalet had known this in her head but now she knew it to be true in her heart.

"I know that thinking of oneself isn't necessarily a negative thing. But I've always run from one person or another on to the next, never really believing in myself. I accepted what others decided for me without putting up a fight. You can't say that about Meryem."

"No, I can't," Isha admitted. "Meryem always knows exactly what she wants and then plots and schemes to get it." Meryem stuck her tongue out at Isha and all three of them laughed.

"I've never done life on my own, but it's something I have to do before I can be with anyone else. It won't be easy without you two, but we'll see what survives. If New York can, then maybe Mark and I can as well. We'll have to see." Adalet got up and hugged both of the young women close to her. "Now I'm going to go into my bedroom and unpack and make some calls. When I come back out, I hope to see two piles instead of twenty piles. If that's the case, we'll all go to get something to eat. I'm starving."

"She's back all right," Meryem said.

Adalet touched Meryem's cheek gently. Perhaps one of the best things about living one's life was the lack of knowing for certain what would come next. Out of the ashes and back into life. Adalet smiled to herself as she walked back to her bedroom to dial Mark's number in New York.

CPSIA information can be obtained
at www.ICGtesting.com
Printed in the USA
FFOW04n0006041216
29994FF

9 780996 999625